P9-CAM-367

PENGUIN TWENTIETH-CENTURY CLASSICS

BETWEEN THE ACTS

Virginia Woolf is now recognized as a major twentieth-century author, a great novelist and essayist, and a key figure in literary history as a feminist and a modernist. Born in 1882, she was the daughter of the editor and critic Leslie Stephen, and suffered a traumatic adolescence after the deaths of her mother, in 1895, and her step-sister Stella, in 1897, leaving her subject to breakdowns for the rest of her life. Her father died in 1904 and two years later her favourite brother Thoby died suddenly of typhoid. With her sister, the painter Vanessa Bell, she was drawn into the company of writers and artists such as Lytton Strachey and Roger Fry, later known as the Bloomsbury Group. Among them she met Leonard Woolf, whom she married in 1912, and together they founded the Hogarth Press in 1917, which was to publish the work of T. S. Eliot, E. M. Forster and Katherine Mansfield as well as the earliest translations of Freud. Woolf lived an energetic life among friends and family, reviewing and writing, and dividing her time between London and the Sussex Downs. In 1941, fearing another attack of mental illness, she drowned herself.

Her first novel, *The Voyage Out*, appeared in 1915, and she then worked through the transitional *Night and Day* (1919) to the highly experimental and impressionistic *Jacob's Room* (1922). From then on her fiction became a series of brilliant and extraordinarily varied experiments, each one searching for a fresh way of presenting the relationship between individual lives and the forces of society and history. She was particularly concerned with women's experience, not only in her novels but also in her essays and her two books of feminist polemic, *A Room of One's Own* (1929) and *Three Guineas* (1938). Her major novels include *Mrs Dalloway* (1925), the historical fantasy *Orlando* (1928), written for Vita Sackville-West, the extraordinarily poetic vision of *The Waves* (1931), the family saga of *The Years* (1937), and *Between the Acts* (1941). All these are published by Penguin, as are her *Diaries*, Volumes I–V, and selections from her essays and short stories.

Gillian Beer is Professor of English at the University of Cambridge and a Fellow of Girton College. Several of her essays on Virginia

Woolf are collected in her *Arguing with the Past: Essays in Narrative from Woolf to Sidney* (1989). Among her other works are *Darwin's Plots* (1983) and *George Eliot* (1986). She is at present working on Woolf's response to waves and wave-theory.

Julia Briggs is General Editor for the works of Virginia Woolf in Penguin Twentieth-Century Classics.

Stella McNichol is a Lecturer in English Literature at Lancaster University. She is the author of a critical study of *To the Lighthouse* (1971) and of *Virginia Woolf and the Poetry of Fiction* (1990), and the editor of a group of Virginia Woolf's stories, *Mrs Dalloway's Party* (1973).

BETWEEN THE ACTS

VIRGINIA WOOLF

WITH AN INTRODUCTION AND
NOTES BY GILLIAN BEER
TEXT EDITED BY STELLA McNICHOL

PENGUIN BOOKS

PENGUIN BOOKS

Published by the Penguin Group
Penguin Books Ltd, 27 Wrights Lane, London w8 5tz, England
Penguin Books USA Inc., 375 Hudson Street, New York, New York 10014, USA
Penguin Books Australia Ltd, Ringwood, Victoria, Australia
Penguin Books Canada Ltd, 10 Alcorn Avenue, Toronto, Ontario, Canada m4v 3b2
Penguin Books (NZ) Ltd, 182–190 Wairau Road, Auckland 10, New Zealand

Penguin Books Ltd, Registered Offices: Harmondsworth, Middlesex, England

Between the Acts first published by The Hogarth Press 1941
This annotated edition published in Penguin Books 1992
1 3 5 7 9 10 8 6 4 2

Introduction and Notes copyright © Gillian Beer, 1992
Other editorial matter copyright © Stella McNichol
All rights reserved

The moral right of the editor has been asserted

Set in 10½/12pt Monophoto Garamond
Printed in England by Clays Ltd, St Ives plc

CONTENTS

Bibliographical Note

The following is a list of abbreviated titles used in this edition.

BA: *Between the Acts*, Virginia Woolf (Hogarth Press, 1941; Penguin Books 1992)

Diary: *The Diary of Virginia Woolf*, 5 vols., ed. Anne Olivier Bell (Hogarth Press, 1977; Penguin Books, 1979).

Letters: *The Letters of Virginia Woolf*, 6 vols. ed. Nigel Nicolson and Joanne Trautmann (Hogarth Press, 1975–80)

Moments of Being: *Moments of Being: Unpublished Autobiographical Writings of Virginia Woolf*, ed. Jeanne Schulkind (Chatto & Windus, 1976).

Introduction

Between the Acts is Woolf's final novel. She imagined, planned, and wrote it through the last days of a peace that seemed at times like a national hallucination, and into the period when England daily expected invasion. As she wrote and revised, the bombers passed nightly overhead. She and Leonard Woolf discussed what they would do if the German parachutes landed. They knew the fate of Jews throughout Europe. They would shut the garage doors and die.[1] When the work was more or less completed she died by her own will, but alone, drowning on 28 March 1941 in that same river where a man she described in a letter to Ethel Smythe shot himself just before the outbreak of war. Such an account of the circumstances of composition suggests a sombre work. But that would be to underestimate Woolf's vitality as a writer.

With *Orlando*, *Between the Acts* is Woolf's most mischievous and playful work, as well as one that muses much upon death and extinction. It is also a work where each word tells – sometimes at odds with its neighbour. Together these disparate words tell a resourceful history that jettisons ideas of development, discovers the remote past in the present moment, celebrates and mocks 'Englishness' and family life – and knows passion in all its improbability.

WAR

The novel is set quite specifically on a mid-June afternoon 1939. The Second World War will start only six weeks later. The characters in the book are preoccupied with the village pageant, with the weather and weather forecasts, with longing and lascivious fantasies: apparently (save for Giles) with anything but the war. But the coming war broods over the whole community, 'the doom of sudden death hanging over us' (p. 70), changing the meaning of past and present, threatening even the possibility of repetition: 'The future shadowed their present, like the sun coming through the many-veined transparent vine leaf: a criss-cross of lines making no pattern' (p. 70).

The playfulness and the holiday atmosphere in the book are partly rituals of defence against that future; a future which in the sentence quoted above is figured pastorally ('like the sun coming through the many-veined transparent vine leaf'), but in words that refer also to the play of searchlights ('a criss-cross of lines making no pattern'). Likewise, the funds raised by the village pageant are to go towards, the vicar says, 'the illumination of our dear old church' (p. 114). But ironically, as Woolf and her first readers well knew, the blackout was about to be imposed, just beyond the book's ending. The novel is sprung on such contingent ironies. The blackout is nowhere mentioned but Woolf wrote in it, her readers read in it, and the work ends in 'the heart of darkness, the fields of night'. Conrad's image of imperialism discovering the savagery at its own heart is combined with a side-long glance at Pope's *Dunciad*, which ends with the return of Chaos as the curtain falls on civilization.

> Thy hand, great Anarch! lets the curtain fall,
> And Universal Darkness buries All.

At the end of Woolf's work, however, the curtain will rise on a future that is also pre-history.

> Left alone together for the first time that day, they were silent. Alone, enmity was bared; also love. Before they slept, they must fight; after they had fought, they would embrace. From that embrace another life might be born. But first they must fight, as the dog fox fights with the vixen, in the heart of darkness, in the fields of night . . . . . . The house had lost its shelter. It was night before roads were made, or houses. It was the night that dwellers in caves had watched from some high place among rocks.
> Then the curtain rose. They spoke.

In those final sentences a new act is set to begin: sexual, theatrical, war-like, yet suggesting continuance. What that communal future will contain the reader must come to know in history beyond the aid of this book.

The work itself humorously, sometimes sardonically, interleaves literature, gossip, and communal events actually occurring in the world beyond the fiction. It dwells on objects and emptiness, skews (and skewers) perceptions through puns and rhymes. The seized fragments of language are robust, demotic, evanescent; many of the people in the work – old Lucy Swithin, her brother Bartholomew, his son Giles, Isa married to Giles, their guests Mrs Manresa and William Dodge, and Miss La Trobe, creator of the pageant – are vividly characterized. The small change of domestic life brims out of a fund of long and deep experience. The book includes the very old as well as new generations: old Mrs Swithin broods on 'the iguanodon, the mammoth, and the mastodon; from whom presumably, she thought, jerking the window open, we descend' (p. 8). Isa 'looked at Mrs. Swithin as if she had been a dinosaur or a very diminutive mammoth. Extinct she must be, since she had lived in the reign of Queen Victoria' (p. 104). All these characters are set in the midst of the voices and names of the village community, whose words are shared, dispersed, and shorn away from particular mouths.

The idea for the book began to stir in April 1938, as Virginia Woolf worked on the proofs of her boldest feminist polemic, *Three Guineas*, and laboured still at her biography of her friend, the art-critic and painter Roger Fry. News came of the ironic death of Ottoline Morell, struck down by a heart-attack on hearing that her husband was ill and might die. Woolf was obliged to write an obituary. She addresses herself in her diary that day:

> So I had to write; the horrid little pellet screwed my brain; leaves it giddy. Yet in spite of that here I am sketching out a new book; only dont please impose that huge burden on me again, I implore. Let it be random and tentative; something I can blow of a morning, to relieve myself of Roger: dont, I implore, lay down a scheme; call in all the cosmic immensities; & force my tired & diffident brain to embrace another whole – all parts contributing – not yet awhile. But to amuse myself, let me note: why not Poyntzet Hall: a centre: all lit. discussed with real little incongruous living humour; & anything that comes into my head; but "I" rejected: 'We' substituted: to whom at the end there shall be an invocation? "We" ... composed of many different things ... we all life, all art, all waifs and strays – a rambling capricious but somehow unified whole – the present state of my mind? And English country; & a scenic old house – & a terrace where nursemaids walk? & people passing – & a perpetual variety & change from intensity to prose. & facts – & notes; & – but eno'. I must read Roger: & go to Ott's memorial service, representing

also T. S. Eliot at his absurd command. 2.30 at Martins in the
Fields.[2]

The impulses set out in this passage are astonishingly close to the
novel that actually emerged, in contrast, for example, to *The Waves*
which underwent many transformations from conception to text.

Woolf's sense that the capricious and the fugitive may be the
only way of holding things together abides throughout the composition of *Between the Acts*. 'Living humour' brings body and language
into irresolute contact. Woolf is amused and irritated in this diary
entry by Eliot's pompous command that she 'represent' him at
Ottoline Morell's memorial service, partly because she sees bodily
difference as more important than symbolic statement. Also she
had, after all, only recently finished *Three Guineas* in which she
mocked the masculine trappings of solemn social rituals. She is *not*
T. S. Eliot: but now there he is, tangled into the start of the new
project. He was to remain so, for *Four Quartets* and *Between the Acts*
cite and sound each other repeatedly.

Ritual in *Between the Acts* emerges from the need for repetition
and recurrence, but its forms are flighty. Woolf was familiar with
the work of the anthropologist Jane Harrison and knew her as a
friend. Harrison's work on ritual, like that of Ruth Benedict whom
Woolf read as she wrote, has its effects in the work, but not, I
would argue, by providing a system of interpretation.[3] Indeed, the
work's partial, fugitive method of allusion and recall characteristically lets the reader brood or skim at will. Things go awry with
interpretation here when the critic seeks, as some have done, to turn
glimpses into systems.

Writing to her friend the composer Ethel Smythe in August
1939, just before the outbreak of the Second World War, Virginia
Woolf describes impasse, dislocation, communal unreality, summer
heat: 'Then there's the war – black outs: a man shot in the river
where I walk; and the Labour party meeting here. I cant make a
song of this, not a consecutive phrase, for I'm too hot.'[4] A few days
later she writes to Vita Sackville-West as she packs up her house:

whatever rung I'm on, the ladder is a great comfort in this kind
of intolerable suspension of all reality – something real.
But isn't it odd? – one cant fold it in any words.[5]

Woolf holds on to prosaic material objects like ladders, finding in them the continuing present. Language seems to promise continuance but, so responsive is it to the multiplicity of the moment, that it cannot be relied upon to provide the comforting sameness of ladders.

Virginia Woolf lingeringly hopes to find songs, phrases, words for overwhelming communal experience; but she knows that they must be words that acknowledge bafflement. Things broken apart, or lightly laid alongside, must take the place of fusion. Heteroglossia is here acted out by recording steadily what's thought, what's said, what's scrappily overheard. Isa, taking a cup of tea, broods on desire and drowning, through a remembered fairy tale:

> 'But what wish should I drop into the well?' She looked round. She could not see the man in grey, the gentleman farmer; nor anyone known to her. 'That the waters should cover me,' she added, 'of the wishing well.'
>
> The noise of china and chatter drowned her murmur. 'Sugar for you?' they were saying. 'Just a spot of milk? And you?' 'Tea without milk or sugar. That's the way I like it.' 'A bit too strong? Let me add water.'
>
> 'That's what I wished,' Isa added, 'when I dropped my pin. Water. Water . . .'
>
> 'I must say,' the voice said behind her, 'it's brave of the King and Queen. They're said to be going to India. She looks such a dear. Someone I know said his hair . . .' (pp. 63–4)

What 'someone I know' said about the King's hair could be readily filled in by the contemporary reader who could join in the glee. Gossip stands in for dialogue. Gossip about the royal family is gleaned from the brouhaha of contemporary talk in the late thirties: 'about the Duke of Windsor. He landed on the south coast. Queen Mary met him. She'd been buying furniture – that's a fact. And the papers say she met him . . .' (p. 64). And so indeed the papers of the time did say, just as Queen Mary's furniture-buying habits were part of ordinary malicious talk outside the fiction. The novel invokes the larger ordinary community of which the reader is a part and makes of that stuff the will to survive.

Dispensing and receiving tea, and the accompanying phrases ('Sugar for you?'), are here the forms that ritual takes, producing surface and depths alike. Woolf eschews grander invocations, of earth mothers or Isis. The community steadies itself through humdrum repetition, whose significance is in saying things again, more than in what is said. Saying things again implies that you are still there to say them. *Between the Acts* is preoccupied with communal survival, even as it glances across individual loss. It does not particularly praise the community it represents. That community typifies the attitudes that have brought the country to the brink of war and of fascism. But neither does the novel suggest any value in the community's possible obliteration.

Screaming past behind the tea-urn and the barn are the swallows who have returned endlessly over the centuries, since before humankind was here. Those same swallows have, by humankind, been made part of myths of rape and violation for which, as I shall show, Woolf uncovers a hideous and absurd recent parallel. This shifting overlay of contemporary life, natural recurrence, phatic language, and literary fragments, is the way Woolf's community survives. She chooses to show them gathered at leisure. That is her method of intensification.

Pastimes – gossip, play-acting, sociable meals – may make tolerable the inevitable passing of time, because they suggest that there is time in abundance. That fiction of time-to-spare becomes more important in periods of crisis. In the community and the historical moment that Woolf writes out of, and into, very little time seemed left. Europe stood on the edge of destruction and by the end of June 1940, a week after the disaster and amateur heroism of Dunkirk, Woolf wrote of the war: 'We pour to the edge of a precipice ... & then? I cant conceive that there will be a 27th June 1941.'[6] For her, there was not. She delayed finishing *Pointz Hall* (the working title of *BA*), as much for the anchoring pleasure its writing gave her, as for any other reason. She toyed with delay to ward off defeat. People were killed nightly in nearby air-raids that passed overhead and she foresaw that she might be one of them. A few days earlier, in a different mood, she wrote in the diary: 'I feel, if this is my last lap, oughn't I to read Shakespeare? But cant. I feel oughn't I to finish off P.H.: oughtn't I to finish something by way of an end? The end gives its vividness, even its gaiety and recklessness to the random daily life.'[7]

Between the Acts comes to no conclusions, but it includes several endings: among them, the end of the village play, the dispersal of the audience, and the end of the day and coming of night with which scene the book itself comes to a close without closure: 'The curtain rose. They spoke.'

At the end of the village pageant that occupies so many pages of the book the audience begins to leave:

> The wheels scurred on the gravel. The cars drove off.
> The gramophone gurgled *Unity – Dispersity*. It gurgled *Un . . . dis . . .* And ceased. (p. 119)

Opposites exist alongside, and cancel each other's meaning. Syllables disjoin. The gramophone runs down, 'And ceased.' At the same time the elements of dispersed words skein together to produce a word of a different sense: *undeceased*.

Throughout the novel the reader works with echoes, wraiths of words and forthright homely statements. Making noises makes sense in this writing. In this passage, for example, the nonce word 'scurred' or 'scrurred' (and its half-rhyme 'gurgled') mimic sounds as if the reader were there now in the drive;[8] the mimesis comes close, and falls pleasurably short, encouraging the reader to try the sounds out with the inner ear, yet acknowledging also that we are reading words and that words will not quite fold round actuality.

WORDS

The fascination with words, their depth and instability of reference, their capacity to survive into new circumstances, their interplay of allusion, is central to Woolf's examination of community. Words are always communal, particularly when set in grammatical relations. Words always include others than the self; they can figure what cannot be performed. People's proper names are quiddities but may express endurance and signify much within a close community:

> Again, had Figgis called the names of the villagers, they too would have answered. Mrs. Sands was born Iliffe; Candish's mother was one of the Perrys. The green mounds in the churchyard had been cast up by their molings, which for centuries had made the earth friable. (p. 47)

In a 1937 essay on 'Craftsmanship' Woolf muses on the street-wise resilience of words:

> Now, this power of suggestion is one of the most mysterious properties of words. Everyone who has ever written a sentence must be conscious or half-conscious of it. Words, English words, are full of echoes, of memories, of associations – naturally. They have been out and about, on people's lips, in their houses, in the streets, in the fields, for many centuries.[9]

Strikingly, this discussion was part of a talk for the BBC, so that it was itself a part of the new oral culture that was rising around the written word. The radio, alongside newspapers, is the new communication system, carrying authoritative pronouncements that are scattered into shards of gossip.

What are the difficulties posed for the writer by the historical freight words carry? 'They are so stored, with meaning, with memories, that they have contracted so many famous marriages.' How to split one word apart from its expected partner is one difficulty, she suggests. Then, 'You cannot use a brand new word in an old language because of the very obvious yet mysterious fact that a word is not a single and separate entity, but part of other words. It is not a word indeed until it is part of a sentence.'[10] Fortunately, as we have already seen, Woolf did not always obey her embargo on new words. More striking is her assertion that words are not fully words until they are set in relationships with other words in a sentence, and that no word is a single or separate entity. Her final question on the same page is: 'How can we combine the old words in new orders so that they survive, so that they create beauty, so that they tell the truth?'

Survival; beauty; truth-telling; her question makes it clear that, for her, lexical play is no lightweight matter, though the play be airily deft. Such play ('combining the old words in new orders') seeks a communal *new order* as well as using the old as a bulwark against ruin. The effect of threnody is strong in much that Woolf writes at this time, sometimes mysteriously so:

> Voices interrupted. People passed the stable yard, talking.
> 'It's a good day, some say, the day we are stripped naked.
> Others, it's the end of the day. They see the Inn and the Inn's

keeper. But none speaks with a single voice. None with a voice free from the old vibrations. Always I hear corrupt murmurs; the chink of gold and metal. Mad music . . .' (p. 94)

Her writing is not nostalgic. It seeks to sustain life in the present, and does so through a singularly free-spoken use of words issuing from unnamed mouths, as gossip and aside. She writes out too the flow of individual half-consciousness in which words whimsically translate themselves, uncovering lateral kinships, saying and changing the unsayable. So Isabella cleanses the foul language of prejudice in the judgement that her husband Giles makes on William Dodge, whose homosexuality is indicated but never named (eg. p. 65):

> Isabella guessed the word that Giles had not spoken. Well, was it wrong if he was that word? Why judge each other? Do we know each other? Not here, not now. But somewhere, this cloud, this crust, this doubt, this dust— She waited for a rhyme, it failed her; but somewhere surely one sun would shine and all, without a doubt, would be clear. (p. 39)

The word 'queer', hinted at in the outer rhyme of 'here' and 'clear' and reinforced a sentence later with 'I think I hear them', is conjured and evaded.

In this book, access to half-consciousness, communal and individual, is given by the anarchic neatness of rhyme, which pins together the unlike, making the ear the arbiter of signification. Woolf uses doggerel as much as high chime, figuring indignant exclamations as the music turns to jazz and the pageant ends without a grand finale:

> What a cackle, a cacophony! Nothing ended. So abrupt. And corrupt. Such an outrage; such an insult; And not plain. Very up to date, all the same. What is her game? To disrupt? (p. 109)

The rhyming game continues on down the page, and on other pages. In part, the effect is a tribute to music which alone, and briefly, can make things whole: 'Music wakes us. Music makes us see the hidden, join the broken. Look and listen' (p. 73). In part, it is a tribute to the human voice, which may belie the sense on the page, registering the tug between oral speech and written language. Woolf is exploring the way words 'cling' together. The effect, though, is often less benign, suggesting the helpless staleness of an old community.

Words in this book also spring apart and re-order themselves in kaleidoscopic comedy (words like *sole*, which in the play of the text shifts vagrantly between fish, crepe soles of shoes, and spirit, and then flips backwards, reversing itself to become *lose* (p. 18), for example). The effect of such transformations is often lackadaisical, eschewing the vigorous urgings of Joycean word-play. The ability of words to come together and produce new ones a little later in the writer's consciousness makes for an easy motion between event and notation. Words shuffle between speech-acts. Frank Kermode has observed, for example, how the words 'prayer' and 'umbrella', contested between Bart Oliver and Lucy Swithin, produce the nurses wheeling a 'perambulator' several lines further on.

Woolf's writing always had this shiftiness at its edge (an ear that heard the auditory likeness between the most improbable concepts, as in *The Waves* the word 'tea-urn' generates 'eternity' a few lines down). But in *Between the Acts* such melding and interruption become crucial to the significance of the work. So Giles can begin a sentence, struggling to recall a line of poetry, and Albert, the idiot, end it (p. 53). Conversely, characters repeatedly break in on each other's reveries. Old Bartholomew dozes:

> seeing as in a glass, its lustre spotted, himself, a young man helmeted; and a cascade falling. But no water; and the hills, like grey stuff pleated; . . . a bullock maggot-eaten in the sun; and in the shadow of the rock, savages; and in his hand a gun . . .
> The door opened.
> 'Am I,' Isa apologized, 'interrupting?' (p. 13)

In this passage fragments of *The Waste Land* shade into Rider Haggard or Rudyard Kipling, the whole seen 'through a glass darkly'. The same sequence of interrupted mind-action is repeated for Mrs Swithin and for Isa. The only character who longs for interruption more than she finds it is Miss La Trobe who needs human company and drink to discover fertile words in the mud of the subconscious. In the pub she listens: 'Words of one syllable sank down into the mud. She drowsed; she nodded. The mud became fertile . . . Words without meaning – wonderful words' (p. 125).

Woolf undoes the canon. Fragments from famous works wind in and out of people's consciousness, half-remembered, often mis-remembered, valued nonetheless. Like single words, single works are not autonomous. In memory they are shards scattered, or shared, among a community. That image of fragmentation becomes also a binding refrain in the book: 'orts, scraps, and fragments'. The lines from Shakespeare's most sceptical play *Troilus and Cressida* are persis-tently referred to, re-arranged, and riffled through the text. They express the scatter of identity, the absence of centre. Where in its original setting the strongest association of the metaphor is with the greasy remnants of a meal, Woolf (and Isa) re-invent the line so that it suggests instead archaeological findings and fragments – and the wisps of speech overheard. The book is not so much studded with quotation and allusion as combed through: sometimes mere sparks of reference remain, sometimes clandestine glories. Shakespeare is dispersed among limber sentences. *Lear*, the sonnets, *Macbeth*, *Troilus* and *The Tempest* all play their parts, in fragments often shorn of context or contextual urgency (never, never, never; the temple-haunting martins; I fear I am not in my perfect mind; this insubst-antial pageant faded). Sometimes streaks of reference are absurdly integrated into apparently inappropriate sentences: Mrs Manresa, flirting with Giles, 'had him in thrall' (p. 68) and her make-up is not sufficiently 'deeply interfused' (p. 120). Wordsworth and Keats are *almost* there, for fun, part of the language of the tribe.

That tribe is capable of terrible things. Once only, when the shower comes as the audience survey themselves uneasily in the mirrors at the end of the pageant, is totality momentarily evoked as language. The rain pours 'like all the people in the world weeping. Tears tears tears'. The 'blots of rain ... were all people's tears, weeping for all people'. A little later an unnamed person remembers the poem (but not that Walt Whitman wrote it): 'There's a poem, *Tears tears tears*, it begins. And goes on *O then the unloosened ocean* ... but I can't remember the rest' (p. 119). Individual authors and whole poems are lost in the oceanic flow of language. Still, frag-ments welter and remain. Accepting the loss of the author is hard but necessary for Woolf. The writing, lightly, forms the figure of 'Anon', (see discussion below, p. xxxiii–iv).

The pageant, like a masque, is performed once only. The day's news is recorded and jettisoned. The flowers fade. But words in their arrangements oddly do survive, often disturbed but called again into life. So, Keats's 'Ode to a Nightingale' can be seamed into a line from *Hamlet*. And when the characters confront the audience at the pageant's end with looking-glasses and reflective scraps of tin, they all simultaneously chant fragments of verse, from music hall songs to Dante (p. 110). The cacophony of western civilization is also a set of talismanic utterances: the flotsam of language absurdly bobbing loose from its moorings is also borne up on an ocean of human grief (p. 107). The unskeining of literature does not disavow it, though it sets it unhierarchically in among all the goings on of human behaviour; that human business which is irrelevant to the sky perpetually passing, the blue 'which resists registration'.

In the mind, things do not keep securely within classifications. In reading, everything is in the mind. In this book, the characters' passions are played out between the acts. Speech-acts and mind-acts create a turbulent medium in which the characters live, enjoy and suffer. The writing shifts under the reader's gaze between third-person narrative and free indirect discourse. In free indirect discourse the terms of the sentence, and its syntax, are recognizably the product of a particular consciousness within the book, though the sentence holds to the form of third-person description. Looking at such sentences the reader often cannot be certain of their provenance: who thinks? or do they speak? perhaps it is she? or they? or I, the generating reader? This casualness about source emphasizes the common tongue, the common reader.

The book is light on the eye. This is no non-stop stream-of-consciousness. Instead the page is slightly pointed with remarks, in which cliché carries as much meaning as does meditation. The fragments shored against ruin here are no grand exotica as at the end of *The Waste Land*; instead they are little phrases, phatic sayings:

> 'He looks blooming,' said Mrs. Swithin.
> 'It's astonishing how they pick up,' said Isa. (p. 17)

The punctuating speech-tags here ('said Mrs. Swithin', 'said Isa') draw attention to the dance being performed between the two characters. Often such speech tags are interposed to disrupt the smooth run of the obvious and re-shape it into the odd:

'Marriages with cousins,' said Mrs. Swithin, 'can't be good for the teeth.' (p. 21)

'What's the origin,' said a voice, 'of the expression "with a flea in his ear"?' (p. 74)

'What's the object,' said Bartholomew, suddenly rousing himself, 'of this entertainment?' (p. 105)

The ritual repetitions that make up so much of the life of speech are likened earlier in the text to church bells: 'The words were like the first peal of a chime of bells. As the first peals, you hear the second; as the second peals, you hear the third' (p. 16). But though reiteration makes for a seemingly unchanging, resonating world, it also highlights change. The harmonics alter. Old Mrs Swithin remembers her mother speaking to her in that same room, 'But in a different world' her brother Bart reminds her. *Between the Acts* is fascinated by change.

Words mean differently – *sound* differently – as they are spoken into new experience. This novel makes clear that though things are said many times they never mean quite the same. As a result, though opposites alternate they never pair simply as disappointment, as slack recurrence. It is not enough, as some recent critics have done, to note alternation as if the matter ended there. Language is capable always of tugging the reader through into unforeseen feeling.

VIOLENCE

Woolf in this novel, as in no other, puts violence near the centre of meaning. For Isa, listening to her elders reiterate their dialogue for the seventh year, the morning newspaper has just made her privy to horror, a horror surrounded by absurdity.

So when Isa heard Mrs. Swithin say: 'I've been nailing the placard on the Barn,' she knew she would say next:
'For the pageant.'
And he would say:
'Today? By Jupiter! I'd forgotten!' . . .
Every summer, for seven summers now, Isa had heard the same words; about the hammer and the nails; the pageant and the weather. Every year they said, would it be wet or fine; and every

year it was – one or the other. The same chime followed the
same chime, only this year beneath the chime she heard: 'The
girl screamed and hit him about the face with a hammer.'
(p. 16)

The steady chime of alternation, the little liturgy of domestic life, is
undermined by violence. The 'hammer and the nails' become also
the instruments of Christ's passion, and the sevenfold repetition
chimes with the seven last words on the cross. Those resonances are
generated partly out of Lucy Swithin's intensely religious life but
they start into consciousness here as Isa broods on an item she has
read in the morning's newspaper.

The events described in the newspaper are, startlingly, not
invented.[11] When Woolf proposed the book to herself she wanted
to include 'facts' and the work hauntingly broods on the question
of what's real: is it what's embodied? what's believed? or what's not
acted? 'Real swallows' swoop across the stage set, 'Reality too
strong,' mutters Miss La Trobe, as her play threatens to collapse
into its artifice of present time and emptiness.

The episode of rape to which Isa flinchingly returns in the quotation above was undeniably real, as I shall explain, and was one of
those 'facts' that Woolf sought. The identification Isa makes with
the victim is altered, I would assert, by the knowledge that the
bodies and persons in the case existed, just as the coming war was a
'real' war, communally experienced.

Isa tries to find in the library of the house a book that will
satisfy her rage to . . . what? understand? participate? be? The need
is not specified. Isa, whose age is the same as the century's,
thirty-nine, is, we are told, part of a generation 'book-shy', 'gun-
shy', for whom literature cannot 'stop her toothache' (pp. 14–15).
Teeth and dentistry form part of the book's debate about what's
savage, what civilized: savages could perform delicate operations,
Isa remembers; while toothache is the most direct experience of
violent pain common in European cultures, and dentistry, when
Woolf wrote, still an excruciating practice. *Between the Acts* refuses
the divisions between high and low examples, reaching instead
for what comes close to hand since that is likely to be shared
experience. So toothache and rape can be laid alongside without
demeaning, and the fantasy of a horse with a green tail (*a green*

tale) leads into real horror. The naïve, green girl believes the tale, and tragedy begins.

> For [Isa's] generation the newspaper was a book; and, as her father-in-law had dropped the *Times*, she took it and read: 'A horse with a green tail . . .' which was fantastic. Next, 'The guard at Whitehall . . .' which was romantic and then, building word upon word, she read: 'The troopers told her the horse had a green tail; but she found it was just an ordinary horse. And they dragged her up to the barrack room where she was thrown upon a bed. Then one of the troopers removed part of her clothing, and she screamed and hit him about the face . . .'
>
> That was real; so real that on the mahogany door panels she saw the Arch in Whitehall; through the Arch the barrack room; in the barrack room the bed, and on the bed the girl was screaming and hitting him about the face, when the door (for in fact it was a door) opened and in came Mrs. Swithin carrying a hammer. (p. 15)

'That was real': that happened beyond fiction to the body and mind of a human woman. In this event, purveyed by a newspaper's account, Isa experiences the empathy she cannot find in literature. 'For in fact it was a door': the Alice-in-Wonderland aside produces an interruption, or juncture, for the reader between Isa's reverie and actuality (which is also our reverie as readers). Is a newspaper different from a book? Is one more real? How does fiction relate to known events? Woolf implicitly places these questions within her own fiction. They are questions intimately connected to a particular brutal happening that occurred, like many other unrecorded brutal happenings, on an April day in 1938.

The very day after Woolf first recorded her project for *Pointz Hall* (in the passage quoted at the start of this essay) a young girl of fourteen was raped by guardsmen, on 27 April 1938. The soldiers asked her if she would like to see a horse with a green tail, lured her into the barracks, and raped her. On 28 April Woolf received the proofs of *Three Guineas*. Woolf's fundamental argument in *Three Guineas* is that men's upbringing and education breeds militarism and makes violence inevitable. The eery contiguity of the conceiving of the novel and the rape would not have been known to Woolf in that moment, but two months later in June of the same year the trial of the soldiers and the girl's testimony was reported in *The Times*:

> The girl said that she was crying and shouting, and he said if she shouted it would be the worse for her. She screamed and tried to push him away and punched him, and he said he would hit her back and hurt her, as he had been a champion boxer.

The girl in the case had no weapons but her hands. The hammer has got into Isa's fantasy enactment from Lucy Swithin's entrance carrying a hammer and interrupting Isa's reverie. The mild old lady becomes momentarily a figure of female vengeance – another of her 'unacted parts'.

The actual case had further consequences. The girl became pregnant and a respected gynaecologist Aleck Bourne performed an abortion and then drew the attention of the police to what he had done. Abortion at that time was illegal, save to preserve the mother's life. So Aleck Bourne was tried at the Old Bailey the month after the soldiers, July 1938, for procuring an abortion. The case became something of a *cause célèbre*. He was acquitted, after the judge extended the phrase 'preserve the mother's life' to mean that 'the probable consequence of the continuance of the pregnancy will be to make the woman a physical or mental wreck'. But the law was not changed until 1967.

Woolf here condenses the actual case of the previous year into the June day of 1939, and associates it with the approach of a war that will send guardsmen into action. The judge in the case had reproached the defendants: 'One would think that every Englishman, especially English soldiers, would be anxious to help her and protect her.' That had not proved to be so. In Miss La Trobe's pageant England is represented as a girl, who forgets her lines.

Woolf makes another condensation in this episode. The newspaper that Isa casually picked up was the one that her father-in-law had used that morning to pretend to be a monster, terrifying her three-year-old son George, and then reproaching him as a cry-baby and a coward. George is absorbed in the flower he is grubbing up out of the earth, and Woolf represents his concentration with febrile intensity, with a mixture of violence and rapture as membranes tear and 'a lambent light under a film of velvet ... filled the caverns behind the eyes with light'. But:

> Then there was a roar and a hot breath and a stream of coarse
> grey hair rushed between him and the flower. Up he leapt, top-
> pling in his fright, and saw coming towards him a terrible peaked
> eyeless monster moving on legs, brandishing arms. (p. 10)

The old man is affronted by the child's fear. The child, further
terrified by his grandfather's Afghan hound, bursts into tears. The
old man is re-living his military days 'as if he were commanding a
regiment' as he cows the 'wild beast' and mocks the 'coward'. The
British Empire, to which old Oliver looks back as his youth, similarly saw itself as disciplining, or subjugating, other 'wild' breeds,
or more 'primitive' peoples, justifying imperialism by the metaphor
of cultural development in which 'other races' were viewed as
children. The analogy is sharply present.

In this episode Woolf conjures the violence that adults' teasing
phlegmatically imposes on children, and makes that insensitivity
work also as a glancing critique of militarism and empire. Her
concurrent reading of Freud's *Moses and Monotheism* may have made
her even more aware of the pre-historic aggressions that, Freud
argues, persist in present-day personality and give insight into early
tribal formations.

The needling recognition forced on the willing or unwilling
reader that militarism plays many parts is, if anything, reinforced by
the suggestion that Bart Oliver is a nice enough old boy. The
episode ends with Bart comforting himself by finding another item
in the paper:

> 'M. Daladier,' he read finding his place in the column, 'has
> been successful in pegging down the franc...' (p. 11)

Again, 'facts' enter the novel. Edouard Daladier, then Prime Minis-
ter of France, was present at the Munich agreement that gave
Europe a delusive hope of peace with Hitler at the end of September
1938. The terms agreed were dishonourable, involving the sacrifice
of Czechoslovakia, though at the time many people were for a while
understandably overwhelmed with relief that the threat of war had
withdrawn. Woolf felt both shame and relief, as her diary records.[12]
In this passage, she draws attention to the market forces at work in
diplomacy, and to the financial interests involved as war approached.
Leonard Woolf in his analysis of the European political scene that

same year, *Barbarians at the Gate* (London, 1939) characterized Daladier as being typical of the forces that weaken civilization, 'not the strength of the dictators and the barbarians' but 'the capitalist who wants liberty, justice, truth, and tolerance'.[13]

Between the Acts, which I earlier characterized as full of play, is, then, also full of violence: the violence of the coming war, of rape, of adults terrorizing children, of snake devouring toad, of Giles stamping on the impasse of toad and snake, of unrealizable passion, '*Vénus tout entière à sa proie attachée*'. The reader experiences also the violence of language awakened from a long sleep of repetition: Giles, outraged by his knowledge that war approaches and that he is powerless to prevent it, refusing to understand his own historical complicity in aggression, hears phrases concerning communal passivity in a new medium.

> 'We remain seated' – 'We are the audience.' Words this afternoon ceased to lie flat in the sentence. They rose, became menacing and shook their fists at you. This afternoon he wasn't Giles Oliver come to see the villagers act their annual pageant; manacled to a rock he was, and forced passively to behold indescribable horror. (p. 38)

He becomes, in his own mind at least, a mythic hero chained to a rock: Prometheus; or, worse, Andromeda?

The work refuses to place these different forms of violence in a hierarchical order. It refuses, too, to privilege violence with the central place in our attention, though it may be central to the order of things in the world. The pageant eschews it altogether, concentrating on reconciliation and accord, save for the absurd figure of the Victorian policeman Budge with his truncheon. The play within the novel sorts language into simpler patterns as a series of copy-book tableaux and pastiches.

The swallows who sweep constantly across the barn recall the myth of Procne and Philomela in Ovid's *Metamorphoses*, but that allusion to rape, violation, and murder is kept as a distant echo, evoking Eliot's 'A Game of Chess' from *The Waste Land*, confirmed by the invocation of the *Pervigilium Veneris* and by the repeated reworking of the opening line of Swinburne's poem 'Itylus', based on the Philomela and Procne legend. Bartholomew murmurs:

> O sister swallow, O sister swallow,
> How can thy heart be full of the spring? (p. 70)

In this novel swallows are not coupled with nightingales – we are told, apparently rather purposively, on the novel's first page as the characters ruminate on sewage, old families, and bird-song, that 'nightingales didn't come so far north'. The swallows' own lives, dipping and wheeling, returning and leaving, are unencumbered by the mythic freight that human beings attach to them though they become for the audience part of the play. Signifying is a limited activity, this work suggests.

Emptiness matters as much. At different times we are told that the nursery is empty, the stage is empty, the barn is empty, the room is empty.

> Empty, empty, empty; silent, silent, silent. The room was a shell, singing of what was before time was; a vase stood in the heart of the house, alabaster, smooth, cold, holding the still, distilled essence of emptiness, silence. (p. 24)

The language of *Four Quartets* is conjured here. Emptiness may be song or distillation. It may also be active, full of all those other, unobserved, non-human inhabitants that human eyes dismiss. Waiting for the tea rush, 'the barn was empty'.

> Mice slid in and out of holes or stood upright, nibbling. Swallows were busy with straw in pockets of earth in the rafters. Countless beetles and insects of various sorts burrowed in the dry wood. A stray bitch had made the dark corner where the sacks stood a lying-in ground for her puppies. All these eyes, expanding and narrowing, some adapted to light, others to darkness, looked from different angles and edges. (pp. 61–2)

Emptiness and silence are the shaping shadows behind language, or even music.

ACTS

Sexuality and desire also pulse through the book. Woolf exempts none of her characters completely from the association with violence: even Mrs Swithin enters with a hammer. William Dodge and Lucy

Swithin, across gender and generation, share a delicately intimate friendship for a single afternoon. Once Giles enters, William Dodge can see only him. Giles knows what William Dodge's 'left hand is doing'. In a world charged with sexuality *eros* is always *agape*. But Woolf does not allow the reader to become besotted with this discovery. Her gossips deal briskly with the question: 'Did she mean, so to speak, something hidden, the unconscious as they call it? But why always drag in sex?' (p. 118) Silence, emptiness, momentary accords, enduring kinships, are also part of the work's exploration, in characterization and in language itself.

One line from Racine's *Phèdre* haunts Isa and flashes across near the end of the book into William Dodge's mind: '"like Venus" he thought, making a rough translation, "to her prey . . ."' (p. 123). Isa's passionate infatuation with Rupert Haines, the 'man in a grey suit' (with whom she scarcely exchanges a word) is as absorbing as Phèdre's tragic love for her stepson. But Isa's love finds neither expression nor outcome. The dart she feels in her flank is felt also by the cows:

> From cow after cow came the same yearning bellow. The whole world was filled with dumb yearning. It was the primeval voice sounding loud in the ear of the present moment. Then the whole herd caught the infection. Lashing their tails, blobbed like pokers, they tossed their heads high, plunged and bellowed, as if Eros had planted his dart in their flanks and goaded them to fury. (p. 85)

The cows' outcry restores the emotion of the stage scene and Miss La Trobe is saved. These parallels between Phèdre, Isa, the cows, are not mock-heroic or demeaning, though serenely absurd. The primal powers of sex and violence, appetite and loss, are always struggling free within the everyday.

In keeping with the seam of reference to Racine that runs through the work, the sequences of the book itself more or less hold to the neo-classical three unities of place, time, and mood. Mrs Swithin argues that:

> 'Actors show us too much. The Chinese, you know, put a dagger on the table and that's a battle. And so Racine . . .'
> 'Yes, they bore one stiff,' Mrs. Manresa interrupted. (p. 85)

Mrs Manresa, the self-conceived 'wild child of nature', the townee whose name is that of a Chelsea street as well as a pun on 'man-raiser' or cock-teaser, is always there to kick over the traces of too intellectual a reading. Her sappy middle-aged sex is mocked and celebrated. She alone of the characters is not confounded when the mirrors turn on them at the end of the play: she powders her nose.

The novel's formal severity of contour contrasts with the plethora of language and event in Miss La Trobe's sprawling, yet stylized, pageant. So Woolf is able to evoke the characteristic forms both of French and English drama – and the experience of play and of audience alike. Miss La Trobe's village pageant displays widely separated moments from English history and literary tradition. Lost heirs discovered, parted lovers united, picnics with a purpose ('O has Mr. Sibthorp a wife'), a final comic unravelling of Victorian domesticity: none of these events matter, Miss La Trobe suggests, save to produce emotion. Love, hate, and, Isa adds, peace. The pastiche languages of the pageant range through lyricism, melo-drama, and comedy without settling on any one of them. By includ-ing the bustling yet static drama of the pageant and the inward, dynamic drama of the audience's thoughts and feelings Woolf is able to achieve a cross-grained play between acts, acting, and the 'unacted part'.

Each of the characters discovers other parts of themselves. Seeing the play makes chaste old Lucy Swithin feel that she 'might have been – Cleopatra' while to William Dodge she appears 'like a girl in a garden in white, among roses, who came running to meet him – an unacted part' (p. 122). In the book's final scene 'For a moment she looked like a tragic figure from another play' (p. 127). The village store-keeper proves to be an imposing Queen Elizabeth; Isa is consumed with desire for the gentleman farmer Haines who merely hands her a cup of tea; William Dodge percipiently acts several parts in relation to the others of the party but experiences himself as 'a half-man'; the idiot is alarmingly himself, always on the verge of shocking the village elders, because for him there is no gap between acts and thought.

The 'acts' of the novel's title are of several kinds: the acts of a play; sexual acts; and the period between the two acts of twentieth-century European history, the First and Second World Wars. The brief time of the book also expands to include in simultaneity pre-history and what Woolf dreaded would prove to be post-history. The book ends with a scene in which present time grows indistinguishable from the remotest past when scarcely a human presence was established in the vastnesses of a natural world without need of the human. '"England," she was reading, "was then a swamp. Thick forests covered the land. On the top of their matted branches birds sang . . ."' (p. 129).

Woolf here draws on a passage from the opening of G. M. Trevelyan's *History of England*, a work she mocked in *Orlando* for the absence of women from its social history. Throughout the book Isa is the medium of brooding awareness and reflexivity. She is also rather silly, as any displayed half-consciousness perhaps would seem. She and her husband address not one remark directly to each other. Only in the final sentence of the book 'They spoke'. What they said the audience is not to hear; but the reader knows that it is prelude to anger and to sexual congress, out of which 'another life might be born'.

The whole action of Woolf's work takes place within twenty-four hours, from evening to evening in mid-June. The place is Pointz Hall, the country house where several of the principal figures live. The mood is more questionable: it remains shifty, vacillating, but equilibrated, able to accommodate love, hate, peace without strident changes of linguistic register and with such slight shifts of pitch that the whole remains, as it were, within an octave. But like any good neo-classical drama, time, place, and mood condense extremes within their apparent constancy. The time zones of the novel range, within the characters' minds, from the pre-historic to the imminent future. Old Mrs Swithin reading her favourite 'Outline of History' has spent the morning hours 'between three and five thinking of rhododendron forests in Piccadilly; when the entire continent, not then, she understood, divided by a channel, was all one' (p. 8). Giles arriving home at lunchtime from the city 'came into the dining-room looking like a cricketer, in flannels, wearing a blue coat with brass buttons; though he was enraged. Had he not read, in the morning paper, in the train, that sixteen men had been shot, others prisoned, just over there, across the gulf in the flat land which divided them from the continent?' (p. 30) Lucy Swithin seeks to resolve divisions and to find 'all one', through space as well as time. Giles is at odds with the pastoral complacency that refuses to recognize that even landscape need not last: 'At any moment guns would rake that land into furrows; planes splinter Bolney Minster into smithereens and blast the Folly. He, too, loved the view' (p. 34). Division, continuity, contiguity: all are phases of time.

Where land earlier joined Britain to the continent, aeroplanes do so now. The vicar's attempted summation of meaning is scattered by the roar of military aircraft overhead. Again, the communal chatter says it: 'I agree – things look worse than ever on the continent. And what's the channel, come to think of it, if they mean to invade us? The aeroplanes, I didn't like to say it, made one think . . .' (p. 118). The outrage of the present burns through but is not allowed predominance within the novel.

The pageant stylizes a peaceable vision of England, re-cast as literature and tableau, landscape and cattle. Its language is busy with the clutter of human desires and their passing. Perhaps there is in its liberalism an allusion to E. M. Forster's village pageant, *England's Pleasant Land*, which was given at Milton Court, near Dorking in July 1938. Certainly the persistent anxiety in *Between the Acts* about a downpour of rain washing out the day (one shared by all organizers of outdoor events in Britain) is borne out by the fate of Forster's pageant: 'Wet, black cold – worst July on record – Morgan's pageant.'[14]

Miss La Trobe's is a revisionary play which cuts out the army and the Grand Ensemble to the discomfiture of some of the audience: 'Also, why leave out the Army, as my husband was saying, if it's history?' (p. 117) The pageant makes few concessions to that ritual patriotism that combines church, state, and armed forces:

> 'What's she keeping us waiting for?' Colonel Mayhew asked irritably . . .
> Mrs. Mayhew agreed. Unless of course she was going to end with a Grand Ensemble. Army; Navy; Union Jack; and behind them perhaps – Mrs. Mayhew sketched what she would have done had it been her pageant – the Church. In cardboard. (p. 106)

Instead, Miss La Trobe confronts her audience with silence and with mirrors: the present moment; emptiness; themselves; dispersal; diaspora.

It is an extraordinary liquidation of the expected triumphalist summary. Present readers, for whom the genre of the Empire Day pageant is unknown, do not perhaps fully grasp the comic and disturbing impertinence of Miss La Trobe's conclusion. While she was first absorbed in imagining *Pointz Hall*, on 3 May 1938, Woolf visited St Albans: '& saw Roman pavements, guarded by men in overcoats, attending upon imbecile sons. Had tea, & heard the local ladies discussing the Empire Day celebrations, which are to include a red white & blue cake decorated with flags. What will they say to 3 Gs?'[15]

Woolf, like La Trobe, is the outsider, averse to imperial celebrations (and also snooty about popular taste). By the next week Woolf had decided that *Pointz Hall* was to be a play: on 9 May she wrote of 'a patchy week': 'cant settle either to my Play (Pointz Hall is to become in the end a play) or to Roger's Cambridge letters.'[16]

Woolf felt herself an outsider in Sussex at the start of the war though she tried to find ways of involving herself in the village community at Rodmell. She was asked by the local Women's Institute to write a play for them. (As most British readers will know, the Women's Institute is a national organization devoted to rural skills within the home for women and at that time much involved in the war effort.) Though she refused to write, Woolf did become embroiled in village rehearsals of dull plays, about which she wrote in her diary with a venomous distaste: 'I'm bored: bored and appalled by the readymade commonplaceness of these plays: which they cant act unless we help. I mean, the minds so cheap, compared with ours, like a bad novel.' Recognizing her own middle-class insolence, she defends herself by arguing that what appals her is 'the simper' ... 'the conventionality'. The battening-down of imagination in the material performed by the Women's Institute is what disgusts her. Elsewhere in the diary at the same time she is writing admiringly about individual workers in the village, picking up scraps of speech for her novel, and commenting on the imaginative power of rumour, which draws on 'a surplus of unused imagination'.[17]

The anger that Woolf experiences is ugly; some of it goes compellingly into Miss La Trobe who is always at odds with her cast, urging them on, gnashing her teeth, crushing her manuscript, hiding in the bushes, a loner who sees because she is separate, pugnacious, imaginative: the one who can imagine community because she is cast out (p. 74). Miss La Trobe has lost her lesbian partner and is distrusted in the village. Her name suggests *trope*, perhaps: those liturgical phrases whose frequent repetition makes it possible to embellish and re-order them without erasing communal meaning. As Mitchell Leaska points out in his useful annotations to the early drafts, her name also suggests a troubadour, and means 'invention'.

Isa at the end of the day broods: 'Love and hate – how they tore her asunder! Surely it was time someone invented a new plot, or that the author came out from the bushes . . .' (pp. 127–8). Neither Miss La Trobe nor Virginia Woolf will come out from the bushes. Woolf works by dispersal. At one moment in the text Miss La Trobe glimpses an idea for a new play, more scattered and domestic than her pageant, but she can't get it and shrugs it off. That other play is very like parts of *Between the Acts*:

> Miss La Trobe stopped her pacing and surveyed the scene. 'It has the makings . . .' she murmured. For another play always lay behind the play she had just written. Shading her eyes, she looked. The butterflies circling; the light changing; the children leaping; the mothers laughing— 'No, I don't get it,' she muttered and resumed her pacing. (p. 40)

In the event, *Between the Acts* includes both play and audience, both acts and intermissions. By this move, Woolf is able to range across many voices, unnamed, and many desires, unknown, even while the play is watched communally in the open air. She recaptures the condition of 'Anon', that communal playwright she described in the new project she was developing alongside *Between the Acts*. But she made room also for the reader: 'There is a long drawn continuity in the book that the play has not. It gives a different pace to the mind. We are in a world where nothing is concluded.' So ends her draft chapter on the reader in her projected work 'Turning the Page'.[18] The resistance to conclusion had a particular political and emotional force at the outbreak of war. She is able to include the anxieties of authorship and the puzzled authority of the audience or reader. She is able also to include the uncontrollable, unforeseeable natural world: the rain that suddenly falls, the cow's bellow, the swallows sweeping between England and Africa.

Woolf wants to explore how England came to be; and how it came to be as she described it in *Three Guineas*, patriarchal, imperialist, and class-ridden. *Between the Acts* acknowledges those characteristics, but faced with the probable obliteration of people, landscape, and history in the war, Woolf sought to produce another idea of England, one which might survive, but survive without portentousness – as mixture and common place.

NOTES

Readers will find detailed bibliographical references and explanation of allusions for passages quoted in the Introduction in the end notes and commentary

1. *Diary*, V, 15 May 1940, p. 284; 7 June 1940, p. 292; 9 June 1940, pp. 292–3.
2. *Diary*, V, 26 April 1938, p. 135.
3. 'I'm reading Ruth Benedict with pressure of suggestions – about Culture patterns – which suggests rather too much' (*Diary*, V, 26 July 1940, p. 306). The influential American anthropologist Ruth Benedict was Woolf's close contemporary (1887–1948). Benedict worked with Franz Boas and influenced Margaret Mead. Woolf here refers to Benedict's *Patterns of Culture* (Houghton Mifflin, 1934). Her later book *Race: Science and Politics* (Modern Age Books, N.Y., 1940) appeared while Woolf was writing *BA*. For extensive discussion of Woolf's possible debts to Jane Harrison see Patricia Maika, *Virginia Woolf's Between the Acts and Jane Harrison's Conspiracy* (U.M.I. Research Press, 1987) and Jane Marcus, *Virginia Woolf and the Languages of Patriarchy* (Indiana University Press, 1987).
4. Letter to Ethel Smyth, 20 August 1939, *Letters*, VI, p. 352.
5. Letter to Vita Sackville-West, 29 August 1939, *Letters*, VI, p. 355.
6. *Diary*, V, 27 June 1940, p. 299.
7. *Diary*, V, 22 June 1940, p. 298.
8. This edition prefers 'scurred' to the first edition's 'scrurred', see Appendix, p. 149. Though 'scrurred' may be happy accident, its

combination of *scrunch* and *whirred* is typical of Woolf's portmanteau words and provides a richer onomatopoeia.

9. 'Craftsmanship', Broadcast on 20 April 1937 in a series called 'Words Fail Me', *The Death of the Moth* (Hogarth Press, 1942, p. 129).

10. ibid. p. 130.

11. Stuart N. Clarke, 'The Horse with a Green Tail', *Virginia Woolf Miscellany*, no. 34, 1990, pp. 3–4. See below, p. 133, note 20, and *The Times*, 28, 29, 30 June, 20, 26, 30 July 1938.

12. *Diary*, V, 29 September–2 October, pp. 176–8.

13. Mitchell Leaska, *Pointz Hall: The Earlier and Later Typescripts* (University Publications, 1983, p. 199).

14. *Diary*, V, 17 July 1938, p. 156 and note.

15. *Diary*, V, 3 May 1938, pp. 138–9.

16. *Diary*, V, 9 May 1938, p. 139.

17. *Diary*, V, 29 May 1940, p. 288; 31 May 1940, p. 291.

18. '"Anon" and "The Reader": Virginia Woolf's Last Essays', edited with an Introduction and Commentary by Brenda Silver, *Twentieth Century Literature*, XXV, 1979, pp. 356–435.

Further Reading

Elizabeth Abel, *Virginia Woolf and the Fictions of Psychoanalysis* (Chicago University Press, 1989).

Gillian Beer, 'Virginia Woolf and Pre-History', *Arguing with the Past* (Routledge, 1989).

'The Island and the Aeroplane: The Case of Virginia Woolf' in *Nation and Narration*, ed. Homi Bhabha (Routledge, 1990).

Mitchell A. Leaska (ed.), *Pointz Hall: The Earlier and Later Typescripts* (University Publications, 1983).

Jane Marcus, *Virginia Woolf and the Languages of Patriarchy* (Indiana University Press, 1987).

J. Hillis Miller, *Fiction and Repetition: Seven English Novels* (Harvard University Press, 1982).

Roger Poole, *The Unknown Virginia Woolf*, 3rd edn (Humanities Press International, 1990).

Sally Sears, 'Theater of War: Virginia Woolf's *Between the Acts*', in *Virginia Woolf: A Feminist Slant*, ed. Jane Marcus (University of Nebraska Press, 1983).

Brenda R. Silver (ed.), '"Anon" and "The Reader": Virginia Woolf's Last Essays', *Twentieth Century Literature*, XXV, 1979.

Alex Zwerdling, *Virginia Woolf and the Real World* (University of California Press, 1986).

A Note on the Text

The text of this edition of *Between the Acts* is based on the original British edition published by The Hogarth Press, London, on 17 July 1941; there was a second impression in July 1941 and a third impression in September 1941. The first American edition was published by Harcourt, Brace & Company, New York, on 2 October 1941.

As usual, the author's final typescript was sent to her British printers (in this case The Garden City Press Ltd, Letchworth, Hertfordshire), who produced two sets of proofs, one of which was to be sent when corrected to Harcourt, Brace & Company in order to serve as copy for the first American edition. At this stage it had been Virginia Woolf's practice to make final revisions to the text of her novel, altering the proofs accordingly, but not doing so consistently in both sets of proofs, with the result that variant authorial readings exist in the British and American editions. However, she having died in March 1941, before her final typescript was sent to the printers, her last novel was seen through the press by Leonard Woolf. Consequently there are very few differences between the two texts; only twenty variants, most of them unimportant, have been selected for listing by James M. Haule and Philip H. Smith, Jr, in their *Concordance to 'Between the Acts'* (Oxford University Press, 1982). In the Appendix to the present edition only such variant readings of the first American edition as have been adopted in this edition have been listed.

The author's final typescript is in the Henry W. and Albert A. Berg Collection of English and American Literature in the New York Public Library. It has not been possible to collate it for the present edition. Mitchell A. Leaska states that it is 'almost identical to the published text'.* He has transcribed and edited the two typescripts (also in the Berg Collection) that preceded it, denoting these as the earlier typescript (*ETS*) and the later typescript (*LTS*) respectively. His edition of these two typescripts has been collated with the first British edition for the present edition, and in nineteen instances (recorded in the Appendix) the readings of *LTS* have warranted substantive emendations. Very few emendations of a non-substantive kind have been made, Virginia Woolf's characteristically light punctuation being usually retained; all such emendations are consistent either with *LTS*'s version of the passage in question or with the first British edition's practice elsewhere. It has not been thought necessary to offer the reader a list of these minor emendations.

Stella McNichol 1991

---

* Mitchell A. Leaska (ed.), *Pointz Hall: The Earlier and Later Typescripts of 'Between the Acts'* (University Publications, New York, 1983), p. 17.

BETWEEN THE ACTS

NOTE

The MS. of this book had been completed, but had not been finally revised for the printer, at the time of Virginia Woolf's death. She would not, I believe, have made any large or material alterations in it, though she would probably have made a good many small corrections or revisions before passing the final proofs.

Leonard Woolf.

It was a summer's night and they were talking, in the big room with the windows open to the garden, about the cesspool. The county council had promised to bring water to the village, but they hadn't.

Mrs. Haines, the wife of the gentleman farmer, a goosefaced woman with eyes protruding as if they saw something to gobble in the gutter, said affectedly: 'What a subject to talk about on a night like this!'

Then there was silence; and a cow coughed; and that led her to say how odd it was, as a child, she had never feared cows, only horses. But, then, as a small child in a perambulator, a great cart-horse had brushed within an inch of her face. Her family, she told the old man in the arm-chair, had lived near Liskeard[1] for many centuries. There were the graves in the churchyard to prove it.

A bird chuckled outside. 'A nightingale?' asked Mrs. Haines. No, nightingales didn't come so far north. It was a daylight bird, chuckling over the substance and succulence of the day, over worms, snails, grit, even in sleep.

The old man in the arm-chair – Mr. Oliver, of the Indian Civil Service, retired – said that the site they had chosen for the cesspool was, if he had heard aright, on the Roman road. From an aeroplane, he said, you could still see, plainly marked, the scars made by the Britons; by the Romans; by the Elizabethan manor house; and by the plough, when they ploughed the hill to grow wheat in the Napoleonic wars.

'But you don't remember . . .' Mrs. Haines began. No, not that. Still he did remember— and he was about to tell them what, when there was a sound outside, and Isa, his son's wife, came in with her hair in pigtails; she was wearing a dressing-gown with faded peacocks on it. She came in like a swan swimming its way; then was checked and stopped; was surprised to find people there; and lights burning. She had been sitting with her little boy who wasn't well, she apologized. What had they been saying?

'Discussing the cesspool,' said Mr. Oliver.

'What a subject to talk about on a night like this!' Mrs. Haines exclaimed again.

What had *he* said about the cesspool; or indeed about anything? Isa wondered, inclining her head towards the gentleman farmer, Rupert Haines. She had met him at a Bazaar; and at a tennis party. He had handed her a cup and a racquet – that was all. But in his ravaged face she always felt mystery; and in his silence, passion. At the tennis party she had felt this, and at the Bazaar. Now a third time, if anything more strongly, she felt it again.

'I remember,' the old man interrupted, 'my mother . . .' Of his mother he remembered that she was very stout; kept her tea-caddy locked; yet had given him in that very room a copy of Byron. It was over sixty years ago, he told them, that his mother had given him the works of Byron in that very room. He paused.

'She walks in beauty like the night,' he quoted.

Then again:

'So we'll go no more a-roving by the light of the moon.'[2]

Isa raised her head. The words made two rings, perfect rings, that floated them, herself and Haines, like two swans down stream. But his snow-white breast was circled with a tangle of dirty duckweed; and she too, in her webbed feet was entangled, by her husband, the stockbroker. Sitting on her three-cornered chair she swayed, with her dark pigtails hanging, and her body like a bolster in its faded dressing-gown.

Mrs. Haines was aware of the emotion circling them, excluding her. She waited, as one waits for the strain of an organ to die out before leaving church. In the car going home to the red villa in the cornfields, she would destroy it, as a thrush pecks the wings off a butterfly. Allowing ten seconds to intervene, she rose; paused; and then, as if she had heard the last strain die out, offered Mrs. Giles Oliver her hand.

But Isa, though she should have risen at the same moment that Mrs. Haines rose, sat on. Mrs. Haines glared at her out of goose-like eyes, gobbling, 'Please, Mrs. Giles Oliver, do me the kindness to recognize my existence . . .' which she was forced to do, rising at last from her chair, in her faded dressing-gown, with the pigtails falling over each shoulder.

Pointz Hall was seen in the light of an early summer morning to be a middle-sized house. It did not rank among the houses that are mentioned in guide books. It was too homely. But this whitish house with the grey roof, and the wing thrown out at right angles, lying unfortunately low on the meadow with a fringe of trees on the bank above it so that smoke curled up to the nests of the rooks, was a desirable house to live in. Driving past, people said to each other: 'I wonder if that'll ever come into the market?' And to the chauffeur: 'Who lives there?'

The chauffeur didn't know. The Olivers, who had bought the place something over a century ago, had no connection with the Warings, the Elveys, the Mannerings or the Burnets; the old families who had all inter-married, and lay in their deaths inter-twisted, like the ivy roots, beneath the churchyard wall.

Only something over a hundred and twenty years the Olivers had been there. Still, on going up the principal staircase – there was another, a mere ladder at the back for the servants – there was a portrait. A length of yellow brocade was visible half-way up; and, as one reached the top, a small powdered face, a great head-dress slung with pearls, came into view; an ancestress of sorts. Six or seven bedrooms opened out of the corridor. The butler had been a soldier; had married a lady's maid; and, under a glass case, there was a watch that had stopped a bullet on the field of Waterloo.

It was early morning. The dew was on the grass. The church clock struck eight times. Mrs. Swithin[3] drew the curtain in her bedroom – the faded white chintz that so agreeably from the outside tinged the window with its green lining. There with her old hands on the hasp, jerking it open, she stood: old Oliver's married sister; a widow. She always meant to set up a house of her own; perhaps in Kensington, perhaps at Kew, so that she could have the benefit of the gardens. But she stayed on all through the summer; and when winter wept its damp upon the panes, and choked the gutters with dead leaves, she said: 'Why, Bart, did they build the house in the hollow, facing north?' Her brother said, 'Obviously to escape from nature. Weren't four horses needed to drag the family coach through the mud?' Then he told her the famous story of the great eighteenth-century winter; when for a whole month the house had been blocked by snow. And the trees had fallen. So every year, when winter came, Mrs. Swithin retired to Hastings.

But it was summer now. She had been waked by the birds. How they sang! attacking the dawn like so many choir boys attacking an iced cake. Forced to listen, she had stretched for her favourite reading – an Outline of History[4] – and had spent the hours between three and five thinking of rhododendron forests in Piccadilly; when the entire continent, not then, she understood, divided by a channel, was all one; populated, she understood, by elephant-bodied, seal-necked, heaving, surging, slowly writhing, and, she supposed, barking monsters; the iguanodon, the mammoth, and the mastodon; from whom presumably, she thought, jerking the window open, we descend.

It took her five seconds in actual time, in mind time ever so much longer, to separate Grace herself, with blue china on a tray, from the leather-covered grunting monster who was about, as the door opened, to demolish a whole tree in the green steaming undergrowth of the primeval forest. Naturally, she jumped, as Grace put the tray down and said: 'Good morning, Ma'am.' 'Batty,' Grace called her, as she felt on her face the divided glance that was half meant for a beast in a swamp, half for a maid in a print frock and white apron.

'How those birds sing!' said Mrs. Swithin, at a venture. The window was open now; the birds certainly were singing. An obliging thrush hopped across the lawn; a coil of pinkish rubber twisted in its beak. Tempted by the sight to continue her imaginative reconstruction of the past, Mrs. Swithin paused; she was given to increasing the bounds of the moment by flights into past or future; or sidelong down corridors and alleys; but she remembered her mother – her mother in that very room rebuking her. 'Don't stand gaping, Lucy, or the wind'll change ...'[5] How often her mother had rebuked her in that very room –

'but in a very different world,' as her brother would remind her. So she sat down to morning tea, like any other old lady with a high nose, thin cheeks, a ring on her finger and the usual trappings of rather shabby but gallant old age, which included in her case a cross gleaming gold on her breast.

The nurses after breakfast were trundling the perambulator up and down the terrace; and as they trundled they were talking – not shaping pellets of information or handing ideas from one to another, but rolling words, like sweets on their tongues; which, as they thinned to transparency, gave off pink, green, and sweetness. This morning that sweetness was: 'How cook had told 'im off about the asparagus; how when she rang I said: how it was a sweet costume with blouse to match;' and that was leading to something about a feller as they walked up and down the terrace rolling sweets, trundling the perambulator.

It was a pity that the man who had built Pointz Hall had pitched the house in a hollow, when beyond the flower garden and the vegetables there was this stretch of high ground. Nature had provided a site for a house; man had built his house in a hollow. Nature had provided a stretch of turf half a mile in length and level, till it suddenly dipped to the lily pool. The terrace was broad enough to take the entire shadow of one of the great trees laid flat. There you could walk up and down, up and down, under the shade of the trees. Two or three grew close together; then there were gaps. Their roots broke the turf, and among those bones were green waterfalls and cushions of grass in which violets grew in spring or in summer the wild purple orchis.

Amy was saying something about a feller when Mabel, with her hand on the pram, turned sharply, her sweet swallowed. 'Leave off grubbing,' she said sharply. 'Come along, George.'

The little boy had lagged and was grouting in the grass. Then the baby, Caro, thrust her fist out over the coverlet and the furry bear was jerked overboard. Amy had to stoop. George grubbed.[6] The flower blazed between the angles of the roots. Membrane after membrane was torn. It blazed a soft yellow, a lambent light under a film of velvet; it filled the caverns behind the eyes with light. All that inner darkness became a hall, leaf smelling, earth smelling, of yellow light. And the tree was beyond the flower; the grass, the flower and the tree were entire. Down on his knees grubbing he held the flower complete. Then there was a roar and a hot breath and a stream of coarse grey hair rushed between him and the flower. Up he leapt, toppling in his fright, and saw coming towards him a terrible peaked eyeless monster moving on legs, brandishing arms.

'Good morning, sir,' a hollow voice boomed at him from a beak of paper.

The old man had sprung upon him from his hiding-place behind a tree.

'Say good morning, George; say "Good morning, Grandpa,"' Mabel urged him, giving him a push towards the man. But George stood gaping. George stood gazing. Then Mr. Oliver crumpled the paper which he had cocked into a snout and appeared in person. A very tall old man, with gleaming eyes, wrinkled cheeks, and a head with no hair on it. He turned.

'Heel!' he bawled, 'heel, you brute!' And George turned; and the nurses turned holding the furry bear; they all turned to look at Sohrab[7] the Afghan hound bounding and bouncing among the flowers.

'Heel!' the old man bawled, as if he were commanding a regiment. It was impressive, to the nurses, the way an old boy of his age could still bawl and make a brute like that obey him. Back came the Afghan hound, sidling, apologetic. And as he cringed at the old man's feet, a string was slipped over his collar; the noose that old Oliver always carried with him.

'You wild beast . . . you bad beast,' he grumbled, stooping. George looked at the dog only. The hairy flanks were sucked in and out; there was a blob of foam on its nostrils. He burst out crying.

Old Oliver raised himself, his veins swollen, his cheeks flushed; he was angry. His little game with the paper hadn't worked. The boy was a cry-baby. He nodded and sauntered on, smoothing out the crumpled paper and muttering, as he tried to find his line in the column, 'A cry-baby — a cry-baby.' But the breeze blew the great sheet out; and over the edge he surveyed the landscape – flowing fields, heath and woods. Framed, they became a picture. Had he been a painter, he would have fixed his easel here, where the country, barred by trees, looked like a picture. Then the breeze fell.

'M. Daladier,'[8] he read finding his place in the column, 'has been successful in pegging down the franc . . .'

Mrs. Giles Oliver drew the comb through the thick tangle of hair which, after giving the matter her best attention, she had never had shingled or bobbed;[9] and lifted the heavily embossed silver brush that had been a wedding present and had its uses in impressing chambermaids in hotels. She lifted it and stood in front of the three-folded mirror, so that she could see three separate versions of her rather heavy, yet handsome, face; and also, outside the glass, a slip of terrace, lawn and tree tops.

Inside the glass, in her eyes, she saw what she had felt over-night for the ravaged, the silent, the romantic gentleman farmer. 'In love,' was in her eyes. But outside, on the washstand, on the dressing-table, among the silver boxes and tooth-brushes, was the other love; love for her husband, the stockbroker – 'The father of my children,' she added, slipping into the cliché conveniently provided by fiction. Inner love was in the eyes; outer love on the dressing-table. But what feeling was it that stirred in her now when above the looking-glass, out of doors, she saw coming across the lawn the perambulator; two nurses; and her little boy George, lagging behind?

She tapped on the window with her embossed hairbrush. They were too far off to hear. The drone of the trees was in their ears; the chirp of birds; other incidents of garden life, inaudible, invisible to her in the bedroom, absorbed them. Isolated on a green island, hedged about with snowdrops, laid with a counterpane of puckered silk, the innocent island floated under her window. Only George lagged behind.

She returned to her eyes in the looking-glass. 'In love,' she must be; since the presence of his body in the room last night could so affect her; since the words he said, handing her a teacup, handing her a tennis racquet, could so attach themselves to a certain spot in her; and thus lie between them like a wire, tingling, tangling, vibrating — she groped, in the depths of the looking-glass, for a word to fit the infinitely quick vibrations of the aeroplane propeller that she had seen once at dawn at Croydon.[10] Faster, faster, faster, it whizzed, whirred, buzzed, till all the flails became one flail and up soared the plane away and away . . .

'Where we know not, where we go not, neither know nor care,' she hummed. 'Flying, rushing through the ambient, incandescent, summer silent . . .'

The rhyme was 'air.' She put down her brush. She took up the telephone.

'Three, four, eight, Pyecombe,' she said.

'Mrs. Oliver speaking . . . What fish have you this morning? Cod? Halibut? Sole? Plaice?'

'There to lose what binds us here,' she murmured. 'Soles. Filleted.[11] In time for lunch please,' she said aloud. 'With a feather, a blue feather . . . flying mounting through the air . . . there to lose what binds us here . . .' The words weren't worth writing in the book bound like an account book in case Giles suspected. 'Abortive,' was the word that expressed her. She never came out of a shop, for example, with the clothes she admired; nor did her figure, seen against the dark roll of trousering in a shop window, please her. Thick of waist, large of limb, and, save for her hair, fashionable in the tight modern way, she never looked like Sappho,[12] or one of the beautiful young men whose photographs adorned the weekly papers. She looked what she was: Sir Richard's daughter; and niece of the two old ladies at Wimbledon who were so proud, being O'Neils, of their descent from the Kings of Ireland.

A foolish, flattering lady, pausing on the threshold of what she once called 'the heart of the house,' the threshold of the library, had once said: 'Next to the kitchen, the library's always the nicest room in the house.' Then she added, stepping across the threshold: 'Books are the mirrors of the soul.'

In this case a tarnished, a spotted soul. For as the train took over three hours to reach this remote village in the very heart of England, no one ventured so long a journey, without staving off possible mind-hunger, without buying a book on a bookstall. Thus the mirror that reflected the soul sublime, reflected also the soul bored. Nobody could pretend, as they looked at the shuffle of shilling shockers that week-enders had dropped, that the looking-glass always reflected the anguish of a Queen or the heroism of King Harry.

At this early hour of a June morning the library was empty. Mrs. Giles had to visit the kitchen. Mr. Oliver still tramped the terrace. And Mrs. Swithin was of course at church. The light but variable breeze,[13] foretold by the weather expert, flapped the yellow curtain, tossing light, then shadow. The fire greyed, then glowed, and the tortoiseshell butterfly beat on the lower pane of the window; beat, beat, beat; repeating that if no human being ever came, never, never, never, the books would be mouldy, the fire out and the tortoiseshell butterfly dead on the pane.

Heralded by the impetuosity of the Afghan hound, the old man entered. He had read his paper; he was drowsy; and so sank down into the chintz-covered chair with the dog at his feet – the Afghan hound. His nose on his paws, his haunches drawn up, he looked a stone dog, a crusader's dog,[14] guarding even in the realms of death the sleep of his master. But the master was not dead; only dreaming; drowsily, seeing as in a glass,[15] its lustre spotted, himself, a young man helmeted; and a cascade falling. But no water;[16] and the hills, like grey stuff pleated; and in the sand a hoop of ribs; a bullock maggot-eaten in the sun; and in the shadow of the rock, savages; and in his hand a gun. The dream hand clenched; the real hand lay on the chair arm, the veins swollen but only with a brownish fluid now.

The door opened.

'Am I,' Isa apologized, 'interrupting?'

Of course she was – destroying youth and India. It was his fault, since she had persisted in stretching his thread of life so fine, so far. Indeed he was grateful to her, watching her as she strolled about the room, for continuing.

Many old men had only their India – old men in clubs, old

men in rooms off Jermyn Street. She in her striped dress continued him, murmuring, in front of the book cases: 'The moor is dark beneath the moon,[17] rapid clouds have drunk the last pale beams of even ... I have ordered the fish,' she said aloud, turning, 'though whether it'll be fresh or not I can't promise. But veal is dear, and everybody in the house is sick of beef and mutton ... Sohrab,' she said, coming to a standstill in front of them, 'What's *he* been doing?'

His tail never wagged. He never admitted the ties of domesticity. Either he cringed or he bit. Now his wild yellow eyes gazed at her, gazed at him. He could outstare them both. Then Oliver remembered:

'Your little boy's a cry-baby,' he said scornfully.

'Oh,' she sighed, pegged down on a chair arm, like a captive balloon, by a myriad of hair-thin ties into domesticity. 'What's been happening?'

'I took the newspaper,' he explained, 'so . . .'

He took it and crumpled it into a beak over his nose. 'So,' he had sprung out from behind a tree on to the children.

'And he howled. He's a coward, your boy is.'

She frowned. He was not a coward, her boy wasn't. And she loathed the domestic, the possessive; the maternal. And he knew it and did it on purpose to tease her, the old brute, her father-in-law.

She looked away.

'The library's always the nicest room in the house,' she quoted, and ran her eyes along the books. 'The mirror of the soul' books were. *The Faerie Queene* and Kinglake's *Crimea*; Keats and the *Kreutzer Sonata*.[18] There they were, reflecting. What? What remedy was there for her at her age – the age of the century, thirty-nine – in books? Book-shy she was, like the rest of her generation; and gun-shy too. Yet as a person with a raging tooth runs her eye in a chemist's shop over green bottles with gilt scrolls on them lest one of them may contain a cure, she considered: Keats and Shelley; Yeats and Donne. Or perhaps not a poem; a life. The life of Garibaldi. The life of Lord Palmerston. Or perhaps not a person's life; a county's. *The Antiquities of Durham*; *The Proceedings of the Archæological Society of Nottingham*. Or not a life at all, but science – Eddington, Darwin, or Jeans.[19]

None of them stopped her toothache. For her generation the newspaper was a book; and, as her father-in-law had dropped the *Times*, she took it and read: 'A horse with a green tail . . .'[20] which was fantastic. Next, 'The guard at Whitehall . . .' which was romantic and then, building word upon word, she read: 'The troopers told her the horse had a green tail; but she found it was just an ordinary horse. And they dragged her up to the barrack room where she was thrown upon a bed. Then one of the troopers removed part of her clothing, and she screamed and hit him about the face . . .'

That was real; so real that on the mahogany door panels she saw the Arch in Whitehall; through the Arch the barrack room; in the barrack room the bed, and on the bed the girl was screaming and hitting him about the face, when the door (for in fact it was a door) opened and in came Mrs. Swithin carrying a hammer.

She advanced, sidling, as if the floor were fluid under her shabby garden shoes, and, advancing, pursed her lips and smiled, sidelong, at her brother. Not a word passed between them as she went to the cupboard in the corner and replaced the hammer, which she had taken without asking leave; together – she unclosed her fist – with a handful of nails.

'Cindy – Cindy,' he growled, as she shut the cupboard door.

Lucy, his sister, was three years younger than he was. The name Cindy, or Sindy, for it could be spelt either way, was short for Lucy. It was by this name that he had called her when they were children; when she had trotted after him as he fished, and had made the meadow flowers into tight little bunches, winding one long grass stalk round and round and round. Once, she remembered, he had made her take the fish off the hook herself. The blood had shocked her – 'Oh!' she had cried – for the gills were full of blood. And he had growled: 'Cindy!' The ghost of that morning in the meadow was in her mind as she replaced the hammer where it belonged on one shelf; and the nails where they belonged on another; and shut the cupboard about which, for he still kept his fishing tackle there, he was still so very particular.

'I've been nailing the placard on the Barn,' she said, giving him a little pat on the shoulder.

The words were like the first peal of a chime of bells. As the first peals, you hear the second; as the second peals, you hear the third. So when Isa heard Mrs. Swithin say: 'I've been nailing the placard on the Barn,' she knew she would say next:

'For the pageant.'

And he would say:

'Today? By Jupiter! I'd forgotten!'

'If it's fine,' Mrs. Swithin continued, 'they'll act on the terrace . . .'

'And if it's wet,' Bartholomew continued, 'in the Barn.'

'And which will it be?' Mrs. Swithin continued. 'Wet or fine?'

Then, for the seventh time in succession, they both looked out of the window.

Every summer, for seven summers now, Isa had heard the same words; about the hammer and the nails; the pageant and the weather. Every year they said, would it be wet or fine; and every year it was — one or the other. The same chime followed the same chime, only this year beneath the chime she heard: 'The girl screamed and hit him about the face with a hammer.'

'The forecast,' said Mr. Oliver, turning the pages till he found it, 'says: Variable winds; fair average temperature; rain at times.'

He put down the paper, and they all looked at the sky to see whether the sky obeyed the meteorologist. Certainly the weather was variable. It was green in the garden one moment; grey the next. Here came the sun — an illimitable rapture of joy, embracing every flower, every leaf. Then in compassion it withdrew, covering its face, as if it forebore to look on human suffering. There was a fecklessness, a lack of symmetry and order in the clouds, as they thinned and thickened. Was it their own law, or no law, they obeyed? Some were wisps of white hair merely. One, high up, very distant, had hardened to golden alabaster; was made of immortal marble. Beyond that was blue, pure blue, black blue; blue that had never filtered down; that had escaped registration. It never fell as sun, shadow, or rain upon the world, but disregarded the little coloured ball of earth entirely. No flower felt it; no field; no garden.

Mrs. Swithin's eyes glazed as she looked at it. Isa thought her gaze was fixed because she saw God there, God on his throne.

But as a shadow fell next moment on the garden Mrs. Swithin loosed and lowered her fixed look and said:

'It's very unsettled. It'll rain, I'm afraid. We can only pray,' she added, and fingered her crucifix.

'And provide umbrellas,' said her brother.

Lucy flushed. He had struck her faith. When she said 'pray,' he added 'umbrellas.' She half covered the cross with her fingers. She shrank; she cowered; but next moment she exclaimed:

'Oh there they are — the darlings!'

The perambulator was passing across the lawn.

Isa looked too. What an angel she was — the old woman! Thus to salute the children; to beat up against those immensities and the old man's irreverences her skinny hands, her laughing eyes! How courageous to defy Bart and the weather!

'He looks blooming,' said Mrs. Swithin.

'It's astonishing how they pick up,' said Isa.

'He ate his breakfast?' Mrs. Swithin asked.

'Every scrap,' said Isa.

'And baby? No sign of measles?'

Isa shook her head. 'Touch wood,' she added, tapping the table.

'Tell me, Bart,' said Mrs. Swithin turning to her brother, 'what's the origin of that? Touch wood . . . Antaeus, didn't he touch earth?'

She would have been, he thought, a very clever woman, had she fixed her gaze. But this led to that; that to the other. What went in at this ear, went out at that. And all were circled, as happens after seventy, by one recurring question. Hers was, should she live at Kensington or at Kew? But every year, when winter came, she did neither. She took lodgings at Hastings.

'Touch wood; touch earth; Antaeus,'[21] he muttered, bringing the scattered bits together. Lemprière would settle it; or the Encyclopædia.[22] But it was not in books the answer to his question — why, in Lucy's skull, shaped so much like his own, there existed a prayable being? She didn't, he supposed, invest it with hair, teeth or toe-nails. It was, he supposed, more of a force or a radiance, controlling the thrush and the worm; the tulip and the hound; and himself, too, an old man with swollen veins. It got her out of bed on a cold morning and sent her down the muddy path to worship it, whose mouthpiece was Streatfield. A good fellow, who smoked cigars in the vestry. He needed some solace, doling out preachments to asthmatic elders, perpetually repairing the perpetually falling steeple, by means of placards nailed to Barns. The love, he was thinking, that they should give to flesh and blood they give to the church ... when Lucy rapping her fingers on the table said:

'What's the origin – the origin – of that?'

'Superstition,' he said.

She flushed, and the little breath too was audible that she drew in as once more he struck a blow at her faith. But, brother and sister, flesh and blood was not a barrier, but a mist. Nothing changed their affection; no argument; no fact; no truth. What she saw he didn't; what he saw she didn't – and so on, *ad infinitum*.

'Cindy,' he growled. And the quarrel was over.

The Barn to which Lucy had nailed her placard was a great building in the farmyard. It was as old as the church, and built of the same stone, but it had no steeple. It was raised on cones of grey stone at the corners to protect it from rats and damp. Those who had been to Greece always said it reminded them of a temple. Those who had never been to Greece – the majority – admired it all the same. The roof was weathered red-orange; and inside it was a hollow hall, sun-shafted, brown, smelling of corn, dark when the doors were shut, but splendidly illuminated when the doors at the end stood open, as they did to let the wagons in – the long low wagons, like ships of the sea, breasting the corn, not the sea, returning in the evening shagged with hay. The lanes caught tufts where the wagons had passed.

Now benches were drawn across the floor of the Barn. If it rained, the actors were to act in the Barn; planks had been laid together at one end to form a stage. Wet or fine, the audience would take tea there. Young men and women – Jim, Iris, David, Jessica – were even now busy with garlands of red and white paper roses left over from the Coronation.[23] The seeds and the dust from the sacks made them sneeze. Iris had a handkerchief bound round her forehead; Jessica wore breeches. The young men worked in shirt sleeves. Pale husks had stuck in their hair, and it was easy to run a splinter of wood into the fingers.

'Old Flimsy' (Mrs. Swithin's nickname) had been nailing another placard on the Barn. The first had been blown down, or the village idiot, who always tore down what had been nailed up, had done it, and was chuckling over the placard under the shade of some hedge. The workers were laughing too, as if old Swithin had left a wake of laughter behind her. The old girl with a wisp of white hair flying, knobbed shoes as if she had claws corned like a canary's, and black stockings wrinkled over the ankles, naturally made David cock his eye and Jessica wink back, as she handed him a length of paper roses. Snobs they were; long enough stationed that is in that one corner of the world to have taken indelibly the print of some three hundred years of customary behaviour. So they laughed; but respected. If she wore pearls, pearls they were.

'Old Flimsy on the hop,' said David. She would be in and out twenty times, and finally bring them lemonade in a great jug and a plate of sandwiches. Jessie held the garland; he hammered. A hen strayed in; a file of cows passed the door; then a sheep dog; then the cowman, Bond,[24] who stopped.

He contemplated the young people hanging roses from one rafter to another. He thought very little of anybody, simples or gentry. Leaning, silent, sardonic, against the door he was like a withered willow, bent over a stream, all its leaves shed, and in his eyes the whimsical flow of the waters.

'Hi–huh!' he cried suddenly. It was cow language presumably, for the particoloured cow, who had thrust her head in at the door, lowered her horns, lashed her tail and ambled off. Bond followed after.

'That's the problem,' said Mrs. Swithin. While Mr. Oliver consulted the Encyclopædia searching under Superstition for the origin of the expression 'Touch Wood,' she and Isa discussed fish: whether, coming from a distance, it would be fresh.

They were so far from the sea. A hundred miles away, Mrs. Swithin said; no, perhaps a hundred and fifty. 'But they do say,' she continued, 'one can hear the waves on a still night. After a storm, they say, you can hear a wave break . . . I like that story,' she reflected. 'Hearing the waves in the middle of the night he saddled a horse and rode to the sea. Who was it, Bart, who rode to the sea?'

He was reading.

'You can't expect it brought to your door in a pail of water,' said Mrs. Swithin, 'as I remember when we were children, living in a house by the sea. Lobsters, fresh from the lobster pots. How they pinched the stick cook gave them! And salmon. You know if they're fresh because they have lice in their scales.'

Bartholomew nodded. A fact that was. He remembered, the house by the sea. And the lobster.

They were bringing up nets full of fish from the sea; but Isa was seeing – the garden, variable as the forecast said, in the light breeze. Again, the children passed, and she tapped on the window and blew them a kiss. In the drone of the garden it went unheeded.

'Are we really,' she said, turning round, 'a hundred miles from the sea?'

'Thirty-five only,' her father-in-law said, as if he had whipped a tape measure from his pocket and measured it exactly.

'It seems more,' said Isa. 'It seems from the terrace as if the land went on for ever and ever.'

'Once there was no sea,' said Mrs. Swithin. 'No sea at all between us and the continent. I was reading that in a book this morning. There were rhododendrons in the Strand; and mammoths in Piccadilly.'

'When we were savages,' said Isa.

Then she remembered; her dentist had told her that savages could perform very skilful operations on the brain. Savages had false teeth, he said. False teeth were invented, she thought he said, in the time of the Pharaohs.

'At least so my dentist told me,' she concluded.

'Which man d'you go to now?' Mrs. Swithin asked her.

'The same old couple; Batty and Bates in Sloane Street.'

'And Mr. Batty told you they had false teeth in the time of the Pharaohs?' Mrs. Swithin pondered.

'Batty? Oh not Batty. Bates,' Isa corrected her.

Batty, she recalled, only talked about Royalty. Batty, she told Mrs. Swithin, had a patient a Princess.

'So he kept me waiting well over an hour. And you know, when one's a child, how long that seems.'

'Marriages with cousins,' said Mrs. Swithin, 'can't be good for the teeth.'

Bart put his finger inside his mouth and projected the upper row outside his lips. They were false. Yet, he said, the Olivers hadn't married cousins. The Olivers couldn't trace their descent for more than two or three hundred years. But the Swithins could. The Swithins were there before the Conquest.[25]

'The Swithins,' Mrs. Swithin began. Then she stopped. Bart would crack another joke about Saints, if she gave him the chance. And she had had two jokes cracked at her already; one about an umbrella; another about superstition.

So she stopped and said, 'How did we begin this talk?' She counted on her fingers. 'The Pharaohs. Dentists. Fish . . . Oh yes, you were saying, Isa, you'd ordered fish; and you were afraid it wouldn't be fresh. And I said "That's the problem . . ."'

The fish had been delivered. Mitchell's boy, holding them in a crook of his arm, jumped off his motor bike. There was no feeding the pony with lumps of sugar at the kitchen door, nor time for gossip, since his round had been increased. He had to deliver right over the hill at Bickley; also go round by Waythorn, Roddam, and Pyeminster, whose names, like his own, were in Domesday Book.[26] But the cook – Mrs. Sands she was called, but by old friends Trixie – had never in all her fifty years been over the hill, nor wanted to.

He dabbed them down on the kitchen table, the filleted soles, the semi-transparent boneless fish. And before Mrs. Sands had time to peel the paper off, he was gone, giving a slap to the very fine yellow cat who rose majestically from the basket chair and advanced superbly to the table, winding the fish.

Were they a bit whiffy? Mrs. Sands held them to her nose. The cat rubbed itself this way, that way against the table legs, against her legs. She would save a slice for Sunny – his drawing-room name Sung-Yen had undergone a kitchen change into Sunny. She took them, the cat attendant, to the larder, and laid them on a plate in that semi-ecclesiastical apartment. For the house before the Reformation,[27] like so many houses in that neighbourhood, had a chapel; and the chapel had become a larder, changing, like the cat's name, as religion changed. The Master (his drawing-room name; in the kitchen they called him Bartie) would bring gentlemen sometimes to see the larder – often when cook wasn't dressed. Not to see the hams that hung from hooks, or the butter on a blue slate, or the joint for tomorrow's dinner, but to see the cellar that opened out of the larder and its carved arch. If you tapped – one gentleman had a hammer – there was a hollow sound; a reverberation; undoubtedly, he said, a concealed passage where once somebody had hid. So it might be. But Mrs. Sands wished they wouldn't come into her kitchen telling stories with the girls about. It put ideas into their silly heads. They heard dead men rolling barrels. They saw a white lady walking under the trees. No one would cross the terrace after dark. If a cat sneezed, 'There's the ghost!'

Sunny had his little bit off the fillet. Then Mrs. Sands took an egg from the brown basket full of eggs; some with yellow fluff sticking to the shells; then a pinch of flour to coat those semi-transparent slips; and a crust from the great earthenware crock full of crusts. Then, returning to the kitchen, she made those quick movements at the oven, cinder raking, stoking, damping, which sent strange echoes through the house, so that in the library, the sitting-room, the dining-room, and the nursery, whatever they were doing, thinking, saying, they knew, they all knew, it was getting on for breakfast, lunch, or dinner.

'The sandwiches . . .' said Mrs. Swithin, coming into the kitchen. She refrained from adding 'Sands' to 'sandwiches,' for Sand and sandwiches clashed. 'Never play,' her mother used to say, 'on people's names.' And Trixie was not a name that suited, as Sands did, the thin, acid woman, red-haired, sharp and clean, who never dashed off masterpieces, it was true; but then never dropped hairpins in the soup. 'What in the name of Thunder?' Bart had said, raising a hairpin in his spoon, in the old days, fifteen years ago, before Sands came, in the time of Jessie Pook.

Mrs. Sands fetched bread; Mrs. Swithin fetched ham. One cut the bread; the other the ham. It was soothing, it was consolidating, this handwork together. The cook's hands cut, cut, cut. Whereas Lucy, holding the loaf, held the knife up. Why's stale bread, she mused, easier to cut than fresh? And so skipped, sidelong, from yeast to alcohol; so to fermentation; so to inebriation; so to Bacchus;[28] and lay under purple lamps in a vineyard in Italy, as she had done, often; while Sands heard the clock tick; saw the cat; noted a fly buzz; and registered, as her lips showed, a grudge she mustn't speak against people making work in the kitchen while they had a high old time hanging paper roses in the barn.

'Will it be fine?' asked Mrs. Swithin, her knife suspended. In the kitchen they humoured old Mother Swithin's fancies.

'Seems like it,' said Mrs. Sands, giving her sharp look out of the kitchen window.

'It wasn't last year,' said Mrs. Swithin. 'D'you remember what a rush we had – when the rain came – getting in the chairs?' She cut again. Then she asked about Billy, Mrs. Sands's nephew, apprenticed to the butcher.

'He's been doing,' Mrs. Sands said, 'what boys shouldn't; cheeking the master.'

'That'll be all right,' said Mrs. Swithin, half meaning the boy, half meaning the sandwich, as it happened a very neat one, trimmed, triangular.

'Mr. Giles may be late,' she added, laying it, complacently, on top of the pile.

For Isa's husband, the stockbrocker,[29] was coming from London. And the local train, which met the express train, arrived by no means punctually, even if he caught the early train which was by no means certain. In which case it meant – but what it meant to Mrs. Sands, when people missed their trains, and she, whatever she might want to do, must wait, by the oven, keeping meat hot, no one knew.

'There!' said Mrs. Swithin, surveying the sandwiches, some

neat, some not. 'I'll take 'em to the barn.' As for the lemonade, she assumed, without a flicker of doubt, that Jane the kitchen-maid would follow after.

Candish paused in the dining-room to move a yellow rose. Yellow, white, carnation red – he placed them. He loved flowers, and arranging them, and placing the green sword or heart shaped leaf that came, fitly, between them. Queerly, he loved them, considering his gambling and drinking. The yellow rose went there. Now all was ready – silver and white, forks and napkins, and in the middle the splashed bowl of variegated roses. So, with one last look, he left the dining-room.

Two pictures hung opposite the window. In real life they had never met, the long lady and the man holding his horse by the rein. The lady was a picture,[30] bought by Oliver because he liked the picture; the man was an ancestor. He had a name. He held the rein in his hand. He had said to the painter:

'If you want my likeness, dang it sir, take it when the leaves are on the trees.' There were leaves on the trees. He had said: 'Ain't there room for Colin as well as Buster?' Colin was his famous hound. But there was only room for Buster. It was, he seemed to say, addressing the company not the painter, a damned shame to leave out Colin whom he wished buried at his feet, in the same grave, about 1750; but that skunk the Reverend Whats-hisname wouldn't allow it.

He was a talk producer, that ancestor. But the lady was a picture. In her yellow robe, leaning, with a pillar to support her, a silver arrow in her hand, and a feather in her hair, she led the eye up, down, from the curve to the straight, through glades of greenery and shades of silver, dun and rose into silence. The room was empty.

Empty, empty, empty; silent, silent, silent. The room was a shell, singing of what was before time was; a vase stood in the heart of the house,[31] alabaster, smooth, cold, holding the still, distilled essence of emptiness, silence.

*

Across the hall a door opened. One voice, another voice, a third voice came wimpling and warbling: gruff – Bart's voice; quavering – Lucy's voice; middle-toned – Isa's voice. Their voices impetuously, impatiently, protestingly came across the hall saying: 'The train's late'; saying: 'Keep it hot'; saying: 'We won't, no Candish, we won't wait.'

Coming out from the library the voices stopped in the hall. They encountered an obstacle evidently; a rock. Utterly impossible was it, even in the heart of the country, to be alone? That was the shock. After that, the rock was raced round, embraced. If it was painful, it was essential. There must be society. Coming out of the library it was painful, but pleasant, to run slap into Mrs. Manresa[32] and an unknown young man with tow-coloured hair and a twisted face. No escape was possible; meeting was inevitable. Uninvited, unexpected, droppers-in, lured off the high road by the very same instinct that caused the sheep and the cows to desire propinquity, they had come. But they had brought a lunch basket. Here it was.

'We couldn't resist when we saw the name on the signpost,'[33] Mrs. Manresa began in her rich fluty voice. 'And this is a friend – William Dodge. We were going to sit all alone in a field. And I said: "Why not ask our dear friends," seeing the signpost, "to shelter us?" A seat at the table – that's all we want. We have our grub. We have our glasses. We ask nothing but—' society apparently, to be with her kind.

And she waved her hand upon which there was a glove, and under the glove it seemed rings, at old Mr. Oliver.

He bowed deep over her hand; a century ago, he would have kissed it. In all this sound of welcome, protestation, apology and again welcome, there was an element of silence, supplied by Isabella, observing the unknown young man. He was of course a gentleman; witness socks and trousers; brainy – tie spotted, waistcoat undone; urban, professional, that is putty coloured, unwholesome; very nervous, exhibiting a twitch at this sudden introduction, and fundamentally infernally conceited, for he deprecated Mrs. Manresa's effusion, yet was her guest.

Isa felt antagonised, yet curious. But when Mrs. Manresa added, to make all shipshape: 'He's an artist,' and when William

Dodge corrected her: 'I'm a clerk in an office'[34] – she thought he said Education or Somerset House – she had her finger on the knot which had tied itself so tightly, almost to the extent of squinting, certainly of twitching, in his face.

Then they went in to lunch, and Mrs. Manresa bubbled up, enjoying her own capacity to surmount, without turning a hair, this minor social crisis – this laying of two more places. For had she not complete faith in flesh and blood? and aren't we all flesh and blood? and how silly to make bones of trifles when we're all flesh and blood under the skin – men and women too! But she preferred men – obviously.

'Or what are your rings for, and your nails, and that really adorable little straw hat?' said Isabella addressing Mrs. Manresa silently and thereby making silence add its unmistakable contribution to talk. Her hat, her rings, her finger nails red as roses, smooth as shells, were there for all to see. But not her life history. That was only scraps and fragments to all of them, excluding perhaps William Dodge, whom she called 'Bill' publicly – a sign perhaps that he knew more than they did. Some of the things that he knew – that she strolled the garden at midnight in silk pyjamas, had the loud speaker playing jazz, and a cocktail bar, of course they knew also. But nothing private; no strict biographical facts.

She had been born, but it was only gossip said so, in Tasmania: her grandfather had been exported for some hanky-panky mid-Victorian scandal; malversation of trusts[35] was it? But the story got no further the only time Isabella heard it than 'exported,' for the husband of the communicative lady – Mrs. Blencowe of the Grange – took exception, pedantically, to 'exported,' said 'expatriated' was more like it, but not the right word, which he had on the tip of his tongue, but couldn't get at. And so the story dwindled away. Sometimes she referred to an uncle, a Bishop. But he was thought to have been a Colonial Bishop only. They forgot and forgave very easily in the Colonies. Also it was said her diamonds and rubies had been dug out of the earth with his own hands by a 'husband' who was not Ralph Manresa. Ralph, a Jew,[36] got up to look the very spit and image of the landed gentry, supplied from directing City companies – that was certain

– tons of money; and they had no child. But surely with George the Sixth on the throne it was old fashioned, dowdy, savoured of moth-eaten furs, bugles, cameos and black-edged notepaper, to go ferreting into people's pasts?

'All I need,' said Mrs. Manresa ogling Candish, as if he were a real man, not a stuffed man, 'is a corkscrew.'[37] She had a bottle of champagne, but no corkscrew.

'Look, Bill,' she continued, cocking her thumb – she was opening the bottle – 'at the pictures. Didn't I tell you you'd have a treat?'

Vulgar she was in her gestures, in her whole person, over-sexed, over-dressed for a picnic. But what a desirable, at least valuable, quality it was – for everybody felt, directly she spoke, 'She's said it, she's done it, not I,' and could take advantage of the breach of decorum, of the fresh air that blew in, to follow like leaping dolphins in the wake of an ice-breaking vessel. Did she not restore to old Bartholomew his spice islands, his youth?

'I told him,' she went on, ogling Bart now, 'that he wouldn't look at our things' (of which they had heaps and mountains) 'after yours. And I promised him you'd show him the – the—' here the champagne fizzed up and she insisted upon filling Bart's glass first. 'What is it all you learned gentlemen rave about? An arch? Norman? Saxon? Who's the last from school? Mrs. Giles?'

She ogled Isabella now, conferring youth upon her; but always when she spoke to women, she veiled her eyes, for they, being conspirators, saw through it.

So with blow after blow, with champagne and ogling, she staked out her claim to be a wild child of nature, blowing into this – she did give one secret smile – sheltered harbour; which did make her smile, after London; yet it did, too, challenge London. For on she went to offer them a sample of her life; a few gobbets of gossip; mere trash; but she gave it for what it was worth; how last Tuesday she had been sitting next so and so; and she added, very casually, a Christian name; then a nick-name; and he'd said – for, as a mere nobody, they didn't mind what they said to her – and 'in strict confidence, I needn't tell you,' she told them. And they all pricked their ears. And then, with a gesture of her hands as if tossing overboard that odious

crackling-under-the-pot London life – so – she exclaimed 'There!
. . . And what's the first thing I do when I come down here?' They
had only come last night, driving through June lanes, alone with
Bill it was understood, leaving London, suddenly become dis-
solute and dirty, to sit down to dinner. 'What do I do? Can I say
it aloud? Is it permitted, Mrs. Swithin? Yes, everything can be
said in this house. I take off my stays' (here she pressed her
hands to her sides – she was stout) 'and roll in the grass. Roll –
you'll believe that . . .' She laughed wholeheartedly. She had
given up dealing with her figure and thus gained freedom.

'That's genuine,' Isa thought. Quite genuine. And her love of
the country too. Often when Ralph Manresa had to stay in town
she came down alone; wore an old garden hat; taught the village
women[38] *not* how to pickle and preserve; but how to weave
frivolous baskets out of coloured straw. Pleasure's what they
want, she said. You often heard her, if you called, yodelling
among the hollyhocks 'Hoity te doity te ray do . . .'

A thorough good sort she was. She made old Bart feel young.
Out of the corner of his eye, as he raised his glass, he saw a flash
of white in the garden. Someone passing.

The scullery maid, before the plates came out, was cooling her
cheeks by the lily pond.

There had always been lilies there, self-sown from wind-
dropped seed, floating red and white on the green plates of their
leaves. Water, for hundreds of years, had silted down into the
hollow, and lay there four or five feet deep over a black cushion
of mud. Under the thick plate of green water, glazed in their self-
centred world, fish swam – gold, splashed with white, streaked
with black or silver. Silently they manœuvred in their water
world, poised in the blue patch made by the sky, or shot silently
to the edge where the grass, trembling, made a fringe of nodding
shadow. On the water-pavement spiders printed their delicate
feet. A grain fell and spiralled down; a petal fell, filled and sank.
At that the fleet of boat-shaped bodies paused; poised; equipped;
mailed; then with a waver of undulation off they flashed.

It was in that deep centre, in that black heart, that the lady had drowned herself.[39] Ten years since the pool had been dredged and a thigh bone recovered. Alas, it was a sheep's, not a lady's. And sheep have no ghosts, for sheep have no souls. But, the servants insisted, they must have a ghost; the ghost must be a lady's; who had drowned herself for love. So none of them would walk by the lily pool at night, only now when the sun shone and the gentry still sat at table.

The flower petal sank; the maid returned to the kitchen; Bartholomew sipped his wine. Happy he felt as a boy; yet reckless as an old man; an unusual, an agreeable sensation. Fumbling in his mind for something to say to the adorable lady, he chose the first thing that came handy; the story of the sheep's thigh. 'Servants,' he said, 'must have their ghost.' Kitchenmaids must have their drowned lady.

'But so must I!' cried the wild child of nature, Mrs. Manresa. She became, of a sudden, solemn as an owl. She *knew*, she said, pinching a bit of bread to make this emphatic, that Ralph, when he was at the war, couldn't have been killed without her seeing him – 'wherever I was, whatever I was doing,' she added, waving her hands so that the diamonds flashed in the sun.

'I don't feel that,' said Mrs. Swithin, shaking her head.

'No,' Mrs. Manresa laughed. 'You wouldn't. None of you would. You see I'm on a level with . . .' she waited till Candish had retired, 'the servants. I'm nothing like so grown up as you are.'

She preened, approving her adolescence. Rightly or wrongly? A spring of feeling bubbled up through her mud. They had laid theirs with blocks of marble. Sheep's bones were sheep's bones to them, not the relics of the drowned Lady Ermyntrude.

'And which camp,' said Bartholomew turning to the unknown guest, 'd'you belong to? The grown, or the ungrown?'

Isabella opened her mouth, hoping that Dodge would open his, and so enable her to place him. But he sat staring. 'I beg your pardon, sir?' he said. They all looked at him. 'I was looking at the pictures.'

The picture looked at nobody. The picture drew them down the paths of silence.

Lucy broke it.

'Mrs. Manresa, I'm going to ask you a favour – If it comes to a pinch this afternoon, will you sing?'

This afternoon? Mrs. Manresa was aghast. Was it the pageant? She had never dreamt it was this afternoon. They would never have thrust themselves in – had they known it was this afternoon. And, of course, once more the chime pealed. Isa heard the first chime; and the second; and the third – If it was wet, it would be in the Barn; if it was fine on the terrace. And which would it be, wet or fine? And they all looked out of the window. Then the door opened. Candish said Mr. Giles had come. Mr. Giles would be down in a moment.

Giles had come. He had seen the great silver-plated car at the door with the initials R. M. twisted so as to look at a distance like a coronet. Visitors, he had concluded, as he drew up behind; and had gone to his room to change. The ghost of convention rose to the surface, as a blush or a tear rises to the surface at the pressure of emotion; so the car touched his training. He must change. And he came into the dining-room looking like a cricketer, in flannels, wearing a blue coat with brass buttons; though he was enraged. Had he not read, in the morning paper, in the train, that sixteen men had been shot, others prisoned, just over there, across the gulf in the flat land which divided them from the continent?[40] Yet he changed. It was Aunt Lucy, waving her hand at him as he came in, who made him change. He hung his grievances on her, as one hangs a coat on a hook, instinctively. Aunt Lucy, foolish, free; always, since he had chosen, after leaving college, to take a job in the city, expressing her amazement, her amusement, at men who spent their lives, buying and selling – ploughs? glass beads was it? or stocks and shares? – to savages who wished most oddly – for were they not beautiful naked? – to dress and live like the English? A frivolous, a malignant statement hers was of a problem which, for he had no special gift, no capital, and had been furiously in love with his wife – he nodded to her across the table – had afflicted him for ten years. Given his choice, he would have chosen to farm. But he was not given his choice. So one thing led to another; and the conglomeration of things pressed you flat; held you fast, like a fish in water. So he came for the week-end, and changed.

'How d'you do?' he said all round; nodded to the unknown guest; took against him; and ate his fillet of sole.

He was the very type of all that Mrs. Manresa adored. His hair curled; far from running away, as many chins did, his was firm; the nose straight, if short; the eyes, of course, with that hair, blue; and finally to make the type complete, there was something fierce, untamed, in the expression which incited her, even at forty-five, to furbish up her ancient batteries.

'He is my husband,' Isabella thought, as they nodded across the bunch of many-coloured flowers. 'The father of my children.' It worked, that old cliché; she felt pride; and affection; then pride again in herself, whom he had chosen. It was a shock to find, after the morning's look in the glass, and the arrow of desire[41] shot through her last night by the gentleman farmer, how much she felt when he came in, not a dapper city gent, but a cricketer, of love; and of hate.

They had met first in Scotland, fishing — she from one rock, he from another. Her line had got tangled; she had given over, and had watched him with the stream rushing between his legs, casting, casting — until, like a thick ingot of silver bent in the middle, the salmon had leapt, had been caught, and she had loved him.

Bartholomew too loved him; and noted his anger — about what? But he remembered his guest. The family was not a family in the presence of strangers. He must, rather laboriously, tell them the story of the pictures at which the unknown guest had been looking when Giles came in.

'That,' he indicated the man with a horse, 'was my ancestor. He had a dog. The dog was famous. The dog has his place in history. He left it on record that he wished his dog to be buried with him.'

They looked at the picture.

'I always feel,' Lucy broke the silence, 'he's saying: "Paint my dog."'

'But what about the horse?' said Mrs. Manresa.

'The horse,' said Bartholomew, putting on his glasses. He looked at the horse. The hindquarters were not satisfactory.

But William Dodge was still looking at the lady.

'Ah,' said Bartholomew who had bought that picture because he liked that picture, 'you're an artist.'

Dodge denied it, for the second time in half an hour, or so Isa noted.

What for did a good sort like the woman Manresa bring these half-breeds in her trail? Giles asked himself. And his silence made its contribution to talk – Dodge, that is, shook his head. 'I like that picture.' That was all he could bring himself to say.

'And you're right,' said Bartholomew. 'A man – I forget his name – a man connected with some Institute,[42] a man who goes about giving advice, gratis, to descendants like ourselves, degenerate descendants, said ... said ...' He paused. They all looked at the lady. But she looked over their heads, looking at nothing. She led them down green glades into the heart of silence.

'Said it was by Sir Joshua?'[43] Mrs. Manresa broke the silence abruptly.

'No, no,' William Dodge said hastily, but under his breath.

'Why's he afraid?' Isabella asked herself. A poor specimen he was; afraid to stick up for his own beliefs – just as she was afraid, of her husband. Didn't she write her poetry in a book bound like an account book lest Giles might suspect? She looked at Giles.

He had finished his fish; he had eaten quickly, not to keep them waiting. Now there was cherry tart. Mrs. Manresa was counting the stones.

'Tinker, tailor, soldier, sailor, apothecary, ploughboy ...[44] that's me!' she cried, delighted to have it confirmed by the cherry stones that she was a wild child of nature.

'You believe,' said the old gentleman, courteously chaffing her, 'in that too?'

'Of course, of course I do!' she cried. Now she was on the rails again. Now she was a thorough good sort again. And they too were delighted; now they could follow in her wake and leave the silver and dun shades that led to the heart of silence.

'I had a father,' said Dodge beneath his breath to Isa who sat next him, 'who loved pictures.'

'Oh, I too!' she exclaimed. Flurriedly, disconnectedly, she explained. She used to stay when she was a child, when she had the whooping cough, with an uncle, a clergyman; who wore a skull cap; and never did anything; didn't even preach; but made up poems, walking in his garden, saying them aloud.

'People thought him mad,' she said. 'I didn't . . .'

She stopped.

'Tinker, tailor, soldier, sailor, apothecary, ploughboy . . . It appears,' said old Bartholomew, laying down his spoon, 'that I am a thief. Shall we take our coffee in the garden?' He rose.

Isa dragged her chair across the gravel, muttering: 'To what dark antre[45] of the unvisited earth, or wind-brushed forest, shall we go now? Or spin from star to star and dance in the maze of the moon? Or . . .'

She held her deck chair at the wrong angle. The frame with the notches was upside down.

'Songs my uncle taught me?' said William Dodge, hearing her mutter. He unfolded the chair and fixed the bar into the right notch.

She flushed, as if she had spoken in an empty room and someone had stepped out from behind a curtain.

'Don't you, if you're doing something with your hands, talk nonsense?' she stumbled. But what did he do with his hands, the white, the fine, the shapely?

Giles went back to the house and brought more chairs and placed them in a semi-circle, so that the view might be shared, and the shelter of the old wall. For by some lucky chance a wall had been built continuing the house, it might be with the intention of adding another wing, on the raised ground in the sun. But funds were lacking; the plan was abandoned, and the wall remained, nothing but a wall. Later, another generation had planted fruit trees, which in time had spread their arms widely across the red-orange weathered brick. Mrs. Sands called it a good year if she could make six pots of apricot jam from them –

the fruit was never sweet enough for dessert. Perhaps three apricots were worth enclosing in muslin bags. But they were so beautiful, naked, with one flushed cheek, one green, that Mrs. Swithin left them naked, and the wasps burrowed holes.

The ground sloped up, so that to quote Figgis's Guide Book (1833),[46] 'it commanded a fine view of the surrounding country . . . The spire of Bolney Minster, Rough Norton woods, and on an eminence rather to the left, Hogben's Folly, so called because . . .'

The Guide Book still told the truth. 1833 was true in 1939. No house had been built; no town had sprung up. Hogben's Folly was still eminent; the very flat, field-parcelled land had changed only in this – the tractor had to some extent superseded the plough. The horse had gone; but the cow remained. If Figgis were here now, Figgis would have said the same. So they always said when in summer they sat there to drink coffee, if they had guests. When they were alone, they said nothing. They looked at the view; they looked at what they knew, to see if what they knew might perhaps be different today. Most days it was the same.

'That's what makes a view so sad,' said Mrs. Swithin, lowering herself into the deck-chair which Giles had brought her. 'And so beautiful. It'll be there,' she nodded at the strip of gauze laid upon the distant fields, 'when we're not.'

Giles nicked his chair into position with a jerk. Thus only could he show his irritation, his rage with old fogies who sat and looked at views over coffee and cream when the whole of Europe – over there – was bristling like . . . He had no command of metaphor. Only the ineffective word 'hedgehog' illustrated his vision of Europe, bristling with guns, poised with planes. At any moment guns would rake that land into furrows; planes splinter Bolney Minster into smithereens and blast the Folly. He, too, loved the view. And blamed Aunt Lucy, looking at views, instead of – doing what? What she had done was to marry a squire now dead; she had borne two children, one in Canada, the other, married, in Birmingham. His father, whom he loved, he exempted from censure; as for himself, one thing followed another; and so he sat, with old fogies, looking at views.

'Beautiful,' said Mrs. Manresa, 'beautiful . . .' she mumbled. She was lighting a cigarette. The breeze blew out her match. Giles hollowed his hand and lit another. She too was exempted – why, he could not say.

'Since you're interested in pictures,' said Bartholomew, turning to the silent guest, 'why, tell me, are we, as a race, so incurious, irresponsive and insensitive' – the champagne had given him a flow of unusual three-decker words – 'to that noble art, whereas Mrs. Manresa, if she'll allow me my old man's liberty, has her Shakespeare by heart?'

'Shakespeare by heart!' Mrs. Manresa protested. She struck an attitude. 'To be, or not to be, that is the question. Whether 'tis nobler . . . Go on!' she nudged Giles, who sat next her.

'Fade far away and quite forget what thou amongst the leaves hast never known . . .'[47] Isa supplied the first words that came into her head by way of helping her husband out of his difficulty.

'The weariness, the torture, and the fret . . .' William Dodge added, burying the end of his cigarette in a grave between two stones.

'There!' Bartholomew exclaimed, cocking his forefinger aloft. 'That proves it! What spring's touched, what secret drawer displays its treasures, if I say' – he raised more fingers – 'Reynolds! Constable! Crome!'[48]

'Why called "Old"?' Mrs. Manresa thrust in.

'We haven't the words – we haven't the words,' Mrs. Swithin protested. 'Behind the eyes; not on the lips; that's all.'

'Thoughts without words,' her brother mused. 'Can that be?'

'Quite beyond me!' cried Mrs. Manresa, shaking her head. 'Much too clever! May I help myself? I know it's wrong. But I've reached the age – and the figure – when I do what I like.'

She took the little silver cream jug and let the smooth fluid curl luxuriously into her coffee, to which she added a shovel full of brown sugar candy. Sensuously, rhythmically, she stirred the mixture round and round.

'Take what you like! Help yourself!' Bartholomew exclaimed. He felt the champagne withdrawing and hastened, before the last trace of geniality was withdrawn, to make the most of it, as if he cast one last look into a lit-up chamber before going to bed.

The wild child, afloat once more on the tide of the old man's benignity, looked over her coffee cup at Giles, with whom she felt in conspiracy. A thread united them – visible, invisible, like those threads, now seen, now not, that unite trembling grass blades in autumn before the sun rises. She had met him once only, at a cricket match. And then had been spun between them an early morning thread before the twigs and leaves of real friendship emerge. She looked before she drank. Looking was part of drinking. Why waste sensation, she seemed to ask, why waste a single drop that can be pressed out of this ripe, this melting, this adorable world? Then she drank. And the air round her became threaded with sensation. Bartholomew felt it; Giles felt it. Had he been a horse, the thin brown skin would have twitched, as if a fly had settled. Isabella twitched too. Jealousy, anger pierced her skin.

'And now,' said Mrs. Manresa, putting down her cup, 'about this entertainment – this pageant, into which we've gone and butted' – she made it, too, seem ripe like the apricot into which the wasps were burrowing – 'Tell me, what's it to be?' She turned. 'Don't I hear?' She listened. She heard laughter, down among the bushes, where the terrace dipped to the bushes.

Beyond the lily pool the ground sank again, and in that dip of the ground, bushes and brambles had mobbed themselves together. It was always shady; sun-flecked in summer, dark and damp in winter. In the summer there were always butterflies; fritillaries darting through; Red Admirals feasting and floating; cabbage whites, unambitiously fluttering round a bush, like muslin milkmaids, content to spend a life there. Butterfly catching, for generation after generation, began there; for Bartholomew and Lucy; for Giles; for George it had begun only the day before yesterday, when, in his little green net, he had caught a cabbage white.

It was the very place for a dressing-room, just as, obviously, the terrace was the very place for a play.

'The very place!' Miss La Trobe[49] had exclaimed the first time she came to call and was shown the grounds. It was a winter's day. The trees were leafless then.

'That's the place for a pageant, Mr. Oliver!' she had exclaimed. 'Winding in and out between the trees ...' She waved her hand at the trees standing bare in the clear light of January.

'There the stage; here the audience; and down there among the bushes a perfect dressing-room for the actors.'

She was always all agog to get things up. But where did she spring from? With that name she wasn't presumably pure English. From the Channel Islands perhaps? Only her eyes and something about her always made Mrs. Bingham suspect that she had Russian blood in her. 'Those deep-set eyes; that very square jaw' reminded her – not that she had been to Russia – of the Tartars. Rumour said that she had kept a tea shop at Winchester; that had failed. She had been an actress. That had failed. She had bought a four-roomed cottage and shared it with an actress. They had quarrelled. Very little was actually known about her. Outwardly she was swarthy, sturdy and thick set; strode about the fields in a smock frock; sometimes with a cigarette in her mouth; often with a whip in her hand; and used rather strong language – perhaps, then, she wasn't altogether a lady? At any rate, she had a passion for getting things up.

The laughter died away.

'Are they going to act?' Mrs. Manresa asked.

'Act; dance; sing; a little bit of everything,' said Giles.

'Miss La Trobe is a lady of wonderful energy,' said Mrs. Swithin.

'She makes everyone do something,' said Isabella.

'Our part,' said Bartholomew, 'is to be the audience. And a very important part too.'

'Also, we provide the tea,' said Mrs. Swithin.

'Shan't we go and help?' said Mrs. Manresa. 'Cut up bread and butter?'

'No, no,' said Mr. Oliver. 'We are the audience.'

'One year we had *Gammer Gurton's Needle*,'[50] said Mrs. Swithin. 'One year we wrote the play ourselves. The son of our blacksmith – Tony? Tommy? – had the loveliest voice. And Elsie at the Crossways – how she mimicked! Took us all off. Bart; Giles;

Old Flimsy – that's me. People are gifted – very. The question is – how to bring it out? That's where she's so clever – Miss La Trobe. Of course, there's the whole of English literature to choose from. But how can one choose? Often on a wet day I begin counting up; what I've read; what I haven't read.'

'And leaving books on the floor,' said her brother. 'Like the pig in the story; or was it a donkey?'

She laughed, tapping him lightly on the knee.

'The donkey who couldn't choose between hay and turnips and so starved,' Isabella explained, interposing – anything – between her aunt and her husband, who hated this kind of talk this afternoon. Books open; no conclusion come to; and he sitting in the audience.

'We remain seated' – 'We are the audience.' Words this afternoon ceased to lie flat in the sentence. They rose, became menacing and shook their fists at you. This afternoon he wasn't Giles Oliver come to see the villagers act their annual pageant; manacled to a rock he was, and forced passively to behold indescribable horror. His face showed it; and Isa, not knowing what to say, abruptly, half purposely, knocked over a coffee cup.

William Dodge caught it as it fell. He held it for a moment. He turned it. From the faint blue mark,[51] as of crossed daggers, in the glaze at the bottom he knew that it was English, made perhaps at Nottingham; date about 1760. His expression, considering the daggers, coming to this conclusion, gave Giles another peg on which to hang his rage as one hangs a coat on a peg, conveniently. A toady; a lickspittle; not a downright plain man of his senses; but a teaser and twitcher; a fingerer of sensations; picking and choosing; dillying and dallying; not a man to have straightforward love for a woman – his head was close to Isa's head – but simply a——[52] At this word, which he could not speak in public, he pursed his lips; and the signet-ring on his little finger looked redder, for the flesh next it whitened as he gripped the arm of his chair.

'Oh what fun!' cried Mrs. Manresa in her fluty voice. 'A little bit of everything. A song; a dance; then a play acted by the villagers themselves. Only,' here she turned with her head on one side to Isabella, 'I'm sure *she's* written it. Haven't you, Mrs. Giles?'

Isa flushed and denied it.

'For myself,' Mrs. Manresa continued, 'speaking plainly, I can't put two words together. I don't know how it is – such a chatterbox as I am with my tongue, once I hold a pen—' She made a face, screwed her fingers as if she held a pen in them. But the pen she held thus on the little table absolutely refused to move.

'And my handwriting – so huge – so clumsy –' She made another face and dropped the invisible pen.

Very delicately William Dodge set the cup in its saucer. 'Now *he*,' said Mrs. Manresa, as if referring to the delicacy with which he did this, and imputing to him the same skill in writing, 'writes beautifully. Every letter perfectly formed.'

Again they all looked at him. Instantly he put his hands in his pockets.

Isabella guessed the word that Giles had not spoken. Well, was it wrong if he was that word? Why judge each other? Do we know each other? Not here, not now. But somewhere, this cloud, this crust, this doubt, this dust— She waited for a rhyme, it failed her; but somewhere surely one sun would shine and all, without a doubt, would be clear.

She started. Again, sounds of laughter reached her.

'I think I hear them,' said said. 'They're getting ready. They're dressing up in the bushes.'

Miss La Trobe was pacing to and fro between the leaning birch trees. One hand was deep stuck in her jacket pocket; the other held a foolscap sheet. She was reading what was written there. She had the look of a commander pacing his deck. The leaning graceful trees with black bracelets circling the silver bark were distant about a ship's length.

Wet would it be, or fine? Out came the sun; and, shading her eyes in the attitude proper to an Admiral on his quarter-deck, she decided to risk the engagement out of doors. Doubts were over. All stage properties, she commanded, must be moved from the Barn to the bushes. It was done. And the actors, while she paced, taking all responsibility and plumping for fine, not wet, dressed among the brambles. Hence the laughter.

The clothes were strewn on the grass. Cardboard crowns, swords made of silver paper, turbans that were sixpenny dish cloths, lay on the grass or were flung on the bushes. There were pools of red and purple in the shade; flashes of silver in the sun. The dresses attracted the butterflies. Red and silver, blue and yellow gave off warmth and sweetness. Red Admirals gluttonously absorbed richness from dish cloths, cabbage whites drank icy coolness from silver paper. Flitting, tasting, returning, they sampled the colours.

Miss La Trobe stopped her pacing and surveyed the scene. 'It has the makings . . .' she murmured. For another play always lay behind the play she had just written. Shading her eyes, she looked. The butterflies circling; the light changing; the children leaping; the mothers laughing— 'No, I don't get it,' she muttered and resumed her pacing.

'Bossy' they called her privately, just as they called Mrs. Swithin 'Flimsy.' Her abrupt manner and stocky figure; her thick ankles and sturdy shoes; her rapid decisions barked out in guttural accents – all this 'got their goat'. No one liked to be ordered about singly. But in little troops they appealed to her. Someone must lead. Then too they could put the blame on her. Suppose it poured?

'Miss La Trobe!' they hailed her now. 'What's the idea about this?'

She stopped. David and Iris each had a hand on the gramophone. It must be hidden; yet must be close enough to the audience to be heard. Well, hadn't she given orders? Where were the hurdles covered in leaves? Fetch them. Mr. Streatfield had said he would see to it. Where was Mr. Streatfield? No clergyman was visible. Perhaps he's in the Barn? 'Tommy, cut along and fetch him.' 'Tommy's wanted in the first scene.' 'Beryl then . . .' The mothers disputed. One child had been chosen; another not. Fair hair was unjustly preferred to dark. Mrs. Ebury had forbidden Fanny to act because of the nettle-rash.[53] There was another name in the village for nettle-rash.

Mrs. Ball's cottage was not what you might call clean. In the last war Mrs. Ball lived with another man while her husband was in the trenches. All this Miss La Trobe knew, but refused to be mixed up in it. She splashed into the fine mesh like a great stone into the lily pool. The criss-cross was shattered. Only the roots beneath water were of use to her. Vanity, for example, made them all malleable. The boys wanted the big parts; the girls wanted the fine clothes. Expenses had to be kept down. Ten pounds was the limit. Thus conventions were outraged. Swathed in conventions, they couldn't see, as she could, that a dish cloth wound round a head in the open looked much richer than real silk. So they squabbled; but she kept out of it. Waiting for Mr. Streatfield, she paced between the birch trees.

The other trees were magnificently straight. They were not too regular; but regular enough to suggest columns in a church; in a church without a roof; in an open-air cathedral, a place where swallows darting seemed, by the regularity of the trees, to make a pattern, dancing, like the Russians, only not to music, but to the unheard rhythm of their own wild hearts.

The laughter died away.

'We must possess our souls in patience,' said Mrs. Manresa again. 'Or could we help?' she suggested, glancing over her shoulder, 'with those chairs?'

Candish, a gardener, and a maid were all bringing chairs – for the audience. There was nothing for the audience to do. Mrs. Manresa suppressed a yawn. They were silent. They stared at the view, as if something might happen in one of those fields to relieve them of the intolerable burden of sitting silent, doing nothing, in company. Their minds and bodies were too close, yet not close enough. We aren't free, each one of them felt separately, to feel or think separately, nor yet to fall asleep. We're too close; but not close enough. So they fidgeted.

The heat had increased. The clouds had vanished. All was sun now. The view laid bare by the sun was flattened, silenced, stilled. The cows were motionless; the brick wall, no longer sheltering, beat back grains of heat. Old Mr. Oliver sighed profoundly. His head jerked; his hand fell. It fell within an inch of the dog's head on the grass by his side. Then up he jerked it again on to his knee.

Giles glared. With his hands bound tight round his knees he stared at the flat fields. Staring, glaring, he sat silent.

Isabella felt prisoned. Through the bars of the prison, through the sleep haze that deflected them, blunt arrows bruised her; of love, then of hate. Through other people's bodies she felt neither love nor hate distinctly. Most consciously she felt — she had drunk sweet wine at luncheon — a desire for water. 'A beaker of cold water, a beaker of cold water,'[54] she repeated, and saw water surrounded by walls of shining glass.

Mrs. Manresa longed to relax and curl in a corner with a cushion, a picture paper, and a bag of sweets.

Mrs. Swithin and William surveyed the view aloofly, and with detachment.

How tempting, how very tempting, to let the view triumph; to reflect its ripple; to let their own minds ripple; to let outlines elongate and pitch over — so — with a sudden jerk.

Mrs. Manresa yielded, pitched, plunged, then pulled herself up.

'What a view!' she exclaimed, pretending to dust the ashes of her cigarette, but in truth concealing her yawn. Then she sighed, pretending to express not her own drowsiness, but something connected with what she felt about views.

Nobody answered her. The flat fields glared green yellow, blue yellow, red yellow, then blue again. The repetition was senseless, hideous, stupefying.

'Then,' said Mrs. Swithin, in a low voice, as if the exact moment for speech had come, as if she had promised, and it was time to fulfil her promise, 'come, come and I'll show you the house.'

She addressed no one in particular. But William Dodge knew she meant him. He rose with a jerk, like a toy suddenly pulled straight by a string.

'What energy!' Mrs. Manresa half sighed, half yawned. 'Have I the courage to go too?' Isabella asked herself. They were going; above all things, she desired cold water, a beaker of cold water; but desire petered out, suppressed by the leaden duty she owed to others. She watched them go — Mrs. Swithin tottering yet tripping; and Dodge unfurled and straightened, as he strode beside her along the blazing tiles under the hot wall, till they reached the shade of the house.

A match-box fell – Bartholomew's. His fingers had loosed it; he had dropped it. He gave up the game; he couldn't be bothered. With his head on one side, his hand dangling above the dog's head, he slept; he snored.

Mrs. Swithin paused for a moment in the hall among the gilt-clawed tables.

'This,' she said, 'is the staircase. And now – up we go.'

She went up, two stairs ahead of her guest. Lengths of yellow satin unfurled themselves on a cracked canvas as they mounted.

'Not an ancestress,' said Mrs. Swithin, as they came level with the head in the picture. 'But we claim her because we've known her – O, ever so many years. Who was she?' she gazed. 'Who painted her?' She shook her head. She looked lit up, as if for a banquet, with the sun pouring over her.

'But I like her best in the moonlight,' Mrs. Swithin reflected, and mounted more stairs.

She panted slightly, going upstairs. Then she ran her hand over the sunk books in the wall on the landing, as if they were pan pipes.

'Here are the poets from whom we descend by way of the mind, Mr. . . .' she murmured. She had forgotten his name. Yet she had singled him out.

'My brother says, they built the house north for shelter, not south for sun. So they're damp in the winter.' She paused. 'And now what comes next?'

She stopped. There was a door.

'The morning room.' She opened the door. 'Where my mother received her guests.'

Two chairs faced each other on either side of a fine fluted mantelpiece. He looked over her shoulder.

She shut the door.

'Now up, now up again.' Again they mounted. 'Up and up they went,' she panted, seeing, it seemed, an invisible procession, 'up and up to bed.'

'A bishop; a traveller; – I've forgotten even their names. I ignore. I forget.'

She stopped at a window in the passage and held back the curtain. Beneath was the garden, bathed in sun. The grass was sleek and shining. Three white pigeons were flirting and tiptoeing as ornate as ladies in ball dresses. Their elegant bodies swayed as they minced with tiny steps on their little pink feet upon the grass. Suddenly, up they rose in a flutter, circled, and flew away.

'Now,' she said, 'for the bedrooms.' She tapped twice very distinctly on a door. With her head on one side, she listened.

'One never knows,' she murmured, 'if there's somebody there.' Then she flung open the door.

He half expected to see somebody there, naked, or half dressed, or knelt in prayer. But the room was empty. The room was tidy as a pin, not slept in for months, a spare room. Candles stood on the dressing-table. The counterpane was straight. Mrs. Swithin stopped by the bed.

'Here,' she said, 'yes, here,' she tapped the counterpane, 'I was born. In this bed.'

Her voice died away. She sank down on the edge of the bed. She was tired, no doubt, by the stairs, by the heat.

'But we have other lives, I think, I hope,' she murmured. 'We live in others, Mr. . . . We live in things.'

She spoke simply. She spoke with an effort. She spoke as if she must overcome her tiredness out of charity towards a stranger, a guest. She had forgotten his name. Twice she had said 'Mr.' and stopped.

The furniture was mid-Victorian, bought at Maples,[55] perhaps, in the forties. The carpet was covered with small purple dots. And a white circle marked the place where the slop pail had stood by the washstand.

Could he say 'I'm William'? He wished to. Old and frail she had climbed the stairs. She had spoken her thoughts, ignoring, not caring if he thought her, as he had, inconsequent, sentimental, foolish. She had lent him a hand to help him up a steep place. She had guessed his trouble. Sitting on the bed he heard her sing, swinging her little legs, 'Come and see my sea weeds, come and see my sea shells, come and see my dicky bird hop upon its perch' – an old child's nursery rhyme to help a child. Standing by the cupboard in the corner he saw her reflected in the glass. Cut off from their bodies, their eyes smiled, their bodiless eyes, at their eyes in the glass.

Then she slipped off the bed.

'Now,' she said, 'what comes next?' and pattered down the corridor. A door stood open. Everyone was out in the garden. The room was like a ship deserted by its crew. The children had been playing – there was a spotted horse in the middle of the carpet. The nurse had been sewing – there was a piece of linen on the table. The baby had been in the cot. The cot was empty.

'The nursery,' said Mrs. Swithin.

Words raised themselves and became symbolical. 'The cradle of our race,' she seemed to say.

Dodge crossed to the fireplace and looked at the New-foundland Dog in the Christmas Annual that was pinned to the wall. The room smelt warm and sweet; of clothes drying; of milk; of biscuits and warm water. 'Good Friends' the picture was called. A rushing sound came in through the open door. He turned. The old woman had wandered out into the passage and leant against the window.

He left the door open for the crew to come back to and joined her.

Down in the courtyard beneath the window cars were assembling. Their narrow black roofs were laid together like the blocks of a floor. Chauffeurs were jumping down; here old ladies gingerly advanced black legs with silver-buckled shoes; old men striped trousers. Young men in shorts leapt out on one side; girls with skin-coloured legs on the other. There was a purring and a churning of the yellow gravel. The audience was assembling. But they, looking down from the window, were truants, detached. Together they leant half out of the window.

And then a breeze blew and all the muslin blinds fluttered out, as if some majestic goddess, rising from her throne among her peers, had tossed her amber-coloured raiment, and the other gods, seeing her rise and go, laughed, and their laughter floated her on.

Mrs. Swithin put her hands to her hair, for the breeze had ruffled it.

'Mr. . . .' she began.

'I'm William,' he interrupted.

At that she smiled a ravishing girl's smile, as if the wind had warmed the wintry blue in her eyes to amber.

'I took you,' she apologized, 'away from your friends, William, because I felt wound tight here . . .' She touched her bony forehead upon which a blue vein wriggled like a blue worm. But her eyes in their caves of bone were still lambent. He saw her eyes only. And he wished to kneel before her, to kiss her hand, and to say: 'At school they held me under a bucket of dirty water, Mrs. Swithin; when I looked up, the world was dirty, Mrs. Swithin; so I married; but my child's not my child, Mrs. Swithin. I'm a half-man, Mrs. Swithin; a flickering, mind-divided little snake in the grass, Mrs. Swithin; as Giles saw; but you've healed me . . .' So he wished to say; but said nothing; and the breeze went lolloping along the corridors, blowing the blinds out.

Once more he looked and she looked down on to the yellow gravel that made a crescent round the door. Pendant from her chain her cross swung as she leant out and the sun struck it. How could she weight herself down by that sleek symbol? How stamp herself, so volatile, so vagrant, with that image? As he looked at it, they were truants no more. The purring of the wheels became vocal. 'Hurry, hurry, hurry,' it seemed to say, 'or you'll be late. Hurry, hurry, hurry, or the best seats'll be taken.'

'O,' cried Mrs. Swithin, 'there's Mr. Streatfield!' And they saw a clergyman, a strapping clergyman, carrying a hurdle,[56] a leafy hurdle. He was striding through the cars with the air of a person of authority, who is awaited, expected, and now comes.

'Is it time,' said Mrs. Swithin, 'to go and join——' She left the sentence unfinished, as if she were of two minds, and they fluttered to right and to left, like pigeons rising from the grass.

The audience was assembling. They came streaming along the paths and spreading across the lawn. Some were old; some were in the prime of life. There were children among them. Among them, as Mr. Figgis might have observed, were representatives of our most respected families – the Dyces of Denton; the Wick-hams of Owlswick; and so on. Some had been there for centuries, never selling an acre. On the other hand there were new-comers, the Manresas, bringing the old houses up to date, adding bath-rooms. And a scatter of odds and ends, like Cobbet of Cobbs Corner, retired, it was understood, on a pension from a tea plantation. Not an asset. He did his own housework and dug in his garden. The building of a car factory[57] and of an aerodrome in the neighbourhood had attracted a number of unattached floating residents. Also there was Mr. Page, the reporter, representing the local paper. Roughly speaking, however, had Figgis been there in person and called a roll call, half the ladies and gentlemen present would have said '*Adsum*;[58] I'm here, in place of my grandfather or great-grandfather,' as the case might be. At this very moment, half-past three on a June day in 1939 they greeted each other, and as they took their seats, finding if possible a seat next one another, they said: 'That hideous new house at Pyes Corner! What an eyesore! And those bungalows! – have you seen 'em?'

Again, had Figgis called the names of the villagers, they too would have answered. Mrs. Sands was born Iliffe; Candish's mother was one of the Perrys. The green mounds in the church-yard had been cast up by their molings, which for centuries had made the earth friable. True, there were absentees when Mr. Streatfield called his roll call in the church. The motor bike, the motor bus, and the movies[59] – when Mr. Streatfield called his roll call, he laid the blame on them.

Rows of chairs, deck chairs, gilt chairs, hired cane chairs, and indigenous garden seats had been drawn up on the terrace. There were plenty of seats for everybody. But some preferred to sit on the ground. Certainly Miss La Trobe had spoken the truth when she said: 'The very place for a pageant!' The lawn was as flat as the floor of a theatre. The terrace, rising, made a natural stage. The trees barred the stage like pillars. And the human figure was seen to great advantage against a background of sky. As for the weather, it was turning out, against all expectation, a very fine day. A perfect summer afternoon.

'What luck!' Mrs. Carter was saying. 'Last year . . .' Then the play began. Was it, or was it not, the play? Chuff, chuff, chuff sounded from the bushes. It was the noise a machine makes when something has gone wrong. Some sat down hastily; others stopped talking guiltily. All looked at the bushes. For the stage was empty. Chuff, chuff, chuff the machine buzzed in the bushes. While they looked apprehensively and some finished their sentences, a small girl, like a rosebud in pink, advanced; took her stand on a mat, behind a conch hung with leaves, and piped:

> *Gentles and simples, I address you all . . .*

So it was the play then. Or was it the prologue?[60]

> *Come hither for our festival* (she continued)
> *This is a pageant, all may see*
> *Drawn from our island history.*
> *England am I . . .*

'She's England,' they whispered. 'It's begun.' 'The prologue,' they added, looking down at the programme.

'*England am I,*' she piped again; and stopped.

She had forgotten her lines.

'Hear! Hear!' said an old man in a white waistcoat briskly. 'Bravo! Bravo!'

'Blast 'em!' cursed Miss La Trobe, hidden behind the tree. She looked along the front row. They glared as if they were exposed to a frost that nipped them and fixed them all at the same level. Only Bond the cowman looked fluid and natural.

'Music!' she signalled. 'Music!' But the machine continued: Chuff, chuff, chuff.

'*A child new born . . .*' she prompted.

'*A child new born,*' Phyllis Jones continued,

> *Sprung from the sea*
> *Whose billows blown by mighty storm*
> *Cut off from France and Germany*
> *This isle.*[61]

She glanced back over her shoulder. Chuff, chuff, chuff, the machine buzzed. A long line of villagers in shirts made of sacking began passing in and out in single file behind her between the trees. They were singing, but not a word reached the audience.

England am I, Phyllis Jones continued, facing the audience,

Now weak and small
A child, as all may see . . .

Her words peppered the audience as with a shower of hard little stones. Mrs. Manresa in the very centre smiled; but she felt as if her skin cracked when she smiled. There was a vast vacancy between her, the singing villagers and the piping child.

Chuff, chuff, chuff, went the machine like a corn-cutter on a hot day.

The villagers were singing, but half their words were blown away.

Cutting the roads . . . up to the hill top . . . we climbed. Down in
the valley . . . sow, wild boar, hog, rhinoceros, reindeer . . . Dug
ourselves in to the hill top . . . Ground roots between stones . . .
Ground corn . . . till we too . . . lay under g—r—o—u—n—d . . .

The words petered away. Chuff, chuff, chuff, the machine ticked. Then at last the machine ground out a tune!

Armed against fate,
The valiant Rhoderick,
Armed and valiant,
Bold and blatant,
Firm, elatant,
See the warriors — here they come . . .

The pompous popular tune brayed and blared. Miss La Trobe watched from behind the tree. Muscles loosened; ice cracked. The stout lady in the middle began to beat time with her hand on her chair. Mrs. Manresa was humming:

My home is at Windsor,[62] close to the Inn.
Royal George is the name of the pub.
And boys you'll believe me,
I don't want no asking . . .

She was afloat on the stream of the melody. Radiating royalty, complacency, good humour, the wild child was Queen of the festival. The play had begun.

But there was an interruption. 'O,' Miss La Trobe growled behind her tree, 'the torture of these interruptions!'

'Sorry I'm so late,' said Mrs. Swithin. She pushed her way through the chairs to a seat beside her brother.

'What's it all about? I've missed the prologue. England? That little girl? Now she's gone . . .'

Phyllis had slipped off her mat.

'And who's this?' asked Mrs. Swithin.

It was Hilda, the carpenter's daughter. She now stood where England had stood.

'O, *England's grown* . . .' Miss La Trobe prompted her.

'O, *England's grown a girl now*,' Hilda sang out.

('What a lovely voice!' someone exclaimed.)

With roses in her hair,
Wild roses, red roses,
She roams the lanes and chooses
A garland for her hair.

'A cushion? Thank you so much,' said Mrs. Swithin, stuffing the cushion behind her back. Then she leant forward.

'That's England in the time of Chaucer, I take it. She's been maying, nutting. She has flowers in her hair . . . But those passing behind her—' she pointed. 'The Canterbury pilgrims? Look!'[63]

All the time the villagers were passing in and out between the trees. They were singing; but only a word or two was audible '. . . *wore ruts in the grass* . . . *built the house in the lane* . . .' The wind blew away the connecting words of their chant, and then, as they reached the tree at the end they sang:

'*To the shrine of the Saint* . . . *to the tomb* . . . *lovers* . . . *believers* . . . *we come* . . .'

They grouped themselves together.

Then there was a rustle and an interruption. Chairs were drawn back. Isa looked behind her. Mr. and Mrs. Rupert Haines, detained by a breakdown on the road, had arrived. He was sitting to the right, several rows back,[64] the man in grey.

Meanwhile the pilgrims, having done their homage to the tomb, were, it appeared, tossing hay on their rakes.

I kissed a girl and let her go,
Another did I tumble,
In the straw and in the hay . . .

– that was what they were singing, as they scooped and tossed
the invisible hay, when she looked round again.

'Scenes from English history,' Mrs. Manresa explained to Mrs.
Swithin. She spoke in a loud cheerful voice, as if the old lady
were deaf. 'Merry England.'

She clapped energetically.

The singers scampered away into the bushes. The tune
stopped. Chuff, chuff, chuff, the machine ticked. Mrs. Manresa
looked at her programme. It would take till midnight unless they
skipped. Early Britons; Plantagenets;[65] Tudors; Stuarts – she
ticked them off, but probably she had forgotten a reign or two.

'Ambitious, ain't it?' she said to Bartholomew, while they
waited. Chuff, chuff, chuff went the machine. Could they talk?
Could they move? No, for the play was going on. Yet the stage
was empty; only the cows moved in the meadows; only the tick
of the gramophone needle was heard. The tick, tick, tick seemed
to hold them together, tranced. Nothing whatsoever appeared
on the stage.

'I'd no notion we looked so nice,' Mrs. Swithin whispered to
William. Hadn't she? The children; the pilgrims; behind the
pilgrims the trees, and behind them the fields – the beauty of the
visible world took his breath away. Tick, tick, tick the machine
continued.

'Marking time,' said old Oliver beneath his breath.

'Which don't exist for us,' Lucy murmured. 'We've only the
present.'

'Isn't that enough?' William asked himself. Beauty – isn't that
enough? But here Isa fidgeted. Her bare brown arms went nervously to her head. She half turned in her seat. 'No, not for us,
who've the future,' she seemed to say. The future disturbing our
present. Who was she looking for? William, turning, following
her eyes, saw only a man in grey.

The ticking stopped. A dance tune was put on the machine. In
time to it, Isa hummed: 'What do I ask? To fly away, from night

and day, and issue where – no partings are – but eye meets eye –
and . . . O,' she cried aloud: 'Look at her!'

Everyone was clapping and laughing. From behind the bushes
issued Queen Elizabeth[66] – Eliza Clark, licensed to sell tobacco.
Could she be Mrs. Clark of the village shop? She was splendidly
made up. Her head, pearl-hung, rose from a vast ruff. Shiny
satins draped her. Sixpenny brooches glared like cats' eyes and
tigers' eyes; pearls looked down; her cape was made of cloth of
silver – in fact swabs used to scour saucepans. She looked the
age in person. And when she mounted the soap box in the
centre, representing perhaps a rock in the ocean, her size made
her appear gigantic. She could reach a flitch of bacon or haul a
tub of oil with one sweep of her arm in the shop. For a moment
she stood there, eminent, dominant, on the soap box with the
blue and sailing clouds behind her. The breeze had risen.

The Queen of this great land . . .

– those were the first words that could be heard above the roar
of laughter and applause.

Mistress of ships and bearded men (she bawled)
Hawkins, Frobisher, Drake,[67]
Tumbling their oranges, ingots of silver,
Cargoes of diamonds, ducats of gold,
Down on the jetty, there in the west land, –
(she pointed her fist at the blazing blue sky)
Mistress of pinnacles, spires and palaces –
(her arm swept towards the house)
For me Shakespeare sang –
(a cow mooed. A bird twittered)
The throstle, the mavis (she continued)
In the green wood, the wild wood,
Carolled and sang, praising England, the Queen,
Then there was heard too
On granite and cobble
From Windsor to Oxford
Loud laughter, low laughter
Of warrior and lover,

The fighter, the singer.
The ashen haired babe
(she stretched out her swarthy, muscular arm)
Stretched his arm in contentment
As home from the Isles came
The sea faring men . . .

Here the wind gave a tug at her head dress. Loops of pearls made it top-heavy. She had to steady the ruffle which threatened to blow away.

'Laughter, loud laughter,' Giles muttered. The tune on the gramophone reeled from side to side as if drunk with merriment. Mrs. Manresa began beating her foot and humming in time to it.

'Bravo! Bravo!' she cried. 'There's life in the old dog yet!' And she trolloped out the words of the song with an abandonment which, if vulgar, was a great help to the Elizabethan age. For the ruff had become unpinned and great Eliza had forgotten her lines. But the audience laughed so loud that it did not matter.

'I fear I am not in my perfect mind,'[68] Giles muttered to the same tune. Words came to the surface – he remembered 'a stricken deer[69] in whose lean flank the world's harsh scorn has struck its thorn . . . Exiled from its festival, the music turned ironical . . . A churchyard haunter at whom the owl hoots and the ivy mocks tap-tap-tapping on the pane . . . For they are dead, and I . . . I . . . I,' he repeated, forgetting the words, and glaring at his Aunt Lucy who sat craned forward, her mouth gaping, and her bony little hands clapping.

What were they laughing at?

At Albert, the village idiot, apparently. There was no need to dress him up. There he came, acting his part to perfection. He came ambling across the grass, mopping and mowing.

I know where the tit nests, he began
In the hedgerow. I know, I know –
What don't I know?
All your secrets, ladies,
And yours, too, gentlemen . . .

He skipped along the front row of the audience, leering at each in turn. Now he was picking and plucking at Great Eliza's skirts. She cuffed him on the ear. He tweaked her back. He was enjoying himself immensely.

'Albert having the time of his life,' Bartholomew muttered.

'Hope he don't have a fit,' Lucy murmured.

'*I know* ... *I know* ...' Albert tittered, skipping round the soap box.

'The village idiot,' whispered a stout black lady — Mrs. Elmhurst — who came from a village ten miles distant where they, too, had an idiot. It wasn't nice. Suppose he suddenly did something dreadful? There he was pinching the Queen's skirts. She half covered her eyes, in case he did do — something dreadful.

> *Hoppety, jiggety*, Albert resumed,
> *In at the window, out at the door,*
> *What does the little bird hear?* (he whistled on his fingers.)
> *And see! There's a mouse* ...
> (he made as if chasing it through the grass)
> *Now the clock strikes!*
> (he stood erect, puffing out his cheeks as if he were blowing a
>   dandelion clock)
> *One, two, three, four* ...

And off he skipped, as if his turn was over.

'Glad that's over,' said Mrs. Elmhurst, uncovering her face. 'Now what comes next? A tableau ... ?'

For helpers, issuing swiftly from the bushes, carrying hurdles, had enclosed the Queen's throne with screens papered to represent walls. They had strewn the ground with rushes. And the pilgrims, who had continued their march and their chant in the background, now gathered round the figure of Eliza on her soap box as if to form the audience at a play.

Were they about to act a play in the presence of Queen Elizabeth? Was this, perhaps, the Globe theatre?[70]

'What does the programme say?' Mrs. Herbert Winthrop asked, raising her lorgnette.

She mumbled through the blurred carbon sheet. Yes; it was a scene from a play.

'About a false Duke; and a Princess disguised as a boy; then the long lost heir turns out to be the beggar, because of a mole on his cheek; and Carinthia[71] – that's the Duke's daughter, only she's been lost in a cave – falls in love with Ferdinando who had been put into a basket as a baby by an aged crone. And they marry. That's I think what happens,' she said, looking up from the programme.

'*Play out the play,*' great Eliza commanded. An aged crone tottered forward.

('Mrs. Otter of the End House,' someone murmured.)

She sat herself on a packing case, and made motions, plucking her dishevelled locks and rocking herself from side to side as if she were an aged beldame in a chimney corner.

('The crone, who saved the rightful heir,' Mrs. Winthrop explained.)

'Twas a winter's night (she croaked out)
I mind me that, I to whom all's one now, summer or winter.
You say the sun shines? I believe you, Sir.
'Oh but it's winter, and the fog's abroad'
All's one to Elsbeth, summer or winter,
By the fireside, in the chimney corner, telling her beads.
I've cause to tell 'em.
Each bead (she held a bead between thumb and finger)
A crime!
'Twas a winter's night, before cockcrow,
Yet the cock did crow ere he left me –
The man with a hood on his face, and the bloody hands
And the babe in the basket.
'Tee hee' he mewed, as who should say 'I want my toy'
Poor witling!
'Tee hee, tee hee!' I could not slay him!
For that, Mary in Heaven, forgive me
The sins I've sinned before cockcrow!
Down to the creek i' the dawn I slipped
Where the gull haunts and the heron stands
Like a stake on the edge of the marshes . . .
Who's here?

(Three young men swaggered on to the stage and accosted her)
— *Are you come to torture me, Sirs?*
There is little blood in this arm,
(she extended her skinny forearm from her ragged shift)
Saints in Heaven preserve me!

She bawled. They bawled. All together they bawled, and so loud that it was difficult to make out what they were saying: apparently it was: *Did she remember concealing a child in a cradle among the rushes some twenty years previously? A babe in a basket, crone! A babe in a basket?* they bawled. *The wind howls and the bittern shrieks*, she replied.

'There is little blood in my arm,' Isabella repeated.

That was all she heard. There was such a medley of things going on, what with the beldame's deafness, the bawling of the youths, and the confusion of the plot that she could make nothing of it.

Did the plot matter? She shifted and looked over her right shoulder. The plot was only there to beget emotion. There were only two emotions: love; and hate. There was no need to puzzle out the plot. Perhaps Miss La Trobe meant that when she cut this knot in the centre?

Don't bother about the plot: the plot's nothing.

But what was happening? The Prince had come.

Plucking up his sleeve, the beldame recognized the mole; and, staggering back in her chair, shrieked:

My child! My child!

Recognition followed. The young Prince (Albert Perry) was almost smothered in the withered arms of the beldame. Then suddenly he started apart.

'*Look where she comes!*' he cried.

They all looked where she came — Sylvia Edwards in white satin.

Who came? Isa looked. The nightingale's song? The pearl in night's black ear? Love embodied.

All arms were raised; all faces stared.

'*Hail, sweet Carinthia!*' said the Prince, sweeping his hat off. And she to him, raising her eyes:

'*My love! My lord!*'

'It was enough. Enough. Enough,' Isa repeated.

All else was verbiage, repetition.

The beldame meanwhile, because that was enough, had sunk back on her chair, the beads dangling from her fingers.

'*Look to the beldame there — old Elsbeth's sick!*'

(They crowded round her)

Dead, Sirs!

She fell back lifeless. The crowd drew away. Peace, let her pass.[72] She to whom all's one now, summer or winter.

Peace was the third emotion. Love. Hate. Peace. Three emotions made the ply of human life. Now the priest, whose cotton wool moustache confused his utterance, stepped forward and pronounced benediction.

From the distaff of life's tangled skein, unloose her hands

(They unloosed her hands)

Of her frailty, let nothing now remembered be.

Call for the robin redbreast and the wren.

And roses fall your crimson pall.

(Petals were strewn from wicker baskets)

Cover the corpse. Sleep well.

(They covered the corpse)

On you, fair Sirs (he turned to the happy couple)

Let Heaven rain benediction!

Haste ere the envying sun

Night's curtain hath undone. Let music sound

And the free air of Heaven waft you to your slumber!

Lead on the dance!

The gramophone blared. Dukes, priests, shepherds, pilgrims, and serving men took hands and danced. The idiot scampered in and out. Hands joined, heads knocking, they danced round the majestic figure of the Elizabethan age personified by Mrs. Clark, licensed to sell tobacco, on her soap box.

It was a mellay;[73] a medley; an entrancing spectacle (to

William) of dappled light and shade on half clothed, fantastically coloured, leaping, jerking, swinging legs and arms. He clapped till his palms stung.

Mrs. Manresa applauded loudly. Somehow she was the Queen; and he (Giles) was the surly hero.

'Bravo! Bravo!' she cried, and her enthusiasm made the surly hero squirm on his seat. Then the great lady in the bath chair, the lady whose marriage with the local peer had obliterated in his trashy title a name that had been a name when there were brambles and briars where the Church now stood – so indigenous was she that even her body, crippled by arthritis, resembled an uncouth, nocturnal animal, now nearly extinct – clapped and laughed loud – the sudden laughter of a startled jay.

'Ha, ha, ha!' she laughed and clutched the arms of her chair with ungloved twisted hands.

A-maying, a-maying, they bawled. *In and out and round about, a-maying, a-maying ...*

It didn't matter what the words were; or who sang what. Round and round they whirled, intoxicated by the music. Then, at a sign from Miss La Trobe behind the tree, the dance stopped. A procession formed. Great Eliza descended from her soap box. Taking her skirts in her hand, striding with long strides, surrounded by Dukes and Princes, followed by the lovers arm in arm, with Albert the idiot playing in and out, and the corpse on its bier concluding the procession, the Elizabethan age passed from the scene.

'Curse! Blast! Damn 'em!' Miss La Trobe in her rage stubbed her toe against a root. Here was her downfall; here was the Interval. Writing this skimble-skamble stuff in her cottage, she had agreed to cut the play here; a slave to her audience, – to Mrs. Sands' grumble – about tea; about dinner; – she had gashed the scene here. Just as she had brewed emotion, she spilt it. So she signalled: Phyllis! And, summoned, Phyllis popped up on the mat again in the middle.

Gentles and simples, I address you all (she piped.)
Our act is done, our scene is over.
Past is the day of crone and lover.

The bud has flowered; the flower has fallen.
But soon will rise another dawning,
For time whose children small we be
Hath in his keeping, you shall see,
You shall see . . .

Her voice petered out. No one was listening. Heads bent, they read 'Interval' on the programme. And, cutting short her words, the megaphone announced in plain English: 'An interval.' Half an hour's interval, for tea. Then the gramophone blared out:

> *Armed against fate,*
> *The valiant Rhoderick,*
> *Bold and blatant,*
> *Firm, elatant, etc., etc.*

At that, the audience stirred. Some rose briskly; others stooped, retrieving walking-sticks, hats, bags. And then, as they raised themselves and turned about, the music modulated. The music chanted: *Dispersed are we.*[74] It moaned: *Dispersed are we*. It lamented: *Dispersed are we*, as they streamed, spotting the grass with colour, across the lawns, and down the paths: *Dispersed are we*.

Mrs. Manresa took up the strain. *Dispersed are we*. 'Freely, boldly, fearing no one' (she pushed a deck chair out of her way). 'Youths and maidens' (she glanced behind her; but Giles had his back turned). 'Follow, follow, follow me . . . Oh Mr. Parker, what a pleasure to see *you* here! I'm for tea!'

'Dispersed are we,' Isabella followed her, humming. 'All is over. The wave has broken. Left us stranded, high and dry. Single, separate on the shingle. Broken is the three-fold ply . . . Now I follow' (she pushed her chair back . . . The man in grey was lost in the crowd by the ilex) 'that old strumpet' (she invoked Mrs. Manresa's tight, flowered figure in front of her) 'to have tea.'

Dodge remained behind. 'Shall I,' he murmured, 'go or stay? Slip out some other way? Or follow, follow, follow the dispersing company?'

Dispersed are we, the music wailed; *dispersed are we*. Giles remained like a stake in the tide of the flowing company.

'Follow?' He kicked his chair back. 'Whom? Where?' He stubbed his light tennis shoes on the wood. 'Nowhere. Anywhere.' Stark still he stood.

Here Cobbet of Cobbs Corner, alone under the monkey puzzle tree, rose and muttered: 'What was in her mind, eh? What idea lay behind, eh? What made her indue the antique with this glamour – this sham lure, and set 'em climbing, climbing, climbing up the monkey puzzle tree?'

Dispersed are we, the music wailed. *Dispersed are we*. He turned and sauntered slowly after the retreating company.

Now Lucy, retrieving her bag from beneath the seat, chirruped to her brother:

'Bart, my dear, come with me . . . D'you remember, when we were children, the play we acted in the nursery?'

He remembered. Red Indians the game was; a reed with a note wrapped up in a pebble.

'But for us, my old Cindy' – he picked up his hat – 'the game's over.' The glare and the stare and the beat of the tom-tom, he meant. He gave her his arm. Off they strolled. And Mr. Page, the reporter, noted, 'Mrs. Swithin: Mr. B. Oliver,' then turning, added further 'Lady Haslip, of Haslip Manor,' as he spied that old lady wheeled in her chair by her footman winding up the procession.

To the valediction of the gramophone hid in the bushes the audience departed. *Dispersed*, it wailed, *Dispersed are we*.

Now Miss La Trobe stepped from her hiding. Flowing, and streaming, on the grass, on the gravel, still for one moment she held them together – the dispersing company. Hadn't she, for twenty-five minutes, made them see? A vision imparted was relief from agony . . . for one moment . . . one moment. Then the music petered out on the last word *we*. She heard the breeze rustle in the branches. She saw Giles Oliver with his back to the audience. Also Cobbet of Cobbs Corner. She hadn't made them see. It was a failure, another damned failure! As usual. Her vision escaped her. And turning, she strode to the actors, undressing, down in the hollow, where butterflies feasted upon swords of silver paper; where the dish cloths in the shadow made pools of yellow.

Cobbet had out his watch. Three hours till seven, he noted; then water the plants. He turned.

Giles, nicking his chair into its notch, turned too, in the other direction. He took the short cut by the fields to the Barn. This dry summer the path was hard as brick across the fields. This dry summer the path was strewn with stones. He kicked – a flinty yellow stone, a sharp stone, edged as if cut by a savage for an arrow. A barbaric stone; a pre-historic. Stone-kicking was a child's game. He remembered the rules. By the rules of the game, one stone, the same stone, must be kicked to the goal. Say a gate, or a tree. He played it alone. The gate was a goal; to be reached in ten. The first kick was Manresa (lust). The second, Dodge (perversion). The third himself (coward). And the fourth and the fifth and all the others were the same.

He reached it in ten. There, couched in the grass, curled in an olive green ring, was a snake. Dead? No, choked with a toad in its mouth. The snake was unable to swallow; the toad was unable to die. A spasm made the ribs contract; blood oozed. It was birth the wrong way round – a monstrous inversion. So, raising his foot, he stamped on them. The mass crushed and slithered. The white canvas on his tennis shoes was bloodstained and sticky. But it was action. Action relieved him. He strode to the Barn, with blood on his shoes.

The Barn, the Noble Barn, the barn that had been built over seven hundred years ago and reminded some people of a Greek temple, others of the middle ages, most people of an age before their own, scarcely anybody of the present moment, was empty.

The great doors stood open. A shaft of light like a yellow banner sloped from roof to floor. Festoons of paper roses, left over from the Coronation, drooped from the rafters. A long table, on which stood an urn, plates and cups, cakes and bread and butter, stretched across one end. The Barn was empty. Mice slid in and out of holes or stood upright, nibbling. Swallows were busy with straw in pockets of earth in the rafters. Countless beetles and insects of various sorts burrowed in the dry wood. A stray bitch had made the dark corner where the sacks stood a lying-in ground for her puppies. All these eyes, expanding and narrowing, some adapted to light, others to darkness, looked from different angles and edges. Minute nibblings and rustlings broke the silence. Whiffs of sweetness and richness veined the air. A blue-bottle had settled on the cake and stabbed its yellow rock with its short drill. A butterfly sunned itself sensuously on a sunlit yellow plate.

But Mrs. Sands was approaching. She was pushing her way through the crowd. She had turned the corner. She could see the great open door. But butterflies she never saw; mice were only black pellets in kitchen drawers; moths she bundled in her hands and put out of the window. Bitches suggested only servant girls misbehaving. Had there been a cat she would have seen it – any cat, a starved cat with a patch of mange on its rump opened the flood gates of her childless heart. But there was no cat. The Barn was empty. And so running, panting, set upon reaching the Barn and taking up her station behind the tea urn before the company came, she reached the Barn. And the butterfly rose and the blue-bottle.

Following her in a scud came the servants and helpers – David, John, Irene, Lois. Water boiled. Steam issued. Cake was sliced. Swallows swooped from rafter to rafter. And the company entered.

'This fine old Barn ...' said Mrs. Manresa, stopping in the doorway. It was not for her to press ahead of the villagers. It was for her, moved by the beauty of the Barn, to stand still; to draw aside; to gaze; to let other people come first.

'We have one, much like it, at Lathom,' said Mrs. Parker, stopping, for the same reasons. 'Perhaps,' she added, 'not quite so large.'

The villagers hung back. Then, hesitating, dribbled past.

'And the decorations ...' said Mrs. Manresa, looking round for someone to congratulate. She stood smiling, waiting. Then old Mrs. Swithin came in. She was gazing up too, but not at the decorations. At the swallows apparently.

'They come every year,' she said, 'the same birds.' Mrs. Manresa smiled benevolently, humouring the old lady's whimsy. It was unlikely, she thought, that the birds were the same.

'The decorations, I suppose, are left over from the Corona-tion,' said Mrs. Parker. 'We kept ours too. We built a village hall.'

Mrs. Manresa laughed. She remembered. An anecdote was on the tip of her tongue, about a public lavatory built to celebrate the same occasion, and how the Mayor . . . Could she tell it? No. The old lady, gazing at the swallows, looked too refined. 'Refeened' – Mrs. Manresa qualified the word to her own ad-vantage, thus confirming her approval of the wild child she was, whose nature was somehow 'just human nature.' Somehow she could span the old lady's 'refeenment,' also the boy's fun – Where was that nice fellow Giles? She couldn't see him; nor Bill either. The villagers still hung back. They must have someone to start the ball rolling.

'Well, I'm dying for my tea!' she said in her public voice; and strode forward. She laid hold of a thick china mug. Mrs. Sands giving precedence, of course, to one of the gentry, filled it at once. David gave her cake. She was the first to drink, the first to bite. The villagers still hung back. 'It's all my eye about democ-racy,' she concluded. So did Mrs. Parker, taking her mug too. The people looked to them. They led; the rest followed.

'What delicious tea!' each exclaimed, disgusting though it was, like rust boiled in water, and the cake fly-blown. But they had a duty to society.

'They come every year,' said Mrs. Swithin, ignoring the fact that she spoke to the empty air. 'From Africa.' As they had come, she supposed, when the Barn was a swamp.

The Barn filled. Fumes rose. China clattered; voices chattered. Isa pressed her way to the table.

'Dispersed are we,' she murmured. And held her cup out to be filled. She took it. 'Let me turn away,' she murmured, turning, 'from the array' – she looked desolately round her – 'of china faces, glazed and hard. Down the ride, that leads under the nut tree and the may tree, away, till I come to the wishing well, where the washer-woman's little boy –' she dropped sugar, two lumps, into her tea, 'dropped a pin. He got his horse, so they say. But what wish should I drop into the well?' She looked round. She could not see the man in grey, the gentleman farmer;

nor anyone known to her. 'That the waters should cover me,' she added, 'of the wishing well.'

The noise of china and chatter drowned her murmur. 'Sugar for you?' they were saying. 'Just a spot of milk? And you?' 'Tea without milk or sugar. That's the way I like it.' 'A bit too strong? Let me add water.'

'That's what I wished,' Isa added, 'when I dropped my pin. Water. Water . . .'

'I must say,' the voice said behind her, 'it's brave of the King and Queen. They're said to be going to India.[75] She looks such a dear. Someone I know said his hair . . .'

'There,' Isa mused, 'would the dead leaf fall, when the leaves fall, on the water. Should I mind not again to see may tree or nut tree? Not again to hear on the trembling spray the thrush sing, or to see, dipping and diving as if he skimmed waves in the air, the yellow woodpecker?'

She was looking at the canary yellow festoons left over from the Coronation.

'I thought they said Canada, not India,' the voice said behind her back. To which the other voice answered: 'D'you believe what the papers say? For instance, about the Duke of Windsor. He landed on the south coast. Queen Mary met him.[76] She'd been buying furniture – that's a fact. And the papers say she met him . . .'

'Alone, under a tree, the withered tree that keeps all day murmuring of the sea, and hears the Rider gallop . . .'[77]

Isa filled in the phrase. Then she started. William Dodge was by her side.

He smiled. She smiled. They were conspirators; each murmuring some song my uncle taught me.

'It's the play,' she said. 'The play keeps running in my head.'

'Hail, sweet Carinthia. My love. My life,' he quoted.

'My lord, my liege,' she bowed ironically.

She was handsome. He wanted to see her, not against the tea urn, but with her glass green eyes and thick body – the neck was broad as a pillar – against an arum lily or a vine. He wished she would say: 'Come along. I'll show you the greenhouse, the pig sty, or the stable.' But she said nothing, and they stood there holding their cups, remembering the play. Then he saw her face change, as if she had got out of one dress and put on another. A small boy battled his way through the crowd, striking against skirts and trousers as if he were swimming blindly.

'Here!' she cried raising her arm.

He made a bee-line for her. He was her little boy, apparently, her son, her George. She gave him cake; then a mug of milk. Then Nurse came up. Then again she changed her dress. This time, from the expression in her eyes it was apparently something in the nature of a strait waistcoat. Hirsute, handsome, virile, the young man in blue jacket and brass buttons, standing in a beam of dusty light, was her husband. And she his wife. Their relations, as he had noted at lunch, were as people say in novels 'strained.' As he had noted at the play, her bare arm had raised itself nervously to her shoulder when she turned – looking for whom? But here he was; and the muscular, the hirsute, the virile plunged him into emotions in which the mind had no share. He forgot how she would have looked against vine leaf in a greenhouse. Only at Giles he looked; and looked and looked. Of whom was he thinking as he stood with his face turned? Not of Isa. Of Mrs. Manresa?

Mrs. Manresa half-way down the Barn had gulped her cup of tea. How can I rid myself, she asked, of Mrs. Parker? If they were of her own class, how they bored her – her own sex! Not the class below – cooks, shopkeepers, farmers' wives; nor the class above – peeresses, countesses; it was the women of her own class that bored her. So she left Mrs. Parker, abruptly.

'Oh Mrs. Moore,' she hailed the keeper's wife. 'What did you think of it? And what did baby think of it?' Here she pinched baby. 'I thought it every bit as good as anything I'd seen in London ... But we mustn't be outdone. We'll have a play of our own. In *our* Barn. We'll show 'em' (here she winked obliquely at the table; so many bought cakes, so few made at home) 'how *we* do it.'

Then cracking her jokes, she turned; saw Giles; caught his eye; and swept him in, beckoning. He came. And what – she looked down – had he done with his shoes? They were blood-stained. Vaguely some sense that he had proved his valour for her admiration flattered her. If vague it was sweet. Taking him in tow, she felt: I am the Queen, he my hero, my sulky hero.

'That's Mrs. Neale!' she exclaimed. 'A perfect marvel of a woman, aren't you, Mrs. Neale! She runs our post office, Mrs. Neale. She can do sums in her head, can't you, Mrs. Neale? Twenty-five halfpenny stamps, two packets of stamped envelopes and a packet of postcards – how much does that come to, Mrs. Neale?'

Mrs. Neale laughed; Mrs. Manresa laughed; Giles too smiled, and looked down at his shoes.

She drew him down the Barn, in and out, from one to another. She knew 'em all. Every one was a thorough good sort. No, she wouldn't allow it, not for a moment – Pinsent's bad leg. 'No, no. We're not going to take that for an excuse, Pinsent.' If he couldn't bowl, he could bat. Giles agreed. A fish on a line meant the same to him and Pinsent; also jays and magpies. Pinsent stayed on the land; Giles went to an office. That was all. And she was a thorough good sort, making him feel less of an audience, more of an actor, going round the Barn in her wake.

Then, at the end by the door, they came upon the old couple, Lucy and Bartholomew, sitting on their Windsor chairs.

Chairs had been reserved for them. Mrs. Sands had sent them tea. It would have caused more bother than it was worth – asserting the democratic principle; standing in the crowd at the table.

'Swallows,' said Lucy, holding her cup, looking at the birds. Excited by the company they were flitting from rafter to rafter. Across Africa, across France they had come to nest here. Year after year they came. Before there was a channel, when the earth, upon which the Windsor chair was planted, was a riot of rhodo-dendrons, and humming birds quivered at the mouths of scarlet trumpets, as she had read that morning in her Outline of History,[78] they had come . . . Here Bart rose from his chair.

But Mrs. Manresa absolutely refused to take his seat. 'Go on sitting, go on sitting,' she pressed him down again. 'I'll squat on the floor.' She squatted. The surly knight remained in attendance.

'And what did you think of the play?' she asked.

Bartholomew looked at his son. His son remained silent.

'And you Mrs. Swithin?' Mrs. Manresa pressed the old lady.

Lucy mumbled, looking at the swallows.

'I was hoping you'd tell me,' said Mrs. Manresa. 'Was it an old play? Was it a new play?'

No one answered.

'Look!' Lucy exclaimed.

'The birds?' said Mrs. Manresa, looking up.

There was a bird with a straw in its beak; and the straw dropped.

Lucy clapped her hands. Giles turned away. She was mocking him as usual, laughing.

'Going?' said Bartholomew. 'Time for the next act?'

And he heaved himself up from his chair. Regardless of Mrs. Manresa and of Lucy, off he strolled too.

'Swallow, my sister, O sister swallow,'[79] he muttered, feeling for his cigar case, following his son.

Mrs. Manresa was nettled. What for had she squatted on the floor then? Were her charms fading? Both were gone. But, woman of action as she was, deserted by the male sex, she was not going to suffer tortures of boredom from the refeened old lady. Up she scrambled, putting her hands to her hair as if it were high time that she went too, though it was nothing of the kind and her hair was perfectly tidy. Cobbet in his corner saw through her little game. He had known human nature in the East. It was the same in the West. Plants remained – the carnation, the zinnia, and the geranium. Automatically he consulted his watch; noted time to water at seven; and observed the little game of the woman following the man to the table in the West as in the East.

William at the table, now attached to Mrs. Parker and Isa, watched him approach. Armed and valiant, bold and blatant, firm, elatant – the popular march tune rang in his head. And the fingers of William's left hand closed firmly, surreptitiously, as the hero approached.

Mrs. Parker was deploring to Isa in a low voice the village idiot.

'Oh that idiot!' she was saying. But Isa was immobile, watching her husband. She could feel the Manresa in his wake. She could hear in the dusk in their bedroom the usual explanation. It made no difference; his infidelity – but hers did.

'The idiot?' William answered Mrs. Parker for her. 'He's in the tradition.'

'But surely,' said Mrs. Parker, and told Giles how creepy the idiot – 'We have one in our village' – had made her feel. 'Surely, Mr. Oliver, we're more civilized?'

'*We?*' said Giles. '*We?*' He looked, once, at William. He knew not his name; but what his left hand was doing.[80] It was a bit of luck – that he could despise him, not himself. Also Mrs. Parker. But not Isa – not his wife. She had not spoken to him, not one word. Nor looked at him either.

'Surely,' said Mrs. Parker, looking from one to the other. 'Surely we are?'

Giles then did what to Isa was his little trick; shut his lips; frowned; and took up the pose of one who bears the burden of the world's woe, making money for her to spend.

'No,' said Isa, as plainly as words could say it. 'I don't admire you,' and looked, not at his face, but at his feet. 'Silly little boy, with blood on his boots.'

Giles shifted his feet. Whom then did she admire? Not Dodge. That he could take for certain. Who else? Some man he knew. Some man, he was sure, in the Barn. Which man? He looked round him.

Then Mr. Streatfield, the clergyman, interrupted. He was carrying cups.

'So I shake hands with my heart!' he exclaimed, nodding his handsome, grizzled head and depositing his burden safely.

Mrs. Parker took the tribute to herself.

'Mr. Streatfield!' she exclaimed. 'Doing all the work! While we stand gossiping!'

'Like to see the greenhouse?' said Isa suddenly, turning to William Dodge.

O not now, he could have cried. But had to follow, leaving Giles to welcome the approaching Manresa, who had him in thrall.[81]

*

The path was narrow. Isa went ahead. And she was broad; she fairly filled the path, swaying slightly as she walked, and plucking a leaf here and there from the hedge.

'Fly then, follow,' she hummed, 'the dappled herds in the cedar grove, who, sporting, play, the red with the roe, the stag with the doe. Fly, away. I grieving stay. Alone I linger, I pluck the bitter herb by the ruined wall, the churchyard wall, and press its sour, its sweet, its sour, long grey leaf, so, twixt thumb and finger . . .'

She threw away the shred of Old Man's Beard that she had picked in passing and kicked open the greenhouse door. Dodge had lagged behind. She waited. She picked up a knife from the plank. He saw her standing against the green glass, the fig tree, and the blue hydrangea, knife in hand.

'She spake,' Isa murmured. 'And from her bosom's snowy antre drew the gleaming blade. "Plunge blade!" she said. And struck. "Faithless!" she cried. Knife, too! It broke. So too my heart,' she said.

She was smiling ironically as he came up.

'I wish the play didn't run in my head,' she said. Then she sat down on a plank under the vine. And he sat beside her. The little grapes above them were green buds; the leaves thin and yellow as the web between birds' claws.

'Still the play?' he asked. She nodded. 'That was your son,' he said, 'in the Barn?'

She had a daughter too, she told him, in the cradle.

'And you – married?' she asked. From her tone he knew she guessed, as women always guessed, everything. They knew at once they had nothing to fear, nothing to hope. At first they resented – serving as statues in a greenhouse. Then they liked it. For then they could say – as she did – whatever came into their heads. And hand him, as she handed him, a flower.

'There's something for your buttonhole, Mr. . . .' she said, handing him a sprig of scented geranium.

'I'm William,' he said, taking the furry leaf and pressing it between thumb and finger.

'I'm Isa,' she answered. Then they talked as if they had known each other all their lives; which was odd, she said, as they always did, considering she'd known him perhaps one hour. Weren't they, though, conspirators, seekers after hidden faces? That confessed, she paused and wondered, as they always did, why they could speak so plainly to each other. And added: 'Perhaps because we've never met before, and never shall again.'[82]

'The doom of sudden death hanging over us,' he said. 'There's no retreating and advancing' – he was thinking of the old lady showing him the house – 'for us as for them.'

The future shadowed their present, like the sun coming through the many-veined transparent vine leaf; a criss-cross of lines making no pattern.

They had left the greenhouse door open, and now music came through it. A.B.C., A.B.C., A.B.C. – someone was practising scales. C.A.T. C.A.T. C.A.T. . . . Then the separate letters made one word 'Cat.' Other words followed. It was a simple tune, like a nursery rhyme –

> The King is in his counting house,
> Counting out his money,
> The Queen is in her parlour
> Eating bread and honey.

They listened. Another voice, a third voice, was saying something simple. And they sat on in the greenhouse, on the plank with the vine over them, listening to Miss La Trobe or whoever it was, practising her scales.

He could not find his son. He had lost him in the crowd. So old Bartholomew left the Barn, and went to his own room, holding his cheroot and murmuring:

> 'O sister swallow, O sister swallow,
> How can thy heart be full of the spring?'

'How can my heart be full of the spring?' he said aloud, standing in front of the book case. Books: the treasured lifeblood of immortal spirits. Poets;[83] the legislators of mankind. Doubtless, it was so. But Giles was unhappy. 'How can my heart, how can my heart,' he repeated, puffing at his cheroot.

'Condemned in life's infernal mine, condemned in solitude to pine . . .'[84] Arms akimbo, he stood in front of his country gentleman's library. Garibaldi; Wellington; Irrigation Officers' Reports; and Hibbert on the Diseases of the Horse.[85] A great harvest the mind had reaped; but for all this, compared with his son, he did not care one damn.

'What's the use, what's the use,' he sank down into his chair muttering, 'O sister swallow, O sister swallow, of singing your song?' The dog, who had followed him, flopped down on to the floor at his feet. Flanks sucked in and out, the long nose resting on his paws, a fleck of foam on the nostril, there he was, his familiar spirit, his Afghan hound.

The door trembled and stood half open. That was Lucy's way of coming in — as if she did not know what she would find. Really! It was her brother! And his dog! She seemed to see them for the first time. Was it that she had no body? Up in the clouds, like an air-ball, her mind touched ground now and then with a shock of surprise. There was nothing in her to weight a man like Giles to the earth.

She perched on the edge of a chair like a bird on a telegraph wire before starting for Africa.

'Swallow, my sister, O sister swallow . . .' he murmured.

From the garden — the window was open — came the sound of someone practising scales. A.B.C. A.B.C. A.B.C. Then the separate letters formed one word. 'Dog.' Then a phrase. It was a simple tune, another voice speaking.

> 'Hark hark, the dogs do bark,
> The beggars are coming to town . . .'

Then it languished and lengthened, and became a waltz. As they listened and looked — out into the garden — the trees tossing and the birds swirling seemed called out of their private lives, out of their separate avocations, and made to take part.

> The lamp of love burns high,[86] over the dark cedar groves,
> The lamp of love shines clear, clear as a star in the sky . . .

Old Bartholomew tapped his fingers on his knee in time to the tune.

Leave your casement and come, lady I love till I die,

He looked sardonically at Lucy, perched on her chair. How, he wondered, had she ever borne children?

For all are dancing, retreating and advancing,
The moth and the dragon-fly . . .

She was thinking, he supposed, God is peace. God is love. For she belonged to the unifiers; he to the separatists.

Then the tune with its feet always on the same spot, became sugared, insipid; bored a hole with its perpetual invocation to perpetual adoration. Had it – he was ignorant of musical terms – gone into the minor key?

For this day and this dance and this merry, merry May
Will be over (he tapped his forefinger on his knee)
With the cutting of the clover this retreating and advancing –

the swifts seemed to have shot beyond their orbits –

Will be over, over, over,
And the ice will dart its splinter, and the winter,
O the winter, will fill the grate with ashes,
And there'll be no glow, no glow on the log.

He knocked the ash off his cheroot and rose.

'So we must,' said Lucy; as if he had said aloud, 'It's time to go.'

The audience was assembling. The music was summoning them. Down the paths, across the lawns they were streaming again. There was Mrs. Manresa, with Giles at her side, heading the procession. In taut plump curves her scarf blew round her shoulders. The breeze was rising. She looked, as she crossed the lawn to the strains of the gramophone, goddess-like, buoyant, abundant, her cornucopia running over. Bartholomew, following, blessed the power of the human body to make the earth fruitful. Giles would keep his orbit so long as she weighted him to the earth. She stirred the stagnant pool of his old heart even –

where bones lay buried, but the dragon-flies shot and the grass trembled as Mrs. Manresa advanced across the lawn to the strains of the gramophone.

Feet crunched the gravel. Voices chattered. The inner voice, the other voice was saying: How can we deny that this brave music, wafted from the bushes, is expressive of some inner harmony? 'When we wake' (some were thinking) 'the day breaks us with its hard mallet blows.' 'The office' (some were thinking) 'compels disparity. Scattered, shattered, hither thither summoned by the bell. "Ping-ping-ping" – that's the phone. "Forward!" "Serving!" – that's the shop.' So we answer to the infernal, agelong and eternal order issued from on high. And obey. 'Working, serving, pushing, striving, earning wages – to be spent – here? Oh dear no. Now? No, by and by. When ears are deaf and the heart is dry.'

Here Cobbet of Cobbs Corner who had stooped – there was a flower – was pressed on by people pushing from behind.

For I hear music, they were saying. Music wakes us. Music makes us see the hidden, join the broken. Look and listen. See the flowers, how they ray their redness, whiteness, silverness and blue. And the trees with their many-tongued much syllabling, their green and yellow leaves hustle us and shuffle us, and bid us, like the starlings, and the rooks, come together, crowd together, to chatter and make merry while the red cow moves forward and the black cow stands still.

The audience had reached their seats. Some sat down; others stood a moment, turned, and looked at the view. The stage was empty; the actors were still dressing up among the bushes. The audience turned to one another and began to talk. Scraps and fragments reached Miss La Trobe where she stood, script in hand, behind the tree.

'They're not ready . . . I hear 'em laughing' (they were saying.) '. . . Dressing up. That's the great thing, dressing up. And it's pleasant now, the sun's not so hot . . . That's one good the war brought us – longer days . . .[87] Where did we leave off? D'you remember? The Elizabethans . . . Perhaps she'll reach the present, if she skips . . . D'you think people change? Their clothes, of course . . . But I meant ourselves . . . Clearing out a cupboard, I found my father's old top hat ... But ourselves – do we change?'

'No, I don't go by politicians. I've a friend who's been to Russia. He says ... And my daughter, just back from Rome, she says the common people, in the cafés, hate Dictators ...[88] Well, different people say different things ...'

'Did you see it in the papers – the case about the dog? D'you believe dogs can't have puppies? ... And Queen Mary[89] and the Duke of Windsor on the south coast? ... D'you believe what's in the papers? I ask the butcher or the grocer ... That's Mr. Streatfield, carrying a hurdle ... The good clergyman, I say, does more work for less pay than all the lot ... It's the wives that make the trouble ...'

'And what about the Jews? The refugees ... the Jews ... People like ourselves, beginning life again[90] ... But it's always been the same ... My old mother, who's over eighty, can remember ... Yes, she still reads without glasses ... How amazing! Well, don't they say, after eighty ... Now they're coming ... No, that's nothing ... I'd make it penal, leaving litter. But then, who's, my husband says, to collect the fines? ... Ah there she is, Miss La Trobe, over there, behind that tree ...'

Over there behind the tree Miss La Trobe gnashed her teeth. She crushed her manuscript. The actors delayed. Every moment the audience slipped the noose; split up into scraps and fragments.

'Music!' she signalled. 'Music!'

'What's the origin,' said a voice, 'of the expression "with a flea in his ear"?'[91]

Down came her hand peremptorily. 'Music, music,' she signalled.

And the gramophone began A.B.C., A.B.C.

> The King is in his counting house
> Counting out his money,
> The Queen is in her parlour
> Eating bread and honey ...[92]

Miss La Trobe watched them sink down peacefully into the nursery rhyme. She watched them fold their hands and compose their faces. Then she beckoned. And at last, with a final touch to her head dress, which had been giving trouble, Mabel Hopkins strode from the bushes, and took her place on the raised ground facing the audience.

Eyes fed on her as fish rise to a crumb of bread on the water. Who was she? What did she represent? She was beautiful – very. Her cheeks had been powdered; her colour glowed smooth and clear underneath. Her grey satin robe (a bedspread), pinned in stone-like folds, gave her the majesty of a statue. She carried a sceptre and a little round orb. England was she? Queen Anne[93] was she? Who was she? She spoke too low at first; all they heard was

. . . reason holds sway.

Old Bartholomew applauded.

'Hear! Hear!' he cried. 'Bravo! Bravo!'

Thus encouraged Reason spoke out.

Time, leaning on his sickle, stands amazed. While Commerce from her cornucopia pours the mingled tribute of her different ores. In distant mines the savage sweats; and from the reluctant earth the painted pot is shaped. At my behest, the armed warrior lays his shield aside; the heathen leaves the Altar steaming with unholy sacrifice. The violet and the eglantine over the riven earth their flowers entwine. No longer fears the unwary wanderer the poisoned snake. And in the helmet, yellow bees their honey make.

She paused. A long line of villagers in sacking were passing in and out of the trees behind her.

Digging and delving, ploughing and sowing they were singing, but the wind blew their words away.

Beneath the shelter of my flowing robe (she resumed, extending her arms) *the arts arise. Music for me unfolds her heavenly harmony. At my behest the miser leaves his hoard untouched; at peace the mother sees her children play . . . Her children play . . .*[94] she repeated, and, waving her sceptre, figures advanced from the bushes.

Let swains and nymphs lead on the play, while Zephyr sleeps, and the unruly tribes of Heaven confess my sway.

A merry little old tune was played on the gramophone. Old

Bartholomew joined his finger tips; Mrs. Manresa smoothed her skirts about her knees.

> *Young Damon said to Cynthia*
> *Come out now with the dawn*
> *And don your azure tippet*
> *And cast your cares adown*
> *For peace has come to England,*
> *And reason now holds sway.*
> *What pleasure lies in dreaming*
> *When blue and green's the day?*
> *Now cast your cares behind you.*
> *Night passes: here is Day.*

Digging and delving, the villagers sang passing in single file in and out between the trees, *for the earth is always the same, summer and winter and spring; and spring and winter again; ploughing and sowing, eating and growing; time passes . . .*

The wind blew the words away.

The dance stopped. The nymphs and swains withdrew. Reason held the centre of the stage alone. Her arms extended, her robes flowing, holding orb and sceptre, Mabel Hopkins stood sublimely looking over the heads of the audience. The audience gazed at her. She ignored the audience. Then while she gazed, helpers from the bushes arranged round her what appeared to be the three sides of a room. In the middle they stood a table. On the table they placed a china tea service. Reason surveyed this domestic scene from her lofty eminence unmoved. There was a pause.

'Another scene from another play, I suppose,' said Mrs. Elmhurst, referring to her programme. She read out for the benefit of her husband, who was deaf: '*Where there's a Will there's a Way*.[95] That's the name of the play. And the characters . . .' She read out: 'Lady Harpy Harraden, in love with Sir Spaniel Lilyliver. Deb, her maid. Flavinda, her niece, in love with Valentine. Sir Spaniel Lilyliver, in love with Flavinda. Sir Smirking Peacebe-with-you-all, a clergyman. Lord and Lady Fribble. Valentine, in love with Flavinda. What names for real people! But look — here they come!'

Out they came from the bushes – men in flowered waistcoats, white stockings and buckled shoes; women wearing brocades tucked up, hooped and draped; glass stars, blue ribands and imitation pearls made them look the very image of Lords and Ladies.

'The first scene,' Mrs. Elmhurst whispered into her husband's ear, 'is Lady Harraden's dressing-room ... That's her ...' She pointed. 'Mrs. Otter, I think, from the End House; but she's wonderfully made up. And that's Deb her maid. Who she is, I don't know.'

'Hush, hush, hush,' someone protested.

Mrs. Elmhurst dropped her programme. The play had begun.

Lady Harpy Harraden entered her dressing-room, followed by Deb her maid.

LADY H. H. ... *Give me the pounce-box. Then the patch. Hand me the mirror, girl. So. Now my wig ... A pox on the girl – she's dreaming!*

DEB ... *I was thinking, my lady, what the gentleman said when he saw you in the Park.*

LADY H. H. (gazing in the glass) *So, so – what was it? Some silly trash! Cupid's dart – hah, hah! lighting his taper – tush – at my eyes ... pooh! That was in milord's time, twenty years since ... But now – what'll he say of me now?* (She looks in the mirror) *Sir Spaniel Lilyliver, I mean ...* (a rap at the door) *Hark! That's his chaise at the door. Run child. Don't stand gaping.*

DEB ... (going to the door) *Say? He'll rattle his tongue as a gambler rattles dice in a box. He'll find no words to fit you. He'll stand like a pig in a poke ... Your servant, Sir Spaniel.*

Enter Sir Spaniel.

SIR S. L. ... *Hail, my fair Saint! What, out o' bed so early? Methought, as I came along the Mall the air was something brighter than usual. Here's the reason ... Venus, Aphrodite, upon my word a very galaxy, a constellation! As I'm a sinner, a very Aurora Borealis!*

(He sweeps his hat off.)

LADY H. H. ... *Oh flatterer, flatterer! I know your ways. But come. Sit down ... A glass of Aqua Vitae. Take this seat, Sir Spaniel. I've something very private and particular to say to you ... You had my letter, Sir?*

Sir S. L. . . . *Pinned to my heart!*

(He strikes his breast.)

Lady H. H. . . . *I have a favour to ask of you, Sir.*

Sir S. L. . . . (singing) *What favour could fair Chloe ask that Damon would not get her? . . . 'A' done with rhymes. Rhymes are still a-bed. Let's speak prose. What can Asphodilla ask of her plain servant Lilyliver? Speak out, Madam. An ape with a ring in his nose, or a strong young jackanapes to tell tales of us when we're no longer here to tell truth about ourselves?*

Lady H. H. (flirting her fan) *Fie, fie, Sir Spaniel. You make me blush — you do indeed. But come closer.* (She shifts her seat nearer to him) *We don't want the whole world to hear us.*

Sir S. L. (aside) *Come closer? A pox on my life! The old hag stinks like a red herring that's been stood over head in a tar barrel!* (Aloud) *Your meaning, Madam? You were saying?*

Lady H. H. *I have a niece, Sir Spaniel, Flavinda by name.*

Sir S. L. (aside) *Why that's the girl I love, to be sure!* (Aloud) *You have a niece, madam? I seem to remember hearing so. An only child, left by your brother, so I've heard, in your Ladyship's charge — him that perished at sea.*

Lady H. H. *The very same Sir. She's of age now and marriageable. I've kept her close as a weevil, Sir Spaniel, wrapped in the sere cloths of her virginity. Only maids about her, never a man to my knowledge, save Clout the serving man, who has a wart on his nose and a face like a nutgrater. Yet some fool has caught her fancy. Some gilded fly — some Harry, Dick; call him what you will.*

Sir S. L. (aside) *That's young Valentine, I warrant. I caught 'em at the play together.* (Aloud) *Say you so, Madam?*

Lady H. H. *She's not so ill favoured, Sir Spaniel — there's beauty in our line — but that a gentleman of taste and breeding like yourself now might take pity on her.*

Sir S. L. *Saving your presence, Madam. Eyes that have seen the sun are not so easily dazzled by the lesser lights — the Cassiopeias, Aldebarans, Great Bears and so on — A fig for them when the sun's up!*

Lady H. H. (ogling him) *You praise my hair-dresser, Sir, or my ear-rings* (she shakes her head).

Sir S. L. (aside) *She jingles like a she-ass at a fair! She's rigged like a barber's pole of a May day.* (Aloud) *Your commands, Madam?*

Lady H. H. *Well Sir, 'twas this way Sir. Brother Bob, for my father was a plain country gentleman and would have none of the fancy names the foreigners brought with 'em — Asphodilla I call myself, but my Christian name's plain Sue — Brother Bob, as I was telling you, ran away to sea; and, so they say, became Emperor of the Indies; where the very stones are emeralds and the sheep crop rubies. Which, for a tenderer-hearted man never lived, he would have brought back with him, Sir, to mend the family fortunes, Sir. But the brig, frigate or what they call it, for I've no head for sea terms, never crossed a ditch without saying the Lord's Prayer backwards, struck a rock. The whale had him. But the cradle was by the bounty of Heaven washed ashore. With the girl in it; Flavinda here. What's more to the point, with the Will in it; safe and sound; wrapped in parchment. Brother Bob's Will. Deb there! Deb I say! Deb!*

(She hollas for Deb)

Sir S. L. (aside) *Ah hah! I smell a rat! A will, quotha! Where there's a Will there's a Way.*

Lady H. H. (bawling) *The Will, Deb! The Will! In the ebony box by the right hand of the escritoire opposite the window . . . A pox on the girl! She's dreaming. It's these romances, Sir Spaniel — these romances. Can't see a candle gutter but it's her heart that's melting, or snuff a wick without reciting all the names in Cupid's Calendar . . .*

(Enter Deb carrying a parchment)

Lady H. H. *So . . . Give it here. The Will. Brother Bob's Will* (she mumbles over the Will).

Lady H. H. *To cut the matter short, Sir, for these lawyers even at the Antipodes are a long-winded race—*

Sir S. L. *To match their ears, Ma'am—*

Lady H. H. *Very true, very true. To cut the matter short, Sir, my brother Bob left all he died possessed of to his only child Flavinda; with this proviso, mark ye. That she marry to her Aunt's liking. Her Aunt;*

that's me. Otherwise, mark ye, all — to wit ten bushels of diamonds; item of rubies; item two hundred square miles of fertile territory bounding the River Amazon to the Nor-Nor-East; item his snuff box; item his flageolet — he was always one to love a tune, sir, Brother Bob; item six Macaws and as many Concubines as he had with him at the time of his decease — all this with other trifles needless to specify he left, mark ye, should she fail to marry to her Aunt's liking — that's me — to found a Chapel, Sir Spaniel, where six poor Virgins should sing hymns in perpetuity for the repose of his soul — which, to speak the truth, Sir Spaniel, poor Brother Bob stands in need of, perambulating the Gulf Stream as he is and consorting with Syrens. But take it; read the Will yourself, Sir.

SIR S. L. (reading) 'Must marry to her Aunt's liking.' *That's plain enough.*

LADY H. H. *Her Aunt, Sir. That's me. That's plain enough.*

SIR S. L. (aside) *She speaks the truth there!* (Aloud) *You would have me understand, Madam . . . ?*

LADY H. H. *Hist! Come closer. Let me whisper in your ear . . . You and I have long entertained a high opinion of one another, Sir Spaniel. Played at ball together. Bound our wrists with daisy chains together. If I mind aright, you called me little bride — 'tis fifty years since. We might have made a match of it, Sir Spaniel, had fortune favoured . . . You take my meaning, Sir?*

SIR S. L. *Had it been written in letters of gold, fifty feet high, visible from Paul's Churchyard to the Goat and Compasses at Peckham, it could have been no plainer . . . Hist, I'll whisper it. I, Sir Spaniel Lilyliver, do hereby bind myself to take thee — what's the name of the green girl that was cast up in a lobster pot covered with seaweed? Flavinda, eh? Flavinda, so — to be my wedded wife . . . O for a lawyer to have it all in writing!*

LADY H. H. *On condition, Sir Spaniel.*

SIR S. L. *On condition, Asphodilla.*

(Both speak together)

That the money is shared between us.

LADY H. H. *We want no lawyer to certify that! Your hand on it, Sir Spaniel!*

SIR S. L. *Your lips Madam!*

(They embrace)

Sɪʀ S. L. *Pah! She stinks!*

'Ha! Ha! Ha!' laughed the indigenous old lady in her bath-chair.

'Reason, begad! Reason!' exclaimed old Bartholomew, and looked at his son as if exhorting him to give over these womanish vapours and be a man, Sir.

Giles sat straight as a dart, his feet tucked under him.

Mrs. Manresa had out her mirror and lipstick and attended to her lips and nose.

The gramophone, while the scene was removed, gently stated certain facts which everybody knows to be perfectly true. The tune said, more or less, how Eve, gathering her robes about her, stands reluctant still to let her dewy mantle fall. The herded flocks, the tune continued, in peace repose. The poor man to his cot returns, and, to the eager ears of wife and child, the simple story of his toil relates: what yield the furrow bears; and how the team the plover on the nest has spared; while Wat her courses ran; and speckled eggs in the warm hollow lay. Meanwhile the good wife on the table spreads her simple fare; and to the shepherd's flute, from toil released, the nymphs and swains join hands and foot it on the green. Then Eve lets down her sombre tresses brown and spreads her lucent veil o'er hamlet, spire, and mead, etc., etc. And the tune repeated itself once more.

The view repeated in its own way what the tune was saying. The sun was sinking; the colours were merging; and the view was saying how after toil men rest from their labours; how coolness comes; reason prevails; and having unharnessed the team from the plough, neighbours dig in cottage gardens and lean over cottage gates.

The cows, making a step forward, then standing still, were saying the same thing to perfection.

Folded in this triple melody, the audience sat gazing; and beheld gently and approvingly without interrogation, for it seemed inevitable, a box tree in a green tub take the place of the lady's dressing-room; while on what seemed to be a wall, was hung a great clock face; the hands pointing to three minutes to the hour; which was seven.

Mrs. Elmhurst roused herself from her reverie; and looked at her programme.

'Scene Two. The Mall,' she read out. 'Time; early morning. Enter Flavinda. Here she comes!'

Here came Millie Loder (shop assistant at Messrs. Hunt and Dicksons, drapery emporium), in sprigged satin, representing Flavinda.

FLAV. *Seven he said, and there's the clock's word for it. But Valentine — where's Valentine? La! How my heart beats! Yet it's not the time o' day, for I'm often afoot before the sun's up in the meadows . . . See — the fine folk passing! All a-tiptoeing like peacocks with spread tails! And I in my petticoat that looked so fine by my Aunt's cracked mirror. Why, here it's a dish clout . . . And they heap their hair up like a birthday cake stuck about with candles . . . That's a diamond — that's a ruby . . . Where's Valentine? The Orange Tree in the Mall, he said. The tree — there. Valentine — nowhere. That's a courtier, I'll warrant, that old fox with his tail between his legs. That's a serving wench out without her master's knowledge. That's a man with a broom to sweep paths for the fine ladies' flounces . . . La! the red in their cheeks! They never got that in the fields, I warrant! O faithless, cruel, hard-hearted Valentine. Valentine! Valentine!*

(She wrings her hands, turning from side to side.)

Didn't I leave my bed a-tiptoe and steal like a mouse in the wainscot for fear of waking Aunt? And lard my hair from her powder box? And scrub my cheeks to make 'em shine? And lie awake watching the stars climb the chimney pots? And give my gold guinea that Godfather hid behind the mistletoe last Twelfth Night to Deb so she shouldn't tell on me? And grease the key in the lock so that Aunt shouldn't wake and shriek Flavvy! Flavvy! Val, I say Val—That's him coming . . . No, I could tell him a mile off the way he strides the waves like what d'you call him in the picture book . . . That's not Val . . . That's a cit; that's a fop; raising his glass, prithee, to have his fill of me . . . I'll be home then . . . No, I won't . . . That's to play the green girl again and sew samplers . . . I'm of age, ain't I, come Michaelmas? Only three turns of the moon and I inherit . . . Didn't I read it in the Will the day the ball bounced on top of the old chest where Aunt keeps her furbelows, and the lid opened? . . . 'All I die possessed of to my Daughter . . .' So far I'd read when the old lady came tapping down the passage like a blind man in an alley . . . I'm no castaway, I'd have you know, Sir; no fishtailed mermaid with a robe of sea weed, at your mercy. I'm a match for any of 'em — the chits you dally with, and bid me meet you at the Orange Tree when you're drowsing the night off spent in their arms . . . Fie upon you, Sir, making sport with a poor girl so . . . I'll not cry, I swear I won't. I'll not brew a drop of the salt liquid for a man who's served me so . . . Yet to think on't — how we hid in the dairy the day the cat jumped. And read romances under the holly tree. La! how I cried when the Duke left poor Polly . . . And my Aunt found me with eyes like red jellies. 'What stung, niece?' says she. And cried 'Quick Deb, the blue bag.' I told ye . . . La, to think I read it all in a book and cried for another! . . . Hist, what's there among the trees? It's come — it's gone. The breeze is it? In the shade now — in the sun now . . . Valentine on my life! It's he! Quick, I'll hide. Let the tree conceal me!

(Flavinda hides behind the tree.)

He's here . . . He turns . . . He casts about . . . He's lost the scent . . . He gazes — this way, that way . . . Let him feast his eyes on the fine faces — taste 'em, sample 'em, say: 'That's the fine lady I danced with . . . that I lay with . . . that I kissed under the mistletoe . . .' Ha! How he spews 'em out! Brave Valentine! How he casts his eyes upon the ground! How his frowns become him! 'Where's Flavinda?' he sighs. 'She I love like the heart in my breast.' See him pull his watch out! 'O faithless wretch!' he sighs. See how he stamps the earth! Now turns on his heel . . . He sees me — no, the sun's in his eyes. Tears fill 'em . . . Lord, how he fingers his sword! He'll run it through his breast like the Duke in the story book! . . . Stop, Sir, stop!

(She reveals herself)

VALENTINE . . . *O Flavinda, O!*
FLAVINDA . . . *O Valentine, O!*

(They embrace)

The clock strikes nine.

'All that fuss about nothing!' a voice exclaimed. People laughed. The voice stopped. But the voice had seen; the voice had heard. For a moment Miss La Trobe behind her tree glowed with glory. The next, turning to the villagers who were passing in and out between the trees, she barked:

'Louder! Louder!'

For the stage was empty; the emotion must be continued; the only thing to continue the emotion was the song; and the words were inaudible.

'Louder! Louder!' She threatened them with her clenched fists.

Digging and delving (they sang), *hedging and ditching, we pass . . . Summer and winter, autumn and spring return . . . All passes but we, all changes . . . but we remain forever the same . . .* (the breeze blew gaps between their words.)

'Louder, louder!' Miss La Trobe vociferated.

Palaces tumble down (they resumed), *Babylon, Nineveh, Troy . . . And Cæsar's great house . . . all fallen they lie . . . Where the plover nests was the arch . . . through which the Romans trod . . . Digging and delving we break with the share of the plough the clod . . . Where Clytemnestra watched for her Lord . . . saw the beacons blaze on the hills . . . we see only the clod . . . Digging and delving we pass . . . and the Queen and the Watch Tower fall . . . for Agamemnon has ridden away . . . Clytemnestra is nothing but . . .*

The words died away. Only a few great names – Babylon,[96] Nineveh, Clytemnestra, Agamemnon,[97] Troy – floated across the open space. Then the wind rose, and in the rustle of the leaves even the great words became inaudible; and the audience sat staring at the villagers, whose mouths opened, but no sound came.

And the stage was empty. Miss La Trobe leant against the tree, paralyzed. Her power had left her. Beads of perspiration broke on her forehead. Illusion had failed. 'This is death,' she murmured, 'death.'

Then suddenly, as the illusion petered out, the cows took up the burden. One had lost her calf. In the very nick of time she lifted her great moon-eyed head and bellowed. All the great moon-eyed heads laid themselves back. From cow after cow came the same yearning bellow. The whole world was filled with dumb yearning. It was the primeval voice sounding loud in the ear of the present moment. Then the whole herd caught the infection. Lashing their tails, blobbed like pokers, they tossed their heads high, plunged and bellowed, as if Eros had planted his dart in their flanks and goaded them to fury. The cows annihilated the gap; bridged the distance; filled the emptiness and continued the emotion.

Miss La Trobe waved her hand ecstatically at the cows.

'Thank Heaven!' she exclaimed.

Suddenly the cows stopped; lowered their heads, and began browsing. Simultaneously the audience lowered their heads and read their programmes.

'The producer,' Mrs. Elmhurst read out for her husband's benefit, 'craves the indulgence of the audience. Owing to lack of time a scene has been omitted; and she begs the audience to imagine that in the interval Sir Spaniel Lilyliver has contracted an engagement with Flavinda; who had been about to plight her troth; when Valentine, hidden inside the grandfather's clock, steps forward; claims Flavinda as his bride; reveals the plot to rob her of her inheritance; and, during the confusion that ensues, the lovers fly together, leaving Lady Harpy and Sir Spaniel alone together.'

'We're asked to imagine all that,' she said, putting down her glasses.

'That's very wise of her,' said Mrs. Manresa, addressing Mrs. Swithin. 'If she'd put it all in, we should have been here till midnight. So we've got to imagine, Mrs. Swithin.' She patted the old lady on the knee.

'Imagine?' said Mrs. Swithin. 'How right! Actors show us too much. The Chinese, you know, put a dagger on the table and that's a battle. And so Racine . . .'[98]

'Yes, they bore one stiff,' Mrs. Manresa interrupted, scenting culture, resenting the snub to the jolly human heart. 'T'other day I took my nephew – such a jolly boy at Sandhurst – to *Pop Goes the Weasel*.[99] Seen it?' She turned to Giles.

'Up and down the City Road,' he hummed by way of an answer.

'Did your Nanny sing that!' Mrs. Manresa exclaimed. 'Mine did. And when she said "Pop" she made a noise like a cork being drawn from a ginger-beer bottle. Pop!'

She made the noise.

'Hush, hush,' someone whispered.

'Now I'm being naughty and shocking your aunt,' she said. 'We must be good and attend. This is Scene Three. Lady Harpy Harraden's Closet. The sound of horses' hooves is heard in the distance.'

The sound of horses' hooves, energetically represented by Albert the idiot with a wooden spoon on a tray, died away.

LADY H. H. *Half-way to Gretna Green already! O my deceitful niece! You that I rescued from the brine and stood on the hearthstone dripping! O that the whale had swallowed you whole! Perfidious porpoise, O! Didn't the Horn book teach you Honour thy Great Aunt? How have you misread it and misspelt it, learnt thieving and cheating and reading of wills in old boxes and hiding of rascals in honest time-pieces that have never missed a second since King Charles's day! O Flavinda! O porpoise, O!*

SIR S. L. (trying to pull on his jack boots) *Old – old – old. He called me 'old' – 'To your bed, old fool, and drink hot posset!'*

LADY H. H. *And she, stopping at the door and pointing the finger of scorn at me said 'old,' Sir – 'woman' Sir – I that am in the prime of life and a lady!*

SIR S. L. (tugging at his boots) *But I'll be even with him. I'll have the law on' em! I'll run 'em to earth . . .*

(He hobbles up and down, one boot on, one boot off)

LADY H. H. (laying her hand on his arm) *Have mercy on your gout, Sir Spaniel. Bethink you, Sir – let's not run mad, we that are on the sunny side of fifty. What's this youth they prate on? Nothing but a goose feather blown on a north wind. Sit you down, Sir Spaniel. Rest your leg – so—*

(She pushes a cushion under his leg)

SIR S. L. *'Old' he called me . . . jumping from the clock like a jack-in-the-box . . . And she, making mock of me, points to my leg and cries 'Cupid's darts, Sir Spaniel, Cupid's darts.' O that I could braise 'em in a mortar and serve 'em up smoking hot on the altar of — O my gout, O my gout!*

LADY H. H. *This talk, Sir, ill befits a man of sense. Bethink you, Sir, only t'other day you were invoking — ahem — the Constellations. Cassiopeia, Aldebaran; the Aurora Borealis . . . It's not to be denied that one of 'em has left her sphere, has shot, has eloped, to put it plainly, with the entrails of a time-piece, the mere pendulum of a grandfather's clock. But, Sir Spaniel, there are some stars that — ahem — stay fixed; that shine, to put it in a nutshell, never so bright as by a sea-coal fire on a brisk morning.*

SIR S. L. *O that I were five and twenty with a sharp sword at my side!*

LADY H. H. (bridling) *I take your meaning, Sir. Te hee — To be sure, I regret it as you do. But youth's not all. To let you into a secret, I've passed the meridian myself. Am on t'other side of the Equator too. Sleep sound o' nights without turning. The dog days are over . . . But bethink you, Sir. Where there's a will there's a way.*

SIR S. L. *God's truth Ma'am . . . ah my foot's like a burning, burning horseshoe on the devil's anvil ah! — what's your meaning?*

LADY H. H. *My meaning, Sir? Must I disrupt my modesty and unquilt that which has been laid in lavender since my lord, peace be to his name — 'tis twenty years since — was lapped in lead? In plain words, Sir, Flavinda's flown. The cage is empty. But we that have bound our wrists with cowslips might join 'em with a stouter chain. To have done with fallals and figures. Here am I, Asphodilla — but my plain name Sue. No matter what my name is — Asphodilla or Sue — here am I, hale and hearty, at your service. Now that the plot's out, Brother Bob's bounty must go to the virgins. That's plain. Here's Lawyer Quill's word for it. 'Virgins . . . in perpetuity . . . sing for his soul.' And I warrant you, he has need of it . . . But no matter. Though we have thrown that to the fishes that might have wrapped us in lamb's-wool, I'm no beggar. There's messuages; tenements; napery; cattle; my dowry; an inventory. I'll show you; engrossed on parchment; enough I'll warrant you to keep us handsomely, for what's to run of our time, as husband and wife.*

SIR S. L. *Husband and wife! So that's the plain truth of it! Why, Madam, I'd rather lash myself to a tar barrel, be bound to a thorn tree in a winter's gale. Faugh!*

LADY H. H. ... *A tar barrel, quotha! A thorn tree — quotha! You that were harping on galaxies and milky ways! You that were swearing I outshone 'em all! A pox on you — you faithless! You shark, you! You serpent in jack boots, you! So you won't have me? Reject my hand do you?*

(She proffers her hand; he strikes it from him.)

SIR S. L. ... *Hide your chalk stones in a woollen mit! pah! I'll none of 'em! Were they diamond, pure diamond, and half the habitable globe and all its concubines strung in string round your throat I'd none of it ... none of it. Unhand me, scritch owl, witch, vampire! Let me go!*

LADY H. H. ... *So all your fine words were tinsel wrapped round a Christmas cracker!*

SIR S. L. ... *Bells hung on an ass's neck! Paper roses on a barber's pole ... O my foot, my foot ... Cupid's darts, she mocked me ... Old, old, he called me old ...*

(He hobbles away)

LADY H. H. (left alone) *All gone. Following the wind. He's gone; she's gone; and the old clock that the rascal made himself into a pendulum for is the only one of 'em all to stop. A pox on 'em — turning an honest woman's house into a brothel. I that was Aurora Borealis[100] am shrunk to a tar barrel. I that was Cassiopeia am turned to a she-ass. My head turns. There's no trusting man nor woman; nor fine speeches; nor fine looks. Off comes the sheep's skin; out creeps the serpent. Get ye to Gretna Green;[101] couch on the wet grass and breed vipers. My head spins ... Tar barrels, quotha. Cassiopeia ... Chalk stones ... Andromeda ... Thorn trees ... Deb, I say, Deb (She holloas) Unlace me. I'm fit to burst ... Bring me my green baize table and set the cards ... And my fur lined slippers, Deb. And a dish of chocolate ... I'll be even with 'em ... I'll outlive 'em all ... Deb, I say! Deb! A pox on the girl! Can't she hear me? Deb, I say, you gipsy's spawn that I snatched from the hedge and taught to sew samplers! Deb! Deb!*

(She throws open the door leading to the maid's closet)

Empty! She's gone too! . . . Hist, what's that on the dresser?

(She picks up a scrap of paper and reads)

'*What care I for your goose-feather bed? I'm off with the raggle-taggle gipsies, O! Signed: Deborah, one time your maid.*' *So! She that I fed on apple parings and crusts from my own table, she that I taught to play cribbage and sew chemises . . . she's gone too. O ingratitude, thy name is Deborah! Who's to wash the dishes now; who's to bring me my posset now, suffer my temper and unlace my stays? . . . All gone. I'm alone then. Sans niece, sans lover; and sans maid.*

> *And so to end the play, the moral is,*
> *The God of love is full of tricks;*
> *Into the foot his dart he sticks,*
> *But the way of the will is plain to see;*
> *Let holy virgins hymn perpetually:*
> '*Where there's a will there's a way.*'
> *Good people all, farewell.*
> (dropping a curtsey, Lady H. H. withdrew)

The scene ended. Reason descended from her plinth. Gathering her robes about her, serenely acknowledging the applause of the audience, she passed across the stage; while Lords and Ladies in stars and garters followed after; Sir Spaniel limping escorted Lady Harraden smirking; and Valentine and Flavinda arm in arm bowed and curtsied.

'God's truth!' cried Bartholomew, catching the infection of the language. 'There's a moral for you!'

He threw himself back in his chair and laughed, like a horse whinnying.

A moral. What? Giles supposed it was: Where there's a Will there's a Way. The words rose and pointed a finger of scorn at him. Off to Gretna Green with his girl; the deed done. Damn the consequences.

'Like to see the greenhouse?' he said abruptly, turning to Mrs. Manresa.

'Love to!' she exclaimed, and rose.

Was there an interval? Yes, the programme said so. The machine in the bushes went chuff, chuff, chuff. And the next scene?

'The Victorian age,'[102] Mrs. Elmhurst read out. Presumably there was time then for a stroll round the gardens, even for a look over the house. Yet somehow they felt – how could one put it – a little not quite here or there. As if the play had jerked the ball out of the cup; as if what I call myself was still floating unattached, and didn't settle. Not quite themselves, they felt. Or was it simply that they felt clothes conscious? Skimpy out-of-date voile dresses; flannel trousers; panama hats; hats wreathed with raspberry-coloured net in the style of the Royal Duchess's hat at Ascot seemed flimsy somehow.

'How lovely the clothes were,' said someone, casting a last look at Flavinda disappearing. 'Most becoming. I wish . . .'

Chuff, chuff, chuff went the machine in the bushes, accurately, insistently.

Clouds were passing across the sky. The weather looked a little unsettled. Hogben's Folly was for a moment ashen white. Then the sun struck the gilt vane of Bolney Minster.

'Looks a little unsettled,' said someone.

'Up you get . . . Let's stretch our legs,' said another voice. Soon the lawns were floating with little moving islands of coloured dresses. Yet some of the audience remained seated.

'Major and Mrs. Mayhew,' Page the reporter noted, licking his pencil. As for the play, he would collar Miss Whatshername and ask for a synopsis. But Miss La Trobe had vanished.

Down among the bushes she worked like a nigger. Flavinda was in her petticoats. Reason had thrown her mantle on a holly hedge. Sir Spaniel was tugging at his jack boots. Miss La Trobe was scattering and foraging.

'The Victorian mantle with the bead fringe . . . Where is the damned thing? Chuck it here . . . Now the whiskers . . .'

Ducking up and down she cast her quick bird's eye over the bushes at the audience. The audience was on the move. The audience was strolling up and down. They kept their distance from the dressing-room; they respected the conventions. But if they wandered too far, if they began exploring the grounds, going over the house, then ... Chuff, chuff, chuff went the machine. Time was passing. How long would time hold them together? It was a gamble; a risk ... And she laid about her energetically, flinging clothes on the grass.

Over the tops of the bushes came stray voices, voices without bodies, symbolical voices they seemed to her, half hearing, seeing nothing, but still, over the bushes, feeling invisible threads connecting the bodiless voices.

'It all looks very black.'

'No one wants it – save those damned Germans.'

There was a pause.

'I'd cut down those trees ...'

'How they get their roses to grow!'

'They say there's been a garden here for five hundred years ...'

'Why even old Gladstone, to do him justice ...'

Then there was silence. The voices passed the bushes. The trees rustled. Many eyes, Miss La Trobe knew, for every cell in her body was absorbent, looked at the view. Out of the corner of her eye she could see Hogben's Folly; then the vane flashed.

'The glass is falling,' said a voice.

She could feel them slipping through her fingers, looking at the view.

'Where's that damned woman, Mrs. Rogers? Who's seen Mrs. Rogers?' she cried, snatching up a Victorian mantle.

Then, ignoring the conventions, a head popped up between the trembling sprays: Mrs. Swithin's.

'Oh Miss La Trobe!' she exclaimed; and stopped. Then she began again; 'Oh Miss La Trobe, I do congratulate you!'

She hesitated. 'You've given me ...' She skipped, then alighted – 'Ever since I was a child I've felt ...' A film fell over her eyes, shutting off the present. She tried to recall her childhood; then gave it up; and, with a little wave of her hand, as if asking Miss La Trobe to help her out, continued: 'This daily round; this going up and down stairs; this saying "What am I going for? My specs? I have 'em on my nose" ...'

She gazed at Miss La Trobe with a cloudless old-aged stare. Their eyes met in a common effort to bring a common meaning to birth. They failed; and Mrs. Swithin, laying hold desperately of a fraction of her meaning, said: 'What a small part I've had to play! But you've made me feel I could have played ... Cleopatra!'[103]

She nodded between the trembling bushes and ambled off.

The villagers winked. 'Batty' was the word for old Flimsy, breaking through the bushes.

'I might have been – Cleopatra,' Miss La Trobe repeated. 'You've stirred in me my unacted part,' she meant.

'Now for the skirt, Mrs. Rogers,' she said.

Mrs. Rogers stood grotesque in her black stockings. Miss La Trobe pulled the voluminous flounces of the Victorian age over her head. She tied the tapes. 'You've twitched the invisible strings,' was what the old lady meant; and revealed – of all people – Cleopatra! Glory possessed her. Ah, but she was not merely a twitcher of individual strings; she was one who seethes wandering bodies and floating voices in a cauldron, and makes rise up from its amorphous mass a re-created world. Her moment was on her – her glory.

'There!' she said, tying the black ribbons under Mrs. Rogers' chin. 'That's done it! Now for the gentleman. Hammond!'

She beckoned Hammond. Sheepishly he came forward, and submitted to the application of black side whiskers. With his eyes half shut, his head leant back, he looked, Miss La Trobe thought, like King Arthur – noble, knightly, thin.

'Where's the Major's old frock coat?' she asked, trusting to the effect of that to transform him.

Tick, tick, tick, the machine continued. Time was passing. The audience was wandering, dispersing. Only the tick tick of the gramophone held them together. There, sauntering solitary far away by the flower beds, was Mrs. Giles escaping.

'The tune!' Miss La Trobe commanded. 'Hurry up! The tune! The next tune! Number Ten!'

'Now may I pluck,' Isa murmured, picking a rose, 'my single

flower. The white or the pink? And press it so, 'twixt thumb and finger . . .'

She looked among the passing faces for the face of the man in grey. There he was for one second; but surrounded, inaccessible. And now vanished.

She dropped her flower. What single, separate leaf could she press? None. Nor stray by the beds alone. She must go on; and she turned in the direction of the stable.

'Where do I wander?' she mused. 'Down what draughty tunnels? Where the eyeless wind blows? And there grows nothing for the eye. No rose. To issue where? In some harvestless dim field where no evening lets fall her mantle; nor sun rises. All's equal there. Unblowing, ungrowing are the roses there. Change is not; nor the mutable and lovable; nor greetings nor partings; nor furtive findings and feelings, where hand seeks hand and eye seeks shelter from the eye.'

She had come into the stable yard where the dogs were chained; where the buckets stood; where the great pear tree spread its ladder of branches against the wall. The tree, whose roots went beneath the flags, was weighted with hard green pears. Fingering one of them she murmured: 'How am I burdened with what they drew from the earth; memories; possessions. This is the burden that the past laid on me, last little donkey in the long caravanserai crossing the desert. "Kneel down," said the past. "Fill your pannier from our tree. Rise up, donkey. Go your way till your heels blister and your hoofs crack."'

The pear was hard as stone. She looked down at the cracked flags beneath which the roots spread. 'That was the burden,' she mused, 'laid on me in the cradle; murmured by waves; breathed by restless elm trees; crooned by singing women; what we must remember; what we would forget.'

She looked up. The gilt hands of the stable clock pointed inflexibly at two minutes to the hour. The clock was about to strike.

'Now comes the lightning,' she muttered, 'from the stone blue sky. The thongs are burst that the dead tied. Loosed are our possessions.'

Voices interrupted. People passed the stable yard, talking.

'It's a good day, some say, the day we are stripped naked. Others, it's the end of the day. They see the Inn and the Inn's keeper. But none speaks with a single voice. None with a voice free from the old vibrations. Always I hear corrupt murmurs; the chink of gold and metal. Mad music . . .'

More voices sounded. The audience was streaming back to the terrace. She roused herself. She encouraged herself. 'On, little donkey, patiently stumble. Hear not the frantic cries of the leaders who in that they seek to lead desert us. Nor the chatter of china faces glazed and hard. Hear rather the shepherd, coughing by the farmyard wall; the withered tree that sighs when the Rider gallops;[104] the brawl in the barrack room when they stripped her naked; or the cry which in London when I thrust the window open someone cries . . .' She had come out on to the path that led past the greenhouse. The door was kicked open. Out came Mrs. Manresa and Giles. Unseen, Isa followed them across the lawns to the front row of seats.

The chuff, chuff, chuff of the machine in the bushes had stopped. In obedience to Miss La Trobe's command, another tune had been put on the gramophone. Number Ten. London street cries it was called. 'A Pot Pourri.'

'Lavender, sweet lavender, who'll buy my sweet lavender' the tune trilled and tinkled, ineffectively shepherding the audience. Some ignored it. Some still wandered. Others stopped, but stood upright. Some, like Colonel and Mrs. Mayhew, who had never left their seats, brooded over the blurred carbon sheet which had been issued for their information.

'The Nineteenth Century.' Colonel Mayhew did not dispute the producer's right to skip two hundred years in less than fifteen minutes. But the choice of scenes baffled him.

'Why leave out the British Army? What's history without the Army, eh?' he mused. Inclining her head, Mrs. Mayhew protested after all one mustn't ask too much. Besides, very likely there would be a Grand Ensemble,[105] round the Union Jack, to end with. Meanwhile, there was the view. They looked at the view.

'Sweet lavender . . . sweet lavender . . .'[106] Humming the tune old Mrs. Lynn Jones (of the Mount) pushed a chair forward.

'Here Etty,' she said, and plumped down, with Etty Springett, with whom, since both were widows now, she shared a house.

'I remember . . .' she nodded in time to the tune, 'You remember too — how they used to cry it down the streets.' They remembered — the curtains blowing, and the men crying: 'All a blowing, all a growing,' as they came with geraniums, sweet william, in pots, down the street.

'A harp, I remember, and a hansom and a growler. So quiet the street was then. Two for a hansom, was it? One for a growler? And Ellen, in cap and apron, whistling in the street? D'you remember? And the runners, my dear, who followed, all the way from the station, if one had a box.'

The tune changed. 'Any old iron, any old iron to sell?' 'D'you remember? That was what the men shouted in the fog. Seven Dials they came from. Men with red handkerchiefs. Garotters,[107] did they call them? You couldn't walk — O, dear me, no — home from the play. Regent Street. Piccadilly. Hyde Park Corner. The loose women . . . And everywhere loaves of bread in the gutter. The Irish you know round Covent Garden . . . Coming back from a Ball, past the clock at Hyde Park Corner, d'you remember the feel of white gloves? . . . My father remembered the old Duke in the Park. Two fingers like that — he'd touch his hat . . . I've got my mother's album. A lake and two lovers. She'd copied out Byron, I suppose, in what was called then the Italian hand . . .'

'What's that? "Knocked 'em in the Old Kent Road."[108] I remember the bootboy whistled it. O, my dear, the servants . . . Old Ellen . . . Sixteen pound a year wages . . . And the cans of hot water! And the crinolines! And the stays! D'you remember the Crystal Palace, and the fireworks, and how Mira's slipper got lost in the mud?'

'That's young Mrs. Giles . . . I remember her mother. She died in India . . . We wore, I suppose, a great many petticoats then. Unhygienic? I dare say . . . Well, look at my daughter. To the right, just behind you. Forty, but slim as a wand. Each flat has its refrigerator . . . It took my mother half the morning to order dinner . . . We were eleven. Counting servants, eighteen in family . . . Now they simply ring up the Stores . . . That's Giles coming, with Mrs. Manresa. She's a type I don't myself fancy. I may be wrong ... And Colonel Mayhew, as spruce as ever ... And Mr. Cobbet of Cobbs Corner, there, under the monkey puzzle tree. One don't see him often ... That's what's so nice — it brings people together. These days, when we're all so busy, that's what one wants ... The programme? Have you got it? Let's see what comes next ... The Nineteenth Century ... Look, there's the chorus, the villagers, coming on now, between the trees. First, there's a prologue ...'

A great box, draped in red baize festooned with heavy gold tassels, had been moved into the middle of the stage. There was a swish of dresses, a stir of chairs. The audience seated themselves, hastily, guiltily. Miss La Trobe's eye was on them. She gave them ten seconds to settle their faces. Then she flicked her hand. A pompous march tune brayed. 'Firm, elatant, bold and blatant,' etc. ... And once more a huge symbolical figure emerged from the bushes.[109] It was Budge the publican; but so disguised that even cronies who drank with him nightly failed to recognize him; and a little titter of enquiry as to his identity ran about among the villagers. He wore a long black many-caped cloak; waterproof; shiny; of the substance of a statue in Parliament Square; a helmet which suggested a policeman; a row of medals crossed his breast; and in his right hand he held extended a special constable's baton (loaned by Mr. Willert of the Hall). It was his voice, husky and rusty, issuing from a thick black cotton-wool beard that gave him away.

'Budge, Budge. That's Mr. Budge,' the audience whispered.

Budge extended his truncheon and spoke:

It ain't an easy job, directing the traffic at 'Yde Park Corner. Buses and 'ansom cabs. All a-clatter on the cobbles. Keep to the right, can't you? Hi there, Stop!

(He waved his truncheon)

There she goes, the old party with the umbrella, right under the 'orse's nose

(The truncheon pointed markedly at Mrs. Swithin)

She raised her skinny hand as if in truth she had fluttered off the pavement on the impulse of the moment to the just rage of authority. Got her, Giles thought, taking sides with authority against his aunt.

Fog or fine weather, I does my duty (Budge continued). *At Piccadilly Circus; at 'Yde Park Corner, directing the traffic of 'Er Majesty's Empire. The Shah of Persia; Sultan of Morocco; or it may be 'Er Majesty in person; or Cook's tourists; black men; white men; sailors, soldiers; crossing the ocean; to proclaim her Empire; all of 'em Obey the Rule of my truncheon.*

(He flourished it magnificently from right to left)

But my job don't end there. I take under my protection and direction the purity and security of all Her Majesty's minions; in all parts of her dominions; insist that they obey the laws of God and Man.

The laws of God and Man (he repeated and made as if to consult a Statute; engrossed on a sheet of parchment which with great deliberation he now produced from his trouser pocket)

Go to Church on Sunday; on Monday, nine sharp, catch the City Bus. On Tuesday it may be, attend a meeting at the Mansion House for the redemption of the sinner; at dinner on Wednesday attend another — turtle soup. Some bother it may be in Ireland; Famine. Fenians. What not. On Thursday it's the natives of Peru require protection and correction; we give 'em what's due. But mark you, our rule don't end there. It's a Christian country, our Empire; under the White Queen Victoria. Over thought and religion; drink; dress; manners; marriage too, I wield my truncheon. Prosperity and respectability always go, as we know, 'and in 'and. The ruler of an Empire must keep his eye on the cot; spy too in the kitchen; drawing-room; library; wherever one or two, me and you, come together. Purity our watchword; prosperity and respectability. If not, why, let 'em fester in . . .

(He paused — no, he had not forgotten his words)

Cripplegate; St. Giles's; Whitechapel; the Minories. Let 'em sweat at the mines; cough at the looms; rightly endure their lot. That's the price of Empire; that's the white man's burden.[110] *And, I can tell you, to direct the traffic orderly, at 'Yde Park Corner, Piccadilly Circus, is a wholetime, white man's job.*

He paused, eminent, dominant, glaring from his pedestal. A very fine figure of a man he was, everyone agreed, his truncheon extended; his waterproof pendant. It only wanted a shower of rain, a flight of pigeons round his head, and the pealing bells of St. Paul's and the Abbey to transform him into the very spit and image of a Victorian constable; and to transport them to a foggy London afternoon, with the muffin bells ringing and the church bells pealing at the very height of Victorian prosperity.

There was a pause. The voices of the pilgrims singing, as they wound in and out between the trees, could be heard; but the words were inaudible. The audience sat waiting.

'Tut-tut-tut,' Mrs. Lynn Jones expostulated. 'There were grand men among them . . .' Why she did not know, yet somehow she felt that a sneer had been aimed at her father; therefore at herself.

Etty Springett tutted too. Yet, children did draw trucks in mines; there was the basement; yet Papa read Walter Scott aloud after dinner; and divorced ladies were not received at Court. How difficult to come to any conclusion! She wished they would hurry on with the next scene. She liked to leave a theatre knowing exactly what was meant. Of course this was only a village play . . . They were setting another scene, round the red baize box. She read out from her programme:

'The Picnic Party. About 1860. Scene: A Lake. Characters—'

She stopped. A sheet had been spread on the Terrace. It was a lake apparently. Roughly painted ripples represented water. Those green stakes were bulrushes. Rather prettily, real swallows darted across the sheet.

'Look, Minnie!' she exclaimed. 'Those are real swallows!'

'Hush, hush,' she was admonished. For the scene had begun. A young man in peg-top trousers and side whiskers carrying a spiked stick appeared by the lake.

EDGAR T. . . . *Let me help you, Miss Hardcastle! There!*

> (he helps Miss Eleanor Hardcastle, a young lady in crinoline and mushroom hat, to the top. They stand for a moment panting slightly, looking at the view.)

ELEANOR. *How small the Church looks down among the trees!*

EDGAR ... *So this is Wanderer's Well, the trysting place.*

ELEANOR ... *Please Mr. Thorold, finish what you were saying before the others come. You were saying, 'Our aim in life ...'*

EDGAR ... *Should be to help our fellow men.*

ELEANOR (sighing deeply) *How true – how profoundly true!*

EDGAR ... *Why sigh, Miss Hardcastle? – You have nothing to reproach yourself with – you whose whole life is spent in the service of others. It was of myself that I was thinking. I am no longer young. At twenty-four the best days of life are over. My life has passed* (he throws a pebble on to the lake) *like a ripple in water.*

ELEANOR. *Oh Mr. Thorold, you do not know me. I am not what I seem. I too—*

EDGAR ... *Do not tell me, Miss Hardcastle – no, I cannot believe it – You have doubted?*

ELEANOR. *Thank Heaven not that, not that ... But safe and sheltered as I am, always at home, protected as you see me, as you think me – O what am I saying? But yes, I will speak the truth, before Mama comes – I too have longed to convert the heathen!*

EDGAR ... *Miss Hardcastle ... Eleanor ... You tempt me! Dare I ask you? No – so young, so fair, so innocent. Think, I implore you, before you answer.*

ELEANOR ... *I have thought – on my knees!*

EDGAR (taking a ring from his pocket) *Then ... My mother with her last breath charged me to give this ring only to one to whom a lifetime in the African desert among the heathens would be—*

ELEANOR (taking the ring) *Perfect happiness! But hist!* (She slips the ring into her pocket) *Here's Mama!* (They start asunder)

(Enter Mrs. Hardcastle, a stout lady in black bombazine, upon a donkey, escorted by an elderly gentleman in a deer-stalker's cap)

MRS. H. ... *So you stole a march upon us, young people. There was a time, Sir John, when you and I were always first on top. Now ...*

(He helps her to alight. Children, young men, young women, some carrying hampers, others butterfly nets, others spy-glasses, others tin botanical cases arrive. A rug is thrown by the lake and Mrs. H. and Sir John seat themselves on camp stools.)

MRS. H. ... *Now who'll fill the kettles? Who'll gather the sticks? Alfred* (to a small boy), *don't run about chasing butterflies or you'll make yourself sick ... Sir John and I will unpack the hampers, here where the grass is burnt, where we had the picnic last year.*

(The young people scatter off in different directions. Mrs. H. and Sir John begin to unpack the hamper)

MRS. H. ... *Last year poor dear Mr. Beach was with us. It was a blessed release* (She takes out a black-bordered handkerchief and wipes her eyes). *Every year one of us is missing. That's the ham ... That's the grouse ... There in that packet are the game pasties ...* (She spreads the eatables on the grass) *As I was saying, poor dear Mr. Beach ... I do hope the cream hasn't curdled. Mr. Hardcastle is bringing the claret. I always leave that to him. Only when Mr. Hardcastle gets talking with Mr. Pigott about the Romans ... last year they quite came to words ... But it's nice for gentlemen to have a hobby, though they do gather the dust — those skulls and things ... But I was saying— poor dear Mr. Beach ... I wanted to ask you* (she drops her voice) *as a friend of the family, about the new clergyman — they can't hear us, can they? No, they're picking up sticks ... Last year, such a disappointment. Just got the things out ... down came the rain. But I wanted to ask you, about the new clergyman, the one who's come in place of dear Mr. Beach. I'm told the name's Sibthorp. To be sure, I hope I'm right, for I had a cousin who married a girl of that name, and as a friend of the family, we don't stand on ceremony ... And when one has daughters — I'm sure I quite envy you, with only one daughter, Sir John, and I have four! So I was asking you to tell me in confidence, about this young — if that's his name — Sibthorp, for I must tell you the day before yesterday our Mrs. Potts happened to say, as she passed the Rectory, bringing our laundry, they were unpacking the furniture; and what did she see on top of the wardrobe? A tea cosy! But of course she might be mistaken ... But it occurred to me to ask you, as a friend of the family, in confidence, has Mr. Sibthorp a wife?*

Here a chorus composed of villagers in Victorian mantles, side whiskers and top hats sang in concert:

O has Mr. Sibthorp a wife? O has Mr. Sibthorp a wife? That is the hornet, the bee in the bonnet, the screw in the cork and the drill; that whirling and twirling are for ever unfurling the folds of the motherly heart; for a mother must ask, if daughters she has, begot in the feathery billowy fourposter family bed, O did he unpack, with his prayer book and bands; his gown and his cane; his rod and his line; and the family album and gun; did he also display the connubial respectable tea-table token, a cosy with honeysuckle embossed. Has Mr. Sibthorp a wife? O has Mr. Sibthorp a wife?

While the chorus was sung, the picnickers assembled. Corks popped. Grouse, ham, chickens were sliced. Lips munched. Glasses were drained. Nothing was heard but the chump of jaws and the clink of glasses.

'They did eat,' Mrs. Lynn Jones whispered to Mrs. Springett. 'That's true. More than was good for them, I dare say.'

MR. HARDCASTLE ... (brushing flakes of meat from his whiskers) *Now* ...

'Now what?' whispered Mrs. Springett, anticipating further travesty.

Now that we have gratified the inner man, let us gratify the desire of the spirit. I call upon one of the young ladies for a song.

CHORUS OF YOUNG LADIES ... *O not me ... not me ... I really couldn't ... No, you cruel thing, you know I've lost my voice ... I can't sing without the instrument ... etc., etc.*

CHORUS OF YOUNG MEN. *O bosh! Let's have 'The Last Rose of Summer.' Let's have 'I never loved a Dear Gazelle.'*

MRS. H. (authoritatively) *Eleanor and Mildred will now sing 'I'd be a Butterfly.'*

(Eleanor and Mildred rise obediently and sing a duet: 'I'd be a Butterfly.')

MRS. H. *Thank you very much, my dears. And now gentlemen, Our Country!*

(Arthur and Edgar sing 'Rule Britannia.')

MRS. H. ... *Thank you very much. Mr. Hardcastle—*

MR. HARDCASTLE (rising to his feet, clasping his fossil) *Let us pray.*

(the whole company rise to their feet)

'This is too much, too much,' Mrs. Springett protested.

MR. H. . . . *Almighty God, giver of all good things, we thank Thee; for our food and drink; for the beauties of Nature; for the understanding with which Thou hast enlightened us* (he fumbled with his fossil) *And for thy great gift of Peace. Grant us to be thy servants on earth; grant us to spread the light of thy* . . .

Here the hindquarters of the donkey, represented by Albert the idiot, became active. Intentional was it, or accidental? 'Look at the donkey! Look at the donkey!' A titter drowned Mr. Hardcastle's prayer; and then he was heard saying:

. . . *a happy homecoming with bodies refreshed by thy bounty, and minds inspired by thy wisdom. Amen.*

Holding his fossil in front of him, Mr. Hardcastle marched off. The donkey was captured; hampers were loaded; and forming into a procession, the picnickers began to disappear over the hill.

EDGAR (winding up the procession with Eleanor) *To convert the heathen!*

ELEANOR. *To help our fellow men!*

(The actors disappeared into the bushes.)

BUDGE . . . *It's time, gentlemen, time, ladies, time to pack up and be gone. From where I stand, truncheon in hand, guarding respect-ability, and prosperity, and the purity of Victoria's land, I see before me* – (he pointed: there was Pointz Hall; the rooks cawing; the smoke rising)

'*Ome, Sweet 'Ome.*

The gramophone took up the strain: *Through pleasures and palaces, etc. There's no place like Home.*

BUDGE . . . *Home, gentlemen; home, ladies, it's time to pack up and go home. Don't I see the fire* (he pointed: one window blazed red) *blazing ever higher? In kitchen; and nursery; drawing-room and library? That's the fire of 'Ome. And see! Our Jane has brought the tea. Now children where's the toys? Mama, your knitting, quick. For here* (he swept his truncheon at Cobbet of Cobbs Corner) *comes the bread-winner, home from the city, home from the counter, home from the shop. 'Mama, a cup o' tea.' 'Children, gather round my knee. I will read aloud.*

Which shall it be? Sindbad the sailor? Or some simple tale from the Scriptures? And show you the pictures? What none of 'em? Then out with the bricks. Let's build: A conservatory. A laboratory? A mechanics' institute? Or shall it be a tower; with our flag on top; where our widowed Queen, after tea, calls the Royal orphans round her knee? For it's 'Ome, ladies, 'Ome, gentlemen. Be it never so humble, there's no place like 'Ome.'

The gramophone warbled Home, Sweet Home, and Budge, swaying slightly, descended from his box and followed the procession off the stage.

There was an interval.

'Oh but it was beautiful,' Mrs. Lynn Jones protested. Home she meant; the lamplit room; the ruby curtains; and Papa reading aloud.

They were rolling up the lake and uprooting the bulrushes. Real swallows were skimming over real grass. But she still saw the home.

'It was . . .' she repeated, referring to the home.

'Cheap and nasty, I call it,' snapped Etty Springett, referring to the play, and shot a vicious glance at Dodge's green trousers, yellow spotted tie, and unbuttoned waistcoat.

But Mrs. Lynn Jones still saw the home. Was there, she mused, as Budge's red baize pediment was rolled off, something – not impure, that wasn't the word – but perhaps 'unhygienic'[111] about the home? Like a bit of meat gone sour, with whiskers, as the servants called it? Or why had it perished? Time went on and on like the hands of the kitchen clock. (The machine chuffed in the bushes.) If they had met with no resistance, she mused, nothing wrong, they'd still be going round and round and round. The Home would have remained; and Papa's beard, she thought, would have grown and grown; and Mama's knitting – what did she do with all her knitting? – Change had to come, she said to herself, or there'd have been yards and yards of Papa's beard, of Mama's knitting. Nowadays her son-in-law was clean shaven. Her daughter had a refrigerator . . . Dear, how my mind wanders, she checked herself. What she meant was, change had to come, unless things were perfect; in which case she supposed they resisted Time. Heaven was changeless.

'Were they like that?' Isa asked abruptly. She looked at Mrs. Swithin as if she had been a dinosaur or a very diminutive mammoth. Extinct she must be, since she had lived in the reign of Queen Victoria.

Tick, tick, tick, went the machine in the bushes.

'The Victorians,' Mrs. Swithin mused. 'I don't believe,' she said with her odd little smile, 'that there ever were such people. Only you and me and William dressed differently.'

'You don't believe in history,'[112] said William.

The stage remained empty. The cows moved in the field. The shadows were deeper under the trees.

Mrs. Swithin caressed her cross. She gazed vaguely at the view. She was off, they guessed, on a circular tour of the imagination – one-making. Sheep, cows, grass, trees, ourselves – all are one. If discordant, producing harmony – if not to us, to a gigantic ear attached to a gigantic head. And thus – she was smiling benignly – the agony of the particular sheep, cow, or human being is necessary; and so – she was beaming seraphically at the gilt vane in the distance – we reach the conclusion that *all* is harmony, could we hear it. And we shall. Her eyes now rested on the white summit of a cloud. Well, if the thought gave her comfort, William and Isa smiled across her, let her think it.

Tick, tick, tick, the machine reiterated.

'D'you get her meaning?' said Mrs. Swithin alighting suddenly. 'Miss La Trobe's?'

Isa, whose eyes had been wandering, shook her head.

'But you might say the same of Shakespeare,' said Mrs. Swithin.

'Shakespeare and the musical glasses!' Mrs. Manresa intervened. 'Dear, what a barbarian you all make me feel!'

She turned to Giles. She invoked his help against this attack upon the jolly human heart.

'Tosh,' Giles muttered.

Nothing whatever appeared on the stage.

Darts of red and green light flashed from the rings on Mrs. Manresa's fingers. He looked from them at Aunt Lucy. From her to William Dodge. From him to Isa. She refused to meet his eyes. And he looked down at his blood-stained tennis shoes.

He said (without words) 'I'm damnably unhappy.'

'So am I,' Dodge echoed.

'And I too,' Isa thought.

They were all caught and caged; prisoners; watching a spectacle. Nothing happened. The tick of the machine was maddening.

'On, little donkey,' Isa murmured, 'crossing the desert ... bearing your burden ...'

She felt Dodge's eye upon her as her lips moved. Always some cold eye crawled over the surface like a winter blue-bottle! She flicked him off.

'What a time they take!' she exclaimed irritably.

'Another interval,' Dodge read out, looking at the programme.

'And after that, what?' asked Lucy.

'Present time. Ourselves,' he read.

'Let's hope to God that's the end,' said Giles gruffly.

'Now you're being naughty,' Mrs. Manresa reproved her little boy, her surly hero.

No one moved. There they sat, facing the empty stage, the cows, the meadows and the view, while the machine ticked in the bushes.

'What's the object,' said Bartholomew, suddenly rousing himself, 'of this entertainment?'

'The profits,' Isa read out from her blurred carbon copy, 'are to go to a fund for installing electric light in the Church.'[113]

'All our village festivals,' Mr. Oliver snorted, turning to Mrs. Manresa, 'end with a demand for money.'

'Of course, of course,' she murmured, deprecating his severity, and the coins in her bead bag jingled.

'Nothing's done for nothing in England,' the old man continued. Mrs. Manresa protested. It might be true, perhaps, of the Victorians; but surely not of ourselves? Did she really believe that we were disinterested? Mr. Oliver demanded.

'Oh you don't know my husband!' the wild child exclaimed, striking an attitude.

Admirable woman! You could trust her to crow when the hour struck like an alarm clock; to stop like an old bus horse when the bell rang. Oliver said nothing. Mrs. Manresa had out her mirror and attended to her face.

All their nerves were on edge. They sat exposed. The machine ticked. There was no music. The horns of cars on the high road were heard. And the swish of trees. They were neither one thing nor the other; neither Victorians nor themselves. They were suspended, without being, in limbo. Tick, tick, tick, went the machine.

Isa fidgeted: glancing to right and to left over her shoulder.

'Four and twenty blackbirds, strung upon a string,' she muttered.

'Down came an Ostrich, an eagle, an executioner,
"Which of you is ripe," he said, "to bake in my pie?
Which of you is ripe, which of you is ready,
Come my pretty gentleman,
Come my pretty lady" . . .'

How long was she going to keep them waiting? 'The present time. Ourselves.' They read it on the programme. Then they read what came next: 'The profits are to go to a fund for installing electric light in the Church.' Where was the Church? Over there. You could see the spire among the trees.

'Ourselves . . .' They returned to the programme. But what could she know about ourselves? The Elizabethans, yes; the Victorians, perhaps; but ourselves; sitting here on a June day in 1939 – it was ridiculous. 'Myself' – it was impossible. Other people, perhaps . . . Cobbet of Cobbs Corner; the Major; old Bartholomew; Mrs. Swithin – them, perhaps. But she won't get me – no, not me. The audience fidgeted. Sounds of laughter came from the bushes. But nothing whatsoever appeared on the stage.

'What's she keeping us waiting for?' Colonel Mayhew asked irritably. 'They don't need to dress up if it's present time.'

Mrs. Mayhew agreed. Unless of course she was going to end with a Grand Ensemble. Army; Navy; Union Jack; and behind them perhaps – Mrs. Mayhew sketched what she would have done had it been her pageant – the Church. In cardboard. One window, looking east, brilliantly illuminated to symbolize – she could work that out when the time came.

'There she is, behind the tree,' she whispered, pointing at Miss La Trobe.

Miss La Trobe stood there with her eye on her script. 'After Vic.' she had written, 'try ten mins. of present time. Swallows, cows etc.' She wanted to expose them, as it were, to douche them, with present-time reality. But something was going wrong with the experiment. 'Reality too strong,' she muttered. 'Curse 'em!' She felt everything they felt. Audiences were the devil. O to write a play without an audience – *the* play. But here she was fronting her audience. Every second they were slipping the noose. Her little game had gone wrong. If only she'd a backcloth to hang between the trees – to shut out cows, swallows, present time! But she had nothing. She had forbidden music. Grating her fingers in the bark, she damned the audience. Panic seized her. Blood seemed to pour from her shoes. This is death, death, death, she noted in the margin of her mind; when illusion fails. Unable to lift her hand, she stood facing the audience.

And then the shower fell, sudden, profuse.

No one had seen the cloud coming. There it was, black, swollen, on top of them. Down it poured like all the people in the world weeping. Tears, Tears. Tears.

'O that our human pain could here have ending!' Isa murmured. Looking up she received two great blots of rain full in her face. They trickled down her cheeks as if they were her own tears. But they were all people's tears, weeping for all people. Hands were raised. Here and there a parasol opened. The rain was sudden and universal. Then it stopped. From the grass rose a fresh earthy smell.

'That's done it,' sighed Miss La Trobe, wiping away the drops on her cheeks. Nature once more had taken her part. The risk she had run acting in the open air was justified. She brandished her script. Music began – A.B.C. – A.B.C. The tune was as simple as could be. But now that the shower had fallen, it was the other voice speaking, the voice that was no one's voice. And the voice that wept for human pain unending said:

> *The King is in his counting house,*
> *Counting out his money,*

The Queen is in her parlour . . .

'O that my life could here have ending,' Isa murmured (taking care not to move her lips). Readily would she endow this voice with all her treasure if so be tears could be ended. The little twist of sound could have the whole of her. On the altar of the rain-soaked earth she laid down her sacrifice . . .

'O look!' she cried aloud.

That was a ladder. And that (a cloth roughly painted) was a wall. And that a man with a hod on his back. Mr. Page the reporter, licking his pencil, noted: 'With the very limited means at her disposal, Miss La Trobe conveyed to the audience Civilization (the wall) in ruins; rebuilt (witness man with hod) by human effort; witness also woman handing bricks. Any fool could grasp that. Now issued black man in fuzzy wig; coffee-coloured ditto in silver turban; they signify presumably the League of . . .'[114]

A burst of applause greeted this flattering tribute to ourselves. Crude of course. But then she had to keep expenses down. A painted cloth must convey – what the *Times* and *Telegraph* both said in their leaders that very morning.

The tune hummed:

> *The King is in his counting house,*
> *Counting out his money,*
> *The Queen is in her parlour*
> *Eating . . .*

Suddenly the tune stopped. The tune changed. A waltz, was it? Something half known, half not. The swallows danced it. Round and round, in and out they skimmed. Real swallows. Retreating and advancing. And the trees, O the trees, how gravely and sedately like senators in council, or the spaced pillars of some cathedral church . . . Yes, they barred the music, and massed and hoarded; and prevented what was fluid from over-flowing. The swallows – or martins were they? – The temple-haunting martins[115] who come, have always come . . . Yes, perched on the wall, they seemed to foretell what after all the *Times* was saying yesterday. Homes will be built. Each flat with its refrigerator, in the crannied wall. Each of us a free man;

plates washed by machinery; not an aeroplane to vex us; all liberated; made whole . . .

The tune changed; snapped; broke; jagged. Fox-trot was it? Jazz? Anyhow the rhythm kicked, reared, snapped short. What a jangle and a jingle! Well, with the means at her disposal, you can't ask too much. What a cackle, a cacophony! Nothing ended. So abrupt. And corrupt. Such an outrage; such an insult; And not plain. Very up to date, all the same. What is her game? To disrupt? Jog and trot? Jerk and smirk? Put the finger to the nose? Squint and pry? Peek and spy? O the irreverence of the generation which is only momentarily – thanks be – 'the young.' The young, who can't make, but only break; shiver into splinters the old vision; smash to atoms what was whole. What a cackle, what a rattle, what a yaffle – as they call the woodpecker, the laughing bird that flits from tree to tree.

Look! Out they come, from the bushes – the riff-raff. Children? Imps – elves – demons. Holding what? Tin cans? Bedroom candlesticks? Old jars? My dear, that's the cheval glass from the Rectory! And the mirror – that I lent her. My mother's. Cracked. What's the notion? Anything that's bright enough to reflect, presumably, ourselves?

Ourselves! Ourselves!

Out they leapt, jerked, skipped. Flashing, dazzling, dancing, jumping. Now old Bart . . . he was caught. Now Manresa. Here a nose . . . There a skirt . . . Then trousers only . . . Now perhaps a face . . . Ourselves? But that's cruel. To snap us as we are, before we've had time to assume . . . And only, too, in parts . . . That's what's so distorting and upsetting and utterly unfair.

Mopping, mowing, whisking, frisking, the looking glasses darted, flashed, exposed. People in the back rows stood up to see the fun. Down they sat, caught themselves . . . What an awful show-up! Even for the old who, one might suppose, hadn't any longer any care about their faces . . . And Lord! the jangle and the din! The very cows joined in. Walloping, tail lashing, the reticence of nature was undone, and the barriers which should divide Man the Master from the Brute were dissolved. Then the dogs joined in. Excited by the uproar, scurrying and worrying, here they came! Look at them! And the hound, the Afghan hound . . . look at him!

Then once more, in the uproar which by this time has passed quite beyond control, behold Miss Whatshername behind the tree summoned from the bushes – or was it *they* who broke away – Queen Bess; Queen Anne; and the girl in the Mall; and the Age of Reason; and Budge the policeman. Here they came. And the Pilgrims. And the lovers. And the grandfather's clock. And the old man with a beard. They all appeared. What's more, each declaimed some phrase or fragment from their parts . . . *I am not* (said one) *in my perfect mind* . . .[116] Another, *Reason am I . . . And I? I'm the old top hat . . . Home is the hunter, home from the hill . . . Home? Where the miner sweats, and maiden faith is rudely strumpeted . . . Sweet and low; sweet and low, wind of the western sea . . . Is that a dagger that I see before me? . . . The owl hoots and the ivy mocks tap-tap-tapping on the pane . . . Lady I love till I die, leave thy chamber and come . . . Where the worm weaves its winding sheet . . . I'd be a butterfly. I'd be a butterfly . . . In thy will is our peace . . . Here, Papa, take your book and read aloud . . . Hark, hark, the dogs do bark and the beggars . . .*

It was the cheval glass that proved too heavy. Young Bonthorp for all his muscle couldn't lug the damned thing about any longer. He stopped. So did they all – hand glasses, tin cans, scraps of scullery glass, harness room glass, and heavily embossed silver mirrors – all stopped. And the audience saw themselves, not whole by any means, but at any rate sitting still.

The hands of the clock had stopped at the present moment. It was now. Ourselves.

So that was her little game! To show us up, as we are, here and now. All shifted, preened, minced; hands were raised, legs shifted. Even Bart, even Lucy, turned away. All evaded or shaded themselves – save Mrs. Manresa who, facing herself in the glass, used it as a glass; had out her mirror; powdered her nose; and moved one curl, disturbed by the breeze, to its place.

'Magnificent!' cried old Bartholomew. Alone she preserved unashamed her identity, and faced without blinking herself. Calmly she reddened her lips.

The mirror bearers squatted; malicious; observant; expectant; expository.

'That's them,' the back rows were tittering. 'Must we submit

passively to this malignant indignity?' the front row demanded.
Each turned ostensibly to say – O whatever came handy – to
his neighbour. Each tried to shift an inch or two beyond the
inquisitive insulting eye. Some made as if to go.

'The play's over, I take it,' muttered Colonel Mayhew, retrieving his hat. 'It's time . . .'

But before they had come to any common conclusion, a voice
asserted itself. Whose voice it was no one knew. It came from
the bushes – a megaphonic, anonymous,[117] loud-speaking affir-
mation. The voice said:

Before we part, ladies and gentlemen, before we go . . . (Those who
had risen sat down) *. . . let's talk in words of one syllable, without
larding, stuffing or cant. Let's break the rhythm and forget the rhyme.
And calmly consider ourselves. Ourselves. Some bony. Some fat.* (The
glasses confirmed this.) *Liars most of us. Thieves too.* (The glasses
made no comment on that.) *The poor are as bad as the rich are.
Perhaps worse. Don't hide among rags. Or let our cloth protect us. Or
for the matter of that book learning; or skilful practice on pianos; or
laying on of paint. Or presume there's innocency in childhood. Consider
the sheep. Or faith in love. Consider the dogs. Or virtue in those that have
grown white hairs. Consider the gun slayers, bomb droppers here or there.
They do openly what we do slyly. Take for example* (here the megaphone adopted a colloquial, conversational tone) *Mr. M's bungalow. A view spoilt for ever. That's murder . . . Or Mrs. E's lipstick
and blood-red nails . . . A tyrant, remember, is half a slave. Item
the vanity of Mr. H. the writer, scraping in the dunghill for sixpenny
fame . . . Then there's the amiable condescension of the lady of the manor
– the upper class manner. And buying shares in the market to sell 'em
. . . O we're all the same. Take myself now. Do I escape my own
reprobation, simulating indignation, in the bush, among the leaves? There's
a rhyme, to suggest, in spite of protestation and the desire for immolation,
I too have had some, what's called, education . . . Look at ourselves,
ladies and gentlemen! Then at the wall; and ask how's this wall, the great
wall, which we call, perhaps miscall, civilization, to be built by* (here
the mirrors flicked and flashed) *orts, scraps and fragments*[118] *like
ourselves?*

*All the same here I change (by way of the rhyme mark ye) to a loftier
strain – there's something to be said: for our kindness to the cat; note too*

in to-day's paper 'Dearly loved by his wife'; and the impulse which leads us — mark you, when no one's looking — to the window at midnight to smell the bean. Or the resolute refusal of some pimpled dirty little scrub in sandals to sell his soul. There is such a thing — you can't deny it. What? You can't descry it? All you can see of yourselves is scraps, orts and fragments? Well then listen to the gramophone affirming . . .

A hitch occurred here. The records had been mixed. Fox trot, Sweet lavender, Home Sweet Home, Rule Britannia — sweating profusely, Jimmy, who had charge of the music, threw them aside and fitted the right one — was it Bach, Handel, Beethoven, Mozart or nobody famous, but merely a traditional tune? Anyhow, thank heaven, it was somebody speaking after the anonymous bray of the infernal megaphone.

Like quicksilver sliding, filings magnetized, the distracted united. The tune began; the first note meant a second; the second a third. Then down beneath a force was born in opposition; then another. On different levels they diverged. On different levels ourselves went forward; flower gathering some on the surface; others descending to wrestle with the meaning; but all comprehending; all enlisted. The whole population of the mind's immeasurable profundity came flocking; from the unprotected, the unskinned; and dawn rose; and azure; from chaos and cacophony measure; but not the melody of surface sound alone controlled it; but also the warring battle-plumed warriors straining asunder: To part? No. Compelled from the ends of the horizon; recalled from the edge of appalling crevasses; they crashed; solved; united. And some relaxed their fingers; and others uncrossed their legs.

Was that voice ourselves? Scraps, orts and fragments, are we, also, that? The voice died away.

As waves withdrawing uncover; as mist uplifting reveals; so, raising their eyes (Mrs. Manresa's were wet; for an instant tears ravaged her powder) they saw, as waters withdrawing leave visible a tramp's old boot, a man in a clergyman's collar surreptitiously mounting a soap-box.

'The Rev. G. W. Streatfield,' the reporter licked his pencil and noted 'then spoke . . .'

All gazed. What an intolerable constriction, contraction, and reduction to simplified absurdity he was to be sure! Of all incongruous sights a clergyman in the livery of his servitude to the summing up was the most grotesque and entire. He opened his mouth. O Lord, protect and preserve us from words the defilers, from words the impure! What need have we of words to remind us? Must I be Thomas, you Jane?

As if a rook had hopped unseen to a prominent bald branch, he touched his collar and hemmed his preliminary croak. One fact mitigated the horror; his forefinger, raised in the customary manner, was stained with tobacco juice. He wasn't such a bad fellow, the Rev. G. W. Streatfield; a piece of traditional church furniture; a corner cupboard; or the top beam of a gate, fashioned by generations of village carpenters after some lost-in-the-mists-of-antiquity model.

He looked at the audience; then up at the sky. The whole lot of them, gentles and simples, felt embarrassed, for him, for themselves. There he stood their representative spokesman; their symbol; themselves; a butt, a clod, laughed at by looking-glasses; ignored by the cows, condemned by the clouds which continued their majestic rearrangement of the celestial landscape; an irrelevant forked stake in the flow and majesty of the summer silent world.

His first words (the breeze had risen; the leaves were rustling) were lost. Then he was heard saying: 'What.' To that word he added another 'Message'; and at last a whole sentence emerged; not comprehensible; say rather audible. 'What message,' it seemed he was asking, 'was our pageant meant to convey?'

They folded their hands in the traditional manner as if they were seated in church.

'I have been asking myself' – the words were repeated – 'what meaning, or message, this pageant was meant to convey?'

If he didn't know, calling himself Reverend, also M.A., who after all could?

'As one of the audience,' he continued (words now put on meaning) 'I will offer, very humbly, for I am not a critic' – and he touched the white gate that enclosed his neck with a yellow forefinger – 'my interpretation. No, that is too bold a word. The gifted lady . . .' He looked round. La Trobe was invisible. He continued: 'Speaking merely as one of the audience, I confess I was puzzled. For what reason, I asked, were we shown these scenes? Briefly, it is true. The means at our disposal this afternoon were limited. Still we were shown different groups. We were shown, unless I mistake, the effort renewed. A few were chosen; the many passed in the background. That surely we were shown. But again, were we not given to understand – am I too presumptuous? Am I treading, like angels, where as a fool I should absent myself? To me at least it was indicated that we are members one of another. Each is part of the whole. Yes, that occurred to me, sitting among you in the audience. Did I not perceive Mr. Hardcastle here' (he pointed) 'at one time a Viking? And in Lady Harridan – excuse me, if I get the names wrong – a Canterbury pilgrim? We act different parts; but are the same. That I leave to you. Then again, as the play or pageant proceeded, my attention was distracted. Perhaps that too was part of the producer's intention? I thought I perceived that nature takes her part. Dare we, I asked myself, limit life to ourselves? May we not hold that there is a spirit that inspires, pervades . . .' (the swallows were sweeping round him. They seemed cognizant of his meaning. Then they swept out of sight.) 'I leave that to you. I am not here to explain. That role has not been assigned me. I speak only as one of the audience, one of ourselves. I caught myself too reflected, as it happened in my own mirror . . .' (Laughter) 'Scraps, orts and fragments! Surely, we should unite?'

'But' ('but' marked a new paragraph) 'I speak also in another capacity. As Treasurer of the Fund. In which capacity' (he consulted a sheet of paper) 'I am glad to be able to tell you that a sum of thirty-six pounds ten shillings and eightpence has been raised by this afternoon's entertainment towards our object: the illumination of our dear old church.'

'Applause,' the reporter reported.

Mr. Streatfield paused. He listened. Did he hear some distant music?

He continued: 'But there is still a deficit' (he consulted his paper) 'of one hundred and seventy-five pounds odd. So that each of us who has enjoyed this pageant has still an opp . . .' The word was cut in two. A zoom severed it. Twelve aeroplanes in perfect formation like a flight of wild duck[119] came overhead.

That was the music. The audience gaped; the audience gazed. Then zoom became drone. The planes had passed.

'. . . portunity,' Mr. Streatfield continued, 'to make a contribution.' He signalled. Instantly collecting boxes were in operation. Hidden behind glasses they emerged. Coppers rattled. Silver jingled. But O what a pity – how creepy it made one feel! Here came Albert, the idiot, jingling his collecting box – an aluminium saucepan without a lid. You couldn't very well deny him, poor fellow. Shillings were dropped. He rattled and sniggered; chattered and jibbered. As Mrs. Parker made her contribution – half a crown as it happened – she appealed to Mr. Streatfield to exorcize this evil, to extend the protection of his cloth.

The good man contemplated the idiot benignly. His faith had room, he indicated, for him too. He too, Mr. Streatfield appeared to be saying, is part of ourselves. But not a part we like to recognize, Mrs. Springett added silently, dropping her sixpence.

Contemplating the idiot, Mr. Streatfield had lost the thread of his discourse. His command over words seemed gone. He twiddled the cross on his watchchain. Then his hand sought his trouser pocket. Surreptitiously he extracted a small silver box. It was plain to all that the natural desire of the natural man was overcoming him. He had no further use for words.

'And now,' he resumed, cuddling the pipe lighter in the palm of his hand, 'for the pleasantest part of my duty. To propose a vote of thanks to the gifted lady . . .' He looked round for an object corresponding to this description. None such was visible. '. . . who wishes it seems to remain anonymous.' He paused. 'And so . . .' He paused again.

It was an awkward moment. How to make an end? Whom to thank? Every sound in nature was painfully audible; the swish of the trees; the gulp of a cow; even the skim of the swallows over the grass could be heard. But no one spoke. Whom could they make responsible? Whom could they thank for their entertainment? Was there no one?

Then there was a scuffle behind the bush; a preliminary premonitory scratching. A needle scraped a disc; chuff, chuff, chuff; then having found the rut, there was a roll and a flutter which portended *God . . .* (they all rose to their feet) *Save the King.*

Standing the audience faced the actors; who also stood with their collecting boxes quiescent, their looking-glasses hidden, and the robes of their various parts hanging stiff.

Happy and glorious,
Long to reign over us
God save the King

The notes died away.

Was that the end? The actors were reluctant to go. They lingered; they mingled. There was Budge the policeman talking to old Queen Bess. And the Age of Reason hobnobbed with the foreparts of the donkey. And Mrs. Hardcastle patted out the folds of her crinoline. And little England, still a child, sucked a peppermint drop out of a bag. Each still acted the unacted part conferred on them by their clothes. Beauty was on them. Beauty revealed them. Was it the light that did it? – the tender, the fading, the uninquisitive but searching light of evening that reveals depths in water and makes even the red brick bungalow radiant?

'Look,' the audience whispered, 'O look, look, look. —' And once more they applauded; and the actors joined hands and bowed.

Old Mrs. Lynn Jones, fumbling for her bag, sighed, 'What a pity – must they change?'

But it was time to pack up and be off.

'Home, gentlemen; home, ladies; it's time to pack up and be off,' the reporter whistled, snapping the band round his note-book. And Mrs. Parker was stooping.

'I'm afraid I've dropped my glove. I'm so sorry to trouble you. Down there, between the seats . . .'

The gramophone was affirming in tones there was no denying, triumphant yet valedictory: *Dispersed are we; who have come together. But,* the gramophone asserted, *let us retain whatever made that harmony.*

O let us, the audience echoed (stooping, peering, fumbling), keep together. For there is joy, sweet joy, in company.

Dispersed are we, the gramophone repeated.

And the audience turning saw the flaming windows, each

daubed with golden sun; and murmured: 'Home, gentlemen; sweet ...' yet delayed a moment, seeing through the golden glory perhaps a crack in the boiler; perhaps a hole in the carpet; and hearing, perhaps, the daily drop of the daily bill.

Dispersed are we, the gramophone informed them. And dismissed them. So, straightening themselves for the last time, each grasping, it might be a hat, or a stick or a pair of suède gloves, for the last time they applauded Budge and Queen Bess; the trees; the white road; Bolney Minster; and the Folly. One hailed another, and they dispersed, across lawns, down paths, past the house to the gravel-strewn crescent, where cars, push bikes and cycles were crowded together.

Friends hailed each other in passing.

'I do think,' someone was saying, 'Miss Whatshername should have come forward and not left it to the rector ... After all, she wrote it ... I thought it brilliantly clever ... O my dear, I thought it utter bosh. Did *you* understand the meaning? Well, he said she meant we all act all parts ... He said, too, if I caught his meaning, Nature takes part ... Then there was the idiot ... Also, why leave out the Army, as my husband was saying, if it's history? And if one spirit animates the whole, what about the aeroplanes? ... Ah, but you're being too exacting. After all, remember, it was only a village play ... For my part, I think they should have passed a vote of thanks to the owners. When we had our pageant, the grass didn't recover till autumn ... Then we had tents ... That's the man, Cobbet of Cobbs Corner, who wins all the prizes at all the shows. I don't myself admire prize flowers, nor yet prize dogs ...'

Dispersed are we, the gramophone triumphed, yet lamented, *Dispersed are we* ...

'But you must remember,' the old cronies chatted, 'they had to do it on the cheap. You can't get people, at this time o' year, to rehearse. There's the hay, let alone the movies ... What we need is a centre. Something to bring us all together ... The Brookes have gone to Italy, in spite of everything. Rather rash? ... If the worst should come – let's hope it won't – they'd hire an aeroplane, so they said ... What amused me was old Streatfield, feeling for his pouch. I like a man to be natural, not always on a perch ... Then those voices from the bushes ... Oracles? You're referring to the Greeks? Were the oracles, if I'm not being irreverent, a foretaste of our own religion? Which is what? ... Crepe soles? That's so sensible ... They last much longer and protect the feet ... But I was saying: can the Christian faith adapt itself? In times like these ... At Larting no one goes to church ... There's the dogs, there's the pictures ... It's odd that science, so they tell me, is making things (so to speak) more spiritual ... The very latest notion, so I'm told, is, nothing's solid[120] ... There, you can get a glimpse of the church through the trees ...

'Mr. Umphelby! How nice to see you! Do come and dine ... No, alas, we're going back to town. The House is sitting ... I was telling them, the Brookes have gone to Italy. They've seen the volcano. Most impressive, so they say – they were lucky – in eruption. I agree – things look worse than ever on the continent. And what's the channel, come to think of it, if they mean to invade us? The aeroplanes, I didn't like to say it, made one think ... No, I thought it much too scrappy. Take the idiot. Did she mean, so to speak, something hidden, the unconscious[121] as they call it? But why always drag in sex ... It's true, there's a sense in which we all, I admit, are savages still. Those women with red nails. And dressing up – what's that? The old savage, I suppose ... That's the bell. Ding dong.[122] Ding ... Rather a cracked old bell ... And the mirrors! Reflecting us ... I call that cruel. One feels such a fool, caught unprotected ... There's Mr. Streatfield, going, I suppose to take the evening service. He'll have to hurry, or he won't have time to change ... He said she meant we all act. Yes, but whose play? Ah, that's the question! And if we're left asking questions, isn't it a failure, as a play? I must say I like to feel sure if I go to the theatre, that I've grasped the meaning ... Or was that, perhaps, what she meant? ... Ding dong. Ding ... that if we don't jump to conclusions, if you think, and I think, perhaps one day, thinking differently, we shall think the same?

'There's dear old Mr. Carfax ... Can't we give you a lift, if you don't mind playing bodkin? We were asking questions, Mr. Carfax, about the play. The looking-glasses now – did they mean the reflection is the dream; and the tune – was it Bach, Handel, or no one in particular – is the truth? Or was it t'other way about?

'Bless my soul, what a dither! Nobody seems to know one car from another. That's why I have a mascot, a monkey ... But I can't see it ... While we're waiting, tell me, did you feel when the shower fell, someone wept for us all? There's a poem, *Tears tears tears*,[123] it begins. And goes on *O then the unloosened ocean* ... but I can't remember the rest.

'Then when Mr. Streatfield said: One spirit animates the whole – the aeroplanes interrupted. That's the worst of playing out of doors ... Unless of course she meant that very thing ... Dear me, the parking arrangements are not what you might call adequate ... I shouldn't have expected either so many Hispano-Suizas ... That's a Rolls ... That's a Bentley ... That's the new type of Ford ... To return to the meaning – Are machines the devil, or do they introduce a discord ... Ding dong, ding ... by means of which we reach the final ... Ding dong ... Here's the car with the monkey ... Hop in ... And good-bye, Mrs. Parker ... Ring us up. Next time we're down don't forget ... Next time ... Next time ...'

The wheels scurred on the gravel. The cars drove off.

The gramophone gurgled *Unity – Dispersity*. It gurgled *Un ... dis* ... And ceased.

The little company who had come together at luncheon were left standing on the terrace. The pilgrims had bruised a lane on the grass. Also, the lawn would need a deal of clearing up. Tomorrow the telephone would ring: 'Did I leave my handbag? ... A pair of spectacles in a red leather case? ... A little old brooch of no value to anyone but me?' Tomorrow the telephone would ring.

Now Mr. Oliver said: 'Dear lady,' and, taking Mrs. Manresa's gloved hand in his, pressed it, as if to say: 'You have given me what you now take from me.' He would have liked to hold on for a moment longer to the emeralds and rubies dug up, so people said, by thin Ralph Manresa in his ragamuffin days. But alas, sunset light was unsympathetic to her make-up; plated it looked, not deeply interfused.[124] And he dropped her hand; and she gave him an arch roguish twinkle, as if to say – but the end of that sentence was cut short. For she turned, and Giles stepped forward; and the light breeze which the meteorologist had foretold fluttered her skirts; and she went, like a goddess, buoyant, abundant, with flower-chained captives following in her wake.

All were retreating, withdrawing and dispersing; and he was left with the ash grown cold and no glow, no glow on the log. What word expressed the sag at his heart, the effusion in his veins, as the retreating Manresa, with Giles attendant, admirable woman, all sensation, ripped the rag doll and let the sawdust stream from his heart?

The old man made a guttural sound, and turned to the right. On with the hobble, on with the limp, since the dance was over. He strolled alone past the trees. It was here, early that very morning, that he had destroyed the little boy's world. He had popped out with his newspaper; the child had cried.

Down in the dell, past the lily pool, the actors were undressing. He could see them among the brambles. In vests and trousers; unhooking; buttoning up: on all fours; stuffing clothes into cheap attaché cases; with silver swords, beards and emeralds on the grass. Miss La Trobe in coat and skirt – too short, for her legs were stout – battled with the billows of a crinoline. He must respect the conventions. So he stopped, by the pool. The water was opaque over the mud.

Then, coming up behind him, 'Oughtn't we to thank her?' Lucy asked him. She gave him a light pat on the arm.

How imperceptive her religion made her! The fumes of that incense obscured the human heart. Skimming the surface, she ignored the battle in the mud. After La Trobe had been excruciated by the Rector's interpretation, by the maulings and the manglings of the actors ... 'She don't want our thanks, Lucy,' he said gruffly. What she wanted, like that carp (something moved in the water) was darkness in the mud; a whisky and soda at the pub; and coarse words descending like maggots through the waters.

'Thank the actors, not the author,' he said. 'Or ourselves, the audience.'

He looked over his shoulder. The old lady, the indigenous, the prehistoric, was being wheeled away by a footman. He rolled her through the arch. Now the lawn was empty. The line of the roof, the upright chimneys, rose hard and red against the blue of the evening. The house emerged; the house that had been obliterated. He was damned glad it was over – the scurry and the scuffle, the rouge and the rings. He stooped and raised a peony that had shed its petals. Solitude had come again. And reason and the lamplit paper . . . But where was his dog? Chained in a kennel? The little veins swelled with rage on his temples. He whistled. And here, released by Candish, racing across the lawn with a fleck of foam on the nostril, came his dog.

Lucy still gazed at the lily pool. 'All gone,' she murmured, 'under the leaves.' Scared by shadows passing, the fish had withdrawn. She gazed at the water. Perfunctorily she caressed her cross. But her eyes went water searching, looking for fish. The lilies were shutting; the red lily, the white lily, each on its plate of leaf. Above, the air rushed; beneath was water. She stood between two fluidities, caressing her cross. Faith required hours of kneeling in the early morning. Often the delight of the roaming eye seduced her – a sunbeam, a shadow. Now the jagged leaf at the corner suggested, by its contours, Europe. There were other leaves. She fluttered her eye over the surface, naming leaves India, Africa, America. Islands of security, glossy and thick.

'Bart . . .' She spoke to him. She had meant to ask him about the dragon-fly – couldn't the blue thread settle, if we destroyed it here, then there? But he had gone into the house.

Then something moved in the water; her favourite fantail. The golden orfe followed. Then she had a glimpse of silver – the great carp himself, who came to the surface so very seldom. They slid on, in and out between the stalks, silver; pink; gold; splashed; streaked; pied.

'Ourselves,' she murmured. And retrieving some glint of faith from the grey waters, hopefully, without much help from reason, she followed the fish; the speckled, streaked, and blotched; seeing in that vision beauty, power, and glory in ourselves.

Fish had faith, she reasoned. They trust us because we've

never caught 'em. But her brother would reply: 'That's greed.'
'Their beauty!' she protested. 'Sex,' he would say. 'Who makes
sex susceptible to beauty?' she would argue. He shrugged who?
Why? Silenced, she returned to her private vision; of beauty
which is goodness; the sea on which we float. Mostly impervious,
but surely every boat sometimes leaks?

He would carry the torch of reason till it went out in the
darkness of the cave. For herself, every morning, kneeling, she
protected her vision. Every night she opened the window and
looked at leaves against the sky. Then slept. Then the random
ribbons of birds' voices woke her.

The fish had come to the surface. She had nothing to give
them – not a crumb of bread. 'Wait, my darlings,' she addressed
them. She would trot into the house and ask Mrs. Sands for
a biscuit. Then a shadow fell. Off they flashed. How vexatious!
Who was it? Dear me, the young man whose name she had
forgotten; not Jones; nor Hodge . . .

Dodge had left Mrs. Manresa abruptly. All over the garden he
had been searching for Mrs. Swithin. Now he found her; and she
had forgotten his name.

'I'm William,' he said. At that she revived, like a girl in a
garden in white, among roses, who came running to meet him –
an unacted part.

'I was going to get a biscuit – no, to thank the actors,' she
stumbled, virginal, blushing. Then she remembered her brother.
'My brother,' she added 'says one mustn't thank the author,
Miss La Trobe.'

It was always 'my brother . . . my brother' who rose from the
depths of her lily pool.

As for the actors, Hammond had detached his whiskers and
was now buttoning up his coat. When the chain was inserted
between the buttons he was off.

Only Miss La Trobe remained, bending over something in the
grass.

'The play's over,' he said. 'The actors have departed.'

'And we mustn't, my brother says, thank the author,' Mrs.
Swithin repeated, looking in the direction of Miss La Trobe.

'So I thank you,' he said. He took her hand and pressed it.

Putting one thing with another, it was unlikely that they would ever meet again.

The church bells always stopped, leaving you to ask: Won't there be another note? Isa, half-way across the lawn, listened . . . Ding, dong, ding . . . There was not going to be another note. The congregation was assembled, on their knees, in the church. The service was beginning. The play was over; swallows skimmed the grass that had been the stage.

There was Dodge, the lip reader, her semblable, her con-spirator,[125] a seeker like her after hidden faces. He was hurrying to rejoin Mrs. Manresa who had gone in front with Giles – 'the father of my children,' she muttered. The flesh poured over her, the hot, nerve wired, now lit up, now dark as the grave physical body. By way of healing the rusty fester of the poisoned dart she sought the face that all day long she had been seeking. Preening and peering, between backs, over shoulders, she had sought the man in grey. He had given her a cup of tea at a tennis party; handed her, once, a racquet. That was all. But, she was crying, had we met before the salmon leapt like a bar of silver . . . had we met, she was crying. And when her little boy came battling through the bodies in the Barn 'Had he been his son,' she had muttered . . . In passing she stripped the bitter leaf that grew, as it happened, outside the nursery window. Old Man's Beard. Shrivelling the shreds in lieu of words, for no words grow there, nor roses either, she swept past her conspirator, her semblable, the seeker after vanished faces – 'like Venus' he thought, making a rough translation, 'to her prey . . .'[126] and followed after.

Turning the corner, there was Giles attached to Mrs. Manresa. She was standing at the door of her car. Giles had his foot on the edge of the running board. Did they perceive the arrows about to strike them?

'Jump in, Bill,' Mrs. Manresa chaffed him.

And the wheels scurred on the gravel, and the car drove off.

At last, Miss La Trobe could raise herself from her stooping position. It had been prolonged to avoid attention. The bells had stopped; the audience had gone; also the actors. She could straighten her back. She could open her arms. She could say to the world, You have taken my gift! Glory possessed her – for one moment. But what had she given? A cloud that melted into the other clouds on the horizon. It was in the giving that the triumph was. And the triumph faded. Her gift meant nothing. If they had understood her meaning; if they had known their parts; if the pearls had been real and the funds illimitable – it would have been a better gift. Now it had gone to join the others.

'A failure,' she groaned, and stooped to put away the records.

Then suddenly the starlings attacked the tree behind which she had hidden. In one flock they pelted it like so many winged stones. The whole tree hummed with the whizz they made, as if each bird plucked a wire. A whizz, a buzz rose from the bird-buzzing, bird-vibrant, bird-blackened tree. The tree became a rhapsody, a quivering cacophony, a whizz and vibrant rapture, branches, leaves, birds syllabling discordantly life, life, life, without measure, without stop devouring the tree. Then up! Then off!

What interrupted? It was old Mrs. Chalmers, creeping through the grass with a bunch of flowers – pinks apparently – to fill the vase that stood on her husband's grave. In winter it was holly, or ivy. In summer, a flower. It was she who had scared the starlings. Now she passed.

Miss La Trobe nicked the lock and hoisted the heavy case of gramophone records to her shoulder. She crossed the terrace and stopped by the tree where the starlings had gathered. It was here that she had suffered triumph, humiliation, ecstasy, despair – for nothing. Her heels had ground a hole in the grass.

It was growing dark. Since there were no clouds to trouble the sky, the blue was bluer, the green greener. There was no longer a view – no Folly, no spire of Bolney Minster. It was land merely, no land in particular. She put down her case and stood looking at the land. Then something rose to the surface.

'I should group them,' she murmured, 'here.' It would be midnight; there would be two figures, half concealed by a rock. The curtain would rise. What would the first words be? The words escaped her.

Again she lifted the heavy suit case to her shoulder. She strode off across the lawn. The house was dormant; one thread of smoke thickened against the trees. It was strange that the earth, with all those flowers incandescent – the lilies, the roses, and clumps of white flowers and bushes of burning green – should still be hard. From the earth green waters seemed to rise over her. She took her voyage away from the shore, and, raising her hand, fumbled for the latch of the iron entrance gate.

She would drop her suit case in at the kitchen window, and then go on up to the Inn. Since the row with the actress who had shared her bed and her purse the need of drink had grown on her. And the horror and the terror of being alone. One of these days she would break – which of the village laws? Sobriety? Chastity? Or take something that did not properly belong to her?

At the corner she ran into old Mrs. Chalmers returning from the grave. The old woman looked down at the dead flowers she was carrying and cut her. The women in the cottages with the red geraniums always did that. She was an outcast. Nature had somehow set her apart from her kind. Yet she had scribbled in the margin of her manuscript: 'I am the slave of my audience.'

She thrust her suit case in at the scullery window and walked on, till at the corner she saw the red curtain at the bar window. There would be shelter; voices; oblivion. She turned the handle of the public house door. The acrid smell of stale beer saluted her; and voices talking. They stopped. They had been talking about Bossy as they called her – it didn't matter. She took her chair and looked through the smoke at a crude glass painting of a cow in a stable; also at a cock and a hen. She raised her glass to her lips. And drank. And listened. Words of one syllable sank down into the mud. She drowsed; she nodded. The mud became fertile. Words rose above the intolerably laden dumb oxen plodding through the mud. Words without meaning – wonderful words.

The cheap clock ticked; smoke obscured the pictures. Smoke became tart on the roof of her mouth. Smoke obscured the earth-coloured jackets. She no longer saw them, yet they upheld her, sitting arms akimbo with her glass before her. There was the high ground at midnight; there the rock; and two scarcely perceptible figures. Suddenly the tree was pelted with starlings. She set down her glass. She heard the first words.

Down in the hollow, at Pointz Hall, beneath the trees, the table was cleared in the dining room. Candish, with his curved brush, had swept the crumbs; had spared the petals and finally left the family to dessert. The play was over, the strangers gone, and they were alone – the family.

Still the play hung in the sky of the mind – moving, diminishing, but still there. Dipping her raspberry in sugar, Mrs. Swithin looked at the play. She said, popping the berry into her mouth, 'What did it mean?' and added: 'The peasants; the kings; the fool and' (she swallowed) 'ourselves?'

They all looked at the play; Isa, Giles and Mr. Oliver. Each of course saw something different. In another moment it would be beneath the horizon, gone to join the other plays. Mr. Oliver, holding out his cheroot, said: 'Too ambitious.' And, lighting his cheroot, he added: 'Considering her means.'

It was drifting away to join the other clouds: becoming invisible. Through the smoke Isa saw not the play but the audience dispersing. Some drove; others cycled. A gate swung open. A car swept up the drive to the red villa in the cornfields. Low hanging boughs of acacia brushed the roof. Acacia petalled the car arrived.

'The looking-glasses and the voices in the bushes,' she murmured. 'What did she mean?'

'When Mr. Streatfield asked her to explain, she wouldn't,' said Mrs. Swithin.

Here, with its sheath sliced in four, exposing a white cone, Giles offered his wife a banana. She refused it. He stubbed his match on the plate. Out it went with a little fizz in the raspberry juice.

'We should be thankful,' said Mrs. Swithin, folding her napkin, 'for the weather, which was perfect, save for one shower.'

Here she rose. Isa followed her across the hall to the big room.

They never pulled the curtains till it was too dark to see, nor shut the windows till it was too cold. Why shut out the day before it was over? The flowers were still bright; the birds chirped. You could see more in the evening often when nothing interrupted, when there was no fish to order, no telephone to answer. Mrs. Swithin stopped by the great picture of Venice – school of Canaletto.[127] Possibly in the hood of the gondola there was a little figure – a woman, veiled; or a man?

Isa, sweeping her sewing from the table, sank, her knee doubled, into the chair by the window. Within the shell of the room she overlooked the summer night. Lucy returned from her voyage into the picture and stood silent. The sun made each pane of her glasses shine red. Silver sparkled on her black shawl. For a moment she looked like a tragic figure from another play.

Then she spoke in her usual voice. 'We made more this year than last, he said. But then last year it rained.'

'This year, last year, next year, never . . .' Isa murmured. Her hand burnt in the sun on the window sill. Mrs. Swithin took her knitting from the table.

'Did you feel,' she asked 'what he said: we act different parts but are the same?'

'Yes,' Isa answered. 'No,' she added. It was Yes, No. Yes, yes, yes, the tide rushed out embracing. No, no, no, it contracted. The old boot appeared on the shingle.

'Orts, scraps and fragments,' she quoted what she remembered of the vanishing play.

Lucy had just opened her lips to reply, and had laid her hand on her cross caressingly, when the gentlemen came in. She made her little chirruping sound of welcome. She shuffled her feet to clear a space. But in fact there was more space than was needed, and great hooded chairs.

They sat down, ennobled both of them by the setting sun. Both had changed. Giles now wore the black coat and white tie of the professional classes, which needed – Isa looked down at his feet – patent leather pumps. 'Our representative, our spokes-man,' she sneered. Yet he was extraordinarily handsome. 'The father of my children, whom I love and hate.' Love and hate –

how they tore her asunder! Surely it was time someone invented a new plot, or that the author came out from the bushes . . .

Here Candish came in. He brought the second post on a silver salver. There were letters; bills; and the morning paper – the paper that obliterated the day before. Like a fish rising to a crumb of biscuit, Bartholomew snapped at the paper. Giles slit the flap of an apparently business document. Lucy read a criss-cross[128] from an old friend at Scarborough. Isa had only bills.

The usual sounds reverberated through the shell; Sands making up the fire; Candish stoking the boiler. Isa had done with her bills. Sitting in the shell of the room she watched the pageant fade.[129] The flowers flashed before they faded. She watched them flash.

The paper crackled. The second hand jerked on. M. Daladier had pegged down the franc. The girl had gone skylarking with the troopers. She had screamed. She had hit him . . . What then?

When Isa looked at the flowers again, the flowers had faded.

Bartholomew flicked on the reading lamp. The circle of the readers, attached to white papers, was lit up. There in that hollow of the sun-baked field were congregated the grasshopper, the ant, and the beetle, rolling pebbles of sun-baked earth through the glistening stubble. In that rosy corner of the sun-baked field Bartholomew, Giles and Lucy polished and nibbled and broke off crumbs. Isa watched them.

Then the newspaper dropped.

'Finished?' said Giles, taking it from his father.

The old man relinquished his paper. He basked. One hand caressing the dog rippled folds of skin towards the collar.

The clock ticked. The house gave little cracks as if it were very brittle, very dry. Isa's hand on the window felt suddenly cold. Shadow had obliterated the garden. Roses had withdrawn for the night.

Mrs. Swithin folding her letter murmured to Isa: 'I looked in and saw the babies, sound asleep, under the paper roses.'

'Left over from the coronation,' Bartholomew muttered, half asleep.

'But we needn't have been to all that trouble with the decorations,' Lucy added, 'for it didn't rain this year.'

'This year, last year, next year, never,' Isa murmured.

'Tinker, tailor, soldier, sailor,' Bartholomew echoed. He was talking in his sleep.

Lucy slipped her letter into its envelope. It was time to read now, her Outline of History. But she had lost her place. She turned the pages looking at pictures – mammoths, mastodons, prehistoric birds. Then she found the page where she had stopped.

The darkness increased. The breeze swept round the room. With a little shiver Mrs. Swithin drew her sequin shawl about her shoulders. She was too deep in the story to ask for the window to be shut. 'England,' she was reading, 'was then a swamp.[130] Thick forests covered the land. On the top of their matted branches birds sang . . .'

The great square of the open window showed only sky now. It was drained of light, severe, stone cold. Shadows fell. Shadows crept over Bartholomew's high forehead; over his great nose. He looked leafless, spectral, and his chair monumental. As a dog shudders its skin, his skin shuddered. He rose, shook himself, glared at nothing, and stalked from the room. They heard the dog's paws padding on the carpet behind him.

Lucy turned the page, quickly, guiltily, like a child who will be told to go to bed before the end of the chapter.

'Prehistoric man,' she read, 'half-human, half-ape, roused himself from his semi-crouching position and raised great stones.'

She slipped the letter from Scarborough between the pages to mark the end of the chapter, rose, smiled, and tiptoed silently out of the room.

The old people had gone up to bed. Giles crumpled the newspaper and turned out the light. Left alone together for the first time that day, they were silent. Alone, enmity was bared; also love. Before they slept, they must fight; after they had fought, they would embrace. From that embrace another life might be born. But first they must fight, as the dog fox fights with the vixen, in the heart of darkness,[131] in the fields of night.

Isa let her sewing drop. The great hooded chairs had become enormous. And Giles too. And Isa too against the window. The window was all sky without colour. The house had lost its shelter. It was night before roads were made, or houses. It was the night that dwellers in caves had watched from some high place among rocks.

Then the curtain rose. They spoke.

Notes

1. *Liskeard*: in Cornwall; the last Celtic area of England.
2. *'She walks in beauty'* ... *'So we'll go no more a-roving'*. First lines of two Byron lyrics. *Byron: Poetical Works*, ed. Frederick Page (Oxford University Press, 1970, pp. 71, 101).
3. *Mrs. Swithin*: according to folklore if it rains on St Swithin's day, 15 July, it will rain for forty days thereafter. Mrs Swithin spends much of the June day worrying about whether it will rain on the outdoor performance of the pageant.
4. *an Outline of History*: H. G. Wells, *The Outline of History: Being a Plain History of Life and Mankind* (Cassell, 1920) is merged with G. M. Trevelyan, *History of England* (Longmans, Green, 1926) in the work Lucy Swithin reads. A passage from Trevelyan, p. 3, is seamed into *BA*, pp. 8, 129. See note 130 and Introduction pp. 30–31.
5. *'the wind'll change'*: the first of many folk sayings and superstitions in the book, representing perhaps anonymous communal beliefs.
6. *George grubbed*: compare *Moments of Being*, p. 71, for a similar, less physically described, episode in Woolf's own childhood: 'I was looking at the flower bed by the front door; "That is the whole," I said. I was looking at a plant with a spread of leaves; and it seemed suddenly plain that the flower itself was part of the earth; that a ring enclosed what was the flower; and that was the real flower; part earth; part flower.'
7. *Sohrab*: named from Matthew Arnold's poem 'Sohrab and Rustum' about a Persian warrior father who unwittingly kills his son.
8. *M. Daladier*: see discussion in Introduction, pp. xxv–vi.
9. *shingled or bobbed*: the fashionable short hair styles of the thirties.
10. *the aeroplane propeller that she had seen once at dawn at Croydon*: Woolf saw her sister Vanessa Bell leave with her young son Quentin, who had tuberculosis, for treatment in Switzerland one early morning from Croydon by plane.

I ought to have made a note on Nessa & the aeroplane – last Friday – no Friday week – at Croydon. We took them there at 7 ... We stood on the top of the roof; saw the aeroplane whirl, till the propellors were lost to sight – simply evaporated:

then the aeroplane takes a slow run, circles & rises. This is death I said, feeling how the human contact was completely severed. Up they went with a sublime air & disappeared like a person dying, the soul going. And we remained. (*Diary*, IV, 12 November 1933, p. 187.)

For the various significations of aeroplanes in *BA* compare Gillian Beer, 'The Island and the Aeroplane: The Case of Virginia Woolf', in *Nation and Narration*, ed. Homi Bhabha (Routledge, 1990). Woolf never flew.

11. *Soles. Filleted:* for discussion, see Introduction, p. xviii.

12. *she never looked like Sappho*: the large-limbed, helplessly heterosexual Isa never looked like Sappho, Greek poet, lover of women and of men; 'celebrated', writes Lemprière, 'for her beauty, her poetical talents, and her amorous disposition, [she] was born in the island of Lesbos, about 600 years before Christ.' *Lemprière's Classical Dictionary*, introd. R. Willets (Routledge, 1984, p. 558). First published 1788.

13. *The light but variable breeze*: the weather forecast was a recent innovation; it is read from *The Times* by Bart Oliver on p. 16. References to meteorological predictions are repeated throughout the novel, e.g. p. 120.

14. *a crusader's dog*: a dog carved on a medieval church monument to a crusader, sculpted at his supine master's feet.

15. *as in a glass*: 'For now we see through a glass, darkly; but then face to face' (I Corinthians, 13:12).

16. *But no water*:

> What are the roots that clutch, what branches grow
> Out of this stony rubbish? Son of man,
> You cannot say, or guess, for you know only
> A heap of broken images, where the sun beats,
> And the dead tree gives no shelter, the cricket no relief,
> And the dry stone no sound of water.

'The Burial of the Dead', lines 19–24, *The Waste Land*. T. S. Eliot, *The Complete Poems and Plays of T. S. Eliot* (Faber and Faber, 1969, p. 61).

And compare the Indian tales of Rudyard Kipling, such as 'The Strange Ride of Morrowbie Jukes' in *The Phantom Rickshaw* (Sampson Low, 1890, p. 56): 'By walking out of the first shallow pool that lay at the foot of the projecting left horn of the horse-shoe, I could wade across, turn the flank of the crater, and made my way inland ... My first step from the tufts of dried grass showed me how utterly futile was any hope of escape ...'

17. *The moor is dark beneath the moon*: Percy Bysshe Shelley, 'Stanzas – April 1814' opens:

> Away, the moor is dark beneath the moon,
> Rapid clouds have drank the last pale beam of even

The Complete Poetical Works of Percy Bysshe Shelley, ed. Thomas Hutchinson (Oxford University Press, 1934, p. 521).

Woolf quotes the first line also in *The Waves*.

18. Edmund Spenser, *The Faerie Queene* (1590, 1596); Alexander Kinglake, *History of the Crimean War* (7 vols., 1863–87); John Keats, poet, 1795–1821; Leo Tolstoy, *The Kreutzer Sonata* (1890).

19. *Eddington, Darwin, or Jeans*: Eddington and Jeans were added in the later draft. Their work of explanation is probably alluded to on p. 16 and on p. 118: 'It's odd that science, so they tell me, is making things (so to speak) more spiritual ... The very latest notion, so I'm told is, nothing's solid.' See James Jeans, *The Universe Around Us* (Cambridge University Press, 1929); *The Mysterious Universe* (Cambridge University Press, 1930); *The New Background of Science* (Cambridge University Press, 1933); Arthur Eddington, *The Nature of the Physical Universe* (Cambridge University Press, 1929); *New Pathways in Science* (Cambridge University Press, 1935); Charles Darwin, *Of the Origin of Species* (Murray, 1859) and, particularly for this novel, *The Descent of Man* (Murray, 1871).

20. *'A horse with a green tail ...'*: Stuart N. Clarke, 'The Horse with a Green Tail', *Virginia Woolf Miscellany*, no. 34, Spring 1990, pp. 3–4 gives a useful account of the case alluded to here. See *The Times*, 28, 29, 30 June, 20, 26, 30 July 1938. See also Aleck Bourne's obituary, *The Times*, 30 December 1974. For discussion, see Introduction pp. xxii–xxiv.

21. *'Touch wood; touch earth; Antaeus,'*: Antaeus, son of Poseidon, gained strength each time he touched earth.

22. *Lemprière ... the Encyclopædia*: John Lemprière, *Bibliotheca Classica or, A Classical Dictionary* (T. Cadell, 1788) went through many editions and is still in print; *The Encyclopaedia Britannica*.

23. *left over from the Coronation*: George VI was crowned in 1937 so the decorations have been kept already for two years. At the end the babies merge with the paper roses, both 'left over from the coronation' (p. 128).

24. *the cowman, Bond*: binding the human and animal worlds he speaks

cow language and 'Only Bond the cowman looked fluid and natural' (p. 48).

25. *before the Conquest*: the Norman Conquest, 1066. This and the following two citations make it clear that the villagers have been there much longer than the current occupants of the manor, as has the house.

26. *in Domesday Book*: the survey ordered by William the Conqueror in 1086 which lists the ownership of lands, buildings, and cattle.

27. *before the Reformation*: with the establishment of the (Protestant) Church of England, private chapels fell into disuse. During the subsequent persecution priests were sometimes hidden by recusant families (p. 22).

28. *Bacchus*: god of wine. Lucy Swithin's recollection of often lying under purple lamps in a vineyard in Italy is another unexpected glimpse: an unacted or acted part?

29. *the stockbroker*: Giles is, reluctantly, part of the financial world of city dealings. See discussion of finances and the coming war: compare p. 30 and Introduction, pp. xxv–vi.

30. *The lady was a picture*: the lady is probably by Thomas Gainsborough (1727–88).

31. *a vase stood in the heart of the house*: compare T. S. Eliot, 'Burnt Norton', section V, *Four Quartets*:

> Only by the form, the pattern,
> Can words or music reach
> The stillness, as a Chinese jar still
> Moves perpetually in its stillness.

Complete Poems, op. cit., p. 175.

32. *Mrs. Manresa*: Manresa is the name of a street in Chelsea; the generic name of many Jesuit novice-houses like the one at Roehampton where Gerard Manley Hopkins lived; and – here – also a pun on 'man-raiser'. Compare Joan Rivière, 'Womanliness as a Masquerade', *International Journal of Psycho-analysis*, 10, 1929, p. 303–11. See Introduction, pp. xxvii–ix.

33. *name on the signpost*: the name is, of course, that of Pointz Hall, not of the family.

34. *a clerk in an office*: a modest self-description by William Dodge who seems to be a higher civil servant in 'Education or Somerset House'.

35. *malversation of trusts*: corrupt administration of trust funds.

36. *Ralph, a Jew*: unattributable prejudice, cast as the voice of gossip, cf. p. 74 and note 90.

37. *a corkscrew*: champagne needs no corkscrew and Mrs Manresa is already opening the bottle, so is this a flirtatious pun?

38. *taught the village women*: unlike the Women's Institute, Mrs Manresa teaches frivolous accomplishments. See Introduction for Woolf's uneasy relations with the local Women's Institute of which, for a time, she was treasurer, p. xxxii.

39. *the lady had drowned herself*: Isa has a wish to drown, p. 64. This founding image of drowning may also be premonitory of Woolf's own end. She records the suicide by drowning of two women locally, *Diary*, V, 17 August 1938, pp. 161–2.

40. This is a mid-June afternoon of 1939, less than three months before Britain entered the Second World War. Since we are told on the first page of the book that nightingales do not come so far north as Pointz Hall (p. 5) the house may be, supposedly, in Lincolnshire or Yorkshire (though it often seems to be in Sussex). Inland far (Lucy Swithin says one hundred miles, Bartholomew thirty-five, p. 20), Pointz Hall faces the North Sea across whose gulf is the flat land of Friesland, a region of Germany. The incident recorded here has the ring of 'fact' (which Woolf wished to include) though the geography of the house's position is shifty.

41. *arrow of desire*: Eros strikes Isa and the cows alike. 'Bring me my arrows of desire' is a line from William Blake's poem, often called 'Jerusalem', at the start of his epic *Milton*. The poem opens:

> And did those feet in ancient time
> Walk upon England's mountains green?
>
> *The Poems of William Blake*, ed. W. H. Stevenson and David Erdman (Longman, 1971, p. 488–9).

The poem was improbably appropriated as its anthem by the Women's Institute. Its vision of England was later interpreted nationalistically, particularly in the choral setting by Sir Hubert Parry. Here, the lady in the picture has an arrow (but so has Diana, goddess of chastity). She is *not* painted by Sir Joshua Reynolds, Blake's enemy (p. 32). This complex of fleeting and conflicting allusions is typical of Woolf's method in the novel.

42. *some Institute*: probably the Courtauld Institute.

43. *Sir Joshua*: Sir Joshua Reynolds (1723–92), compare p. 35.

44. *Tinker, tailor*: this is a rather grand version of the stone-counting game: more ordinarily it runs: tinker, tailor, soldier, sailor, rich man, poor man, beggarman, thief.

45. *antre*: cave, cavern. The *Oxford English Dictionary* records its use only by poets: Shakespeare, Keats, Meredith.
46. *Figgis's Guide Book*: fictional.
47. '*Fade far away*': from stanza three of Keats's 'Ode to a Nightingale', not *Hamlet*. William Dodge misquotes, substituting the word 'torture' for 'fever':

> Fade far away, dissolve, and quite forget
> What thou among the leaves hast never known,
> The weariness, the fever, and the fret
> Here, where men sit and hear each other groan.

   The Poetical Works of John Keats, ed. H. Buxton Forman (Oxford University Press, 1908, p. 231).

48. '*Reynolds! Constable! Crome!*': Sir Joshua Reynolds (1723–92), the most famous artist and theorist of his day in England and First President of the Royal Academy; John Constable (1776–1837), with Turner, the outstanding landscape painter of the English nineteenth century; John Crome (1768–1821), landscape painter of the Norwich school, called 'old' to distinguish him from his son who painted in a similar manner.
49. *Miss La Trobe*: Mitchell A. Leaska, *Pointz Hall: The Earlier and Later Typescripts of 'Between the Acts'* (University Publications, New York, 1983, p. 209), points out that the Larousse *Dictionnaire étymologique des noms de famille et prénoms de France* 'explains that the name "La Trobe" means *invention* and is possibly a troubadour's surname'. In 'Some Sources for *Between the Acts*', *Virginia Woolf Miscellany*, no. 6, 1977, pp. 1–3, Jane Marcus argues that Miss La Trobe is modelled on Edith Craig, Ellen Terry's daughter.
50. *Gammer Gurton's Needle*: the second recorded English comedy in verse, published 1575, authorship disputed.
51. *the faint blue mark*: such marks under the glaze were not necessarily an indication of where the cup was made since they belonged to individual craftsmen who might move about a good deal.
52. *but simply a——*: see discussion in Introduction, p. xvii.
53. *nettle-rash*: impetigo.
54. '*A beaker of cold water*': Isa reverses Keats's desire for wine, recalling another line of the 'Ode to a Nightingale' that she quoted earlier (see note 47):

> 'O for a beaker full of the warm South'

55. *Maples*: Maples Furniture Store, then still in Tottenham Court Road.
56. *a hurdle*: a portable frame, for the gramophone, or for scenery.

57. *a car factory ... an aerodrome*: Woolf lived near Gatwick aerodrome in Sussex.

58. *Adsum*: the traditional response in English public schools to the calling of the register, meaning 'I am present'.

59. *The motor bike, the motor bus, and the movies*: new forms of transport and entertainment are changing the village community irreversibly, quite apart from the approaching war.

60. The pageant, which some of the audience expect to follow the genre of Empire Day pageants, pursues a different course (see Introduction, p. xxxii). Empire Day was celebrated on 24 May.

61. *Cut off from France and Germany | This isle.*: references to the geological and political ties with the continent persist throughout the book, emerging first from Mrs Swithin's reading of Wells's *History* (see note 4).

62. *My home is at Windsor*: the music-hall song mocks the royal family whose castle is at Windsor.

63. The pageant begins with Chaucer's *Canterbury Tales*, *c.* 1387, which Woolf was reading as she wrote. *Diary*, V, 19 December 1938, p. 193; 29 April 1939, p. 217, etc.

64. *several rows back*: Isa's strained backward glance for Rupert Haines is noted at frequent intervals throughout the book (as on pp. 51, 56, 59, 123), though often without any open reference to the object of her gaze. There is no indication that he is answering her glance.

65. *Plantagenets . . .*: royal house.

66. *Queen Elizabeth*: Elizabeth I, Queen of England and Ireland (1558–1603). The pageant is set in the reigns of three queens of England: Elizabeth, Anne, and Victoria. The process of Empire is to be seen in their accrued titles.

67. *Hawkins, Frobisher, Drake*: Elizabethan explorers and empire-builders.

68. '*I fear I am not in my perfect mind*': to the same tune as the triumphal pastiche of Elizabethan exploration and conquest, Giles sings to himself King Lear's line in madness (*King Lear*, IV. vii. 76).

69. '*a stricken deer*':

> I was a stricken deer, that left the herd
> Long since; with many an arrow deep infixt
> My panting side was charged.
> William Cowper, *The Task*, Book III, ll. 108–10.

70. *Globe theatre*: Shakespeare's theatre.

71. The heroine of Meredith's last novel, *The Amazing Marriage*, is called

Carinthia. The plot of the Elizabethan pageant play is somewhat like that of *Cymbeline*.

72. *Peace, let her pass*:

> Vex not his ghost, O let him pass, he hates him,
> That would upon the rack of this tough world
> Stretch him out longer.
> (*King Lear*, V. iii. 351-3)

73. *mellay*: mixture (obsolete and rare, *Oxford English Dictionary*).

74. *Dispersed are we*: Ariel: 'In troops I have dispers'd them 'bout the Isle', Shakespeare, *The Tempest*, I. ii. 258. 'Dispersed', a word of rare occurrence in Shakespeare, appears twice in his *The Rape of Lucrece*. The ensuing *BA* passage is full of rhymes, closed up by the widely separated rhyme words of *we, tea, tree, we, me, nursery* which are taken up again on p. 60, with the word *agony* added. Some rhymes are deliberately grotesque, for example, *glamour – sham lure*.

75. *They're said to be going to India . . . I thought they said Canada*: counter-suggestions here: a visit to India would be an assertion of British imperial authority, a visit to Canada would be flight. Many wealthier people went to Canada at the onset of the war, or evacuated their children there. The King and Queen stayed in London throughout the bombing.

76. *Queen Mary met him*: see Introduction, p. xiii.

77. *the Rider gallop*: see note 104.

78. *her Outline of History*: see note 4.

79. *Swallow, my sister, O sister swallow*: the first line of Swinburne's poem 'Itylus', based on the legend of Procne and Philomela in Ovid's *Metamorphoses*. The poem opens:

> Swallow, my sister, O sister swallow,
> How can thine heart be full of the spring?

Tereus, married to Procne, raped her sister Philomela and cut out her tongue so that she might never declare the crime. She sent to Procne a tapestry woven through with a thread that told her story. In revenge, Procne slaughtered and served up their son Itylus to his father. The sisters fled, Procne being transformed into a swallow and Philomela to a nightingale. Compare pp. 70, 71. Swinburne's poem is uttered by the nightingale and ends with a reproach which, like many allusions in *BA*, suggests the coming end:

> Thou hast forgotten, O summer swallow
> But the world shall end when I forget.

The Poems of Algernon Charles Swinburne, vol. 1
(Chatto and Windus, 1905, p. 54).

The swallow occurs in one of the 'fragments I have shored against my ruins' at the end of *The Waste Land* in a quotation from the *Pervigilium Veneris*:

> *Quando fiam uti chelidon* – O swallow swallow

See discussion in Introduction, pp. xxii–xxvii.

In 'Liberty, Sorority, Misogyny', ed. C. Heilbrun and M. Higgonet, *The Representation of Women in Fiction* (Johns Hopkins Press, 1983) Jane Marcus reads *BA* as 'the modern version of a lost Greek play – Sophocles' play on the myth of Procne and Philomela' (p. 67).

80. *what his left hand was doing*: self-stimulation.
81. *had him in thrall*: John Keats, 'La Belle Dame Sans Merci':

> I saw pale kings, and princes too,
> Pale warriors, death-pale were they all;
> Who cry'd – 'La belle Dame sans merci
> Hath thee in thrall!'

op. cit., p. 356

82. Isa seems to have Phèdre or Lucrece in mind, rather than the pageant.
83. *Books . . . Poets . . .*: famous lines from Milton's *Areopagitica* and Shelley's *A Defense of Poetry*.
84. *How can my heart*: Giles adapts a Swinburne line.

Condemned in life's infernal mine: this may be Bart's adaptation of the opening line from Samuel Johnson's poem, 'On the death of Dr Robert Levet'. The rest of Johnson's stanza answers Bart's mood of despair at ageing:

> Condemn'd to hope's delusive mine,
> As on we toil from day to day,
> By sudden blasts, or slow decline,
> Our social comforts drop away.

Samuel Johnson, *Poems* (Yale Edition of the Works of Samuel Johnson, vol. 6) ed. E. L. McAdam Jr (Yale University Press, 1964, p. 314).

Another example of skeining fragments of poems together.

85. *Garibaldi; Wellington; Irrigation Officers' Reports; and Hibbert on the Diseases of the Horse*: Garibaldi, founder of Italian independence; Wellington, British general and politician; 'Irrigation Reports' perhaps refers back obliquely to the question of the cesspool at the beginning of the novel; Hibbert, probably a fictional writer. The library, which to Isa is full of poets, to Bart is full of history and useful reports.

86. *The lamp of love burns high*: Victorian song?

87. *longer days*: summer time (putting the clocks one hour forward) was introduced as a result of the First World War. Double summer time was temporarily introduced during the Second World War.

88. *the common people . . . hate Dictators*: Mussolini was in power in Italy, Stalin in Russia, Hitler in Germany, and Franco in Spain.

89. *Queen Mary*: cf. p. 64.

90. *The refugees . . . the Jews*: the diaspora of European Jewry in the face of Nazi oppression was in full tide in 1939. Leonard Woolf was Jewish. The repeated phrase 'dispersed are we' may include a particular reference to Jewish experience.

91. *a flea in his ear*: 'said of a stinging or mortifying reproof', *Compact Oxford English Dictionary* (Oxford University Press, 1971, p. 305). *OED* cites examples from *c.* 1430 to Rider Haggard and says the phrase is after French *avoir ou mettre la puce à l'oreille*.

92. *The King is in his counting house*: like *Hark, hark, the dogs do bark* a favourite nursery rhyme of Woolf's, cited elsewhere in her novels. Here caught into the discourse of money, privilege, and the war.

93. *Queen Anne*: Queen of England, Scotland, and Ireland (1702–7) and of Great Britain and Ireland (1707–14).

94. Woolf skeins together words and phrases recognizable from a wide, and multiple, range of poetic contexts. For example, 'heavenly harmony' occurs in Dryden's 'Ode on St Cecilia's Day', owes much to Milton, becomes 'heavenliest harmony' in Southey's *Roderick*, etc. The iambic pentameter, established in the first sentence and played upon throughout the passage, organizes the words and phrases: the rhythm of the verse more even than words indicates the different periods of literature.

95. *Where there's a Will there's a Way*: mock Restoration comedy.

96. *Babylon, Nineveh . . . Troy*: Babylon, twice the seat of a major empire before the birth of Christ, destroyed by Sennacherib in 689 BC; Nineveh, capital of Sennacherib's Assyrian empire before it was sacked by the Medes; Troy, captured and sacked by the Greeks under Agamemnon after a ten-year siege, recounted in Homer's

Iliad. The proleptic reference to the fate of Europe in the coming war is obvious. Compare the images of falling empires in *The Waste Land*, 'What the Thunder said', ll. 373–6, ed. cit., p. 73:

> Falling towers
> Jerusalem Athens Alexandria
> Vienna London
> Unreal

97. *Clytemnestra, Agamemnon*: not only empires but also individuals fall. Clytemnestra murdered her husband Agamemnon on his triumphal return from Troy because he had earlier sacrificed their daughter Iphigenia in return for a fair wind for the expedition.

98. Jean Racine, French tragic playwright. See Introduction, p. xxviii.

99. *Pop Goes the Weasel*: popular nineteenth-century tune, attributed to W. R. Mandale.

100. *Aurora Borealis . . . Cassiopeia . . . Andromeda*: the Northern Lights, a constellation, a star.

101. *Gretna Green*: the first village across the border in Scotland that eloping couples could marry in.

102. *The Victorian age*: Victoria, Queen of Great Britain and Ireland and of dependencies overseas (1837–1901) and from 1876 Empress of India.

103. *Cleopatra*: Lucy Swithin's insight draws on Shakespeare, *Antony and Cleopatra*, and on the idea of Cleopatra as Queen of Fertility in whose domain primeval life began in the mud of the Nile. Lucy Swithin's reading and ruminating on primordial life makes the association closer than at first appears. She has a number of unacted parts, see Introduction, p. xxix, and note 130.

104. *the Rider gallops*: a passage of anti-pastoral: the shepherd coughs, the girl is raped, the Rider gallops; perhaps with an echo of W. H. Auden's menacing poem 'Epilogue' which opens

> 'O where are you going?' said reader to rider
> *The English Auden: Poems, Essays and Dramatic Writing 1927–1939*, ed. Edward Mendelson (Faber, 1977, p. 110)

105. *a Grand Ensemble*: Miss La Trobe flouts the conventions of Empire Day pageants and ends with mirrors.

106. *Sweet lavender . . . Any old iron*: London street cries.

107. *Garotters*: cut-throats.

108. *'Knocked 'em in the Old Kent Road'*: by Albert Chevalier. The music hall songs of Woolf's own youth surface increasingly here, for she,

like Mrs Swithin, grew up in the reign of Queen Victoria (Woolf was born in 1882).

109. This episode mocks British imperialism and the late nineteenth-century growth of Empire as well as class divisions and oppression, particularly the oppression of the Irish ('famine, fenians'). The areas of London are contrasted to make the point economically: e.g. Mansion House splendour as opposed to Whitechapel poverty.

110. *the white man's burden*: Mitchell Leaska, op. cit., p. 237, revealingly points out that Woolf probably has in mind a remark of Arnold Bennett's that she quotes in her biography of *Roger Fry*, p. 207: 'Really the white man's burden isn't the poor blacks but his own incredible idealistic folly.'

111. *unhygienic*: a Victorian coinage.

112. *don't believe in history*: A people without history

> Is not redeemed from time, for history is a pattern
> Of timeless moments. So while the light fails
> On a winter's afternoon, in a secluded chapel
> History is now and England.

'Little Gidding', *Four Quartets*, op. cit., p. 197.
Written after *BA*, this may be part of Eliot's response to Woolf's work.

113. *installing electric light in the Church*: the black-out is about to be imposed. Woolf was herself threatened with prosecution for showing a light after dark (*Diary* V, 3 November 1940, p. 356):
'T'other night cooking alone, Freeth came. Light showing. A plane overhead (It was bright starlight). Later, P.C. Collins. Here I observed the official bully.'

114. *the League of . . .*: Nations. For discussion of Bloomsbury's loss of faith in the League of Nations see Alex Zwerdling's chapter 'Pacifism without Hope' in his *Virginia Woolf and the Real World* (University of California Press, 1986).

115. *The temple-haunting martins*: *Macbeth*, I. vi. 9: 'The temple-haunting martlet doth approve': martins were reputed to nest where the air was pure and were therefore birds of good omen. This omen is set alongside the sanguine *Times* leading article prophesying material prosperity and peace to come. In *Macbeth*, the King is shortly to be murdered in the castle where the martins suggest good health. *The Times* leader may be similarly unreliable prophecy.

116. *my perfect mind*: *King Lear* (see note 68); *I'm the old top hat*, music hall song; *Home is the hunter*: from Robert Louis Stevenson's self-epitaph 'Requiem'; *maiden faith*: 'And maiden virtue rudely strumpeted',

Woolf amends a line from Shakespeare's sonnet 66 to emphasize the raped girl's innocent belief, 'virtue' becomes 'faith'; *Sweet and low*: lullaby from Tennyson, 'The Princess', II, l. 456; *Is that a dagger*: Macbeth, II. i. 46, 'Is this a dagger which I see before me'; *I'd be a butterfly*: song by Thomas Bayly. *In thy will is our peace*: the quotation from Dante, *Paradiso*, III, l. 85 was adopted by Matthew Arnold as one of his 'touchstones' for poetry in 'The Study of Poetry' as 'the simple but perfect line'. The essay proposes to put poetry in the place of religion; its opening sentence is: 'The future of poetry is immense, because in poetry, where it is worthy of its high destinies, our race, as time goes on, will find an ever surer and surer stay.' Matthew Arnold, *English and Irish Politics*, ed. R. H. Super (Ann Arbor: University of Michigan Press, 1973), pp. 169, 176. Woolf in this passage scatters poetry and ironically amends Arnold's hopes without quite forgoing them.

117. *megaphonic, anonymous*: the megaphone suggests both tyranny and mass communication. The anonymous oracular voice comes from the bushes where Miss La Trobe lurks.

118. *orts, scraps, and fragments*: Shakespeare, *Troilus and Cressida*, V. ii. 181–5:

> The bonds of heaven are slipt, dissolv'd, and loos'd,
> And with another knot five finger tied,
> The fractions of her faith, orts of her love,
> The fragments, scraps, the bits, and greasy relics,
> Of her o'er-eaten faith, are bound to Diomed.

Cf. 'Scraps, orts, and fragments, are we, also, that?', p. 112.

119. *like . . . wild duck*: the planes are in battle formation.

120. *nothing's solid*: see note 19.

121. *the unconscious*: in December 1939 Woolf was reading and made notes on 'Freud on Groups', that is his *Group Psychology and the Analysis of the Ego* (Holograph Reading Notes, vol. 21, Berg Collection, New York Public Library); Brenda Silver, *Virginia Woolf's Reading Notebooks* (Princeton University Press, 1983, p. 116). While writing *BA* she also read his *Moses and Monotheism* (*Letters*, VI, p. 346). See Elizabeth Abel, *Virginia Woolf and the Fictions of Psychoanalysis* (University of Chicago Press, 1989).

122. *Ding dong*: cf. nursery rhyme

> Ding dong bell
> Pussy's in the well

and

> Full fathom five thy Father lies
> . . . .
> Sea-nymphs hourly ring his knell.
> Hark now I hear them, ding dong bell.
> Shakespeare, *The Tempest* I, 2, 460, 467-8:

'Sunday is the devils own day at M. H. Dogs, children, bells . . . there they go for evensong . . . Ding dong bell . . . ding dong – why did we settle in a village?' (*Diary*, V, 28 August 1938, p. 164.)

123. *Tears, tears, tears*: Walt Whitman, 'Tears' in *Sea-Drift*. The last lines of this short poem exactly express the sense in *BA* of the gap between social surface and inner desolation:

> O shade so sedate and decorous by day, with calm
> countenance and regulated pace,
> But away at night as you fly, none looking – O then
> the unloosen'd ocean,
> Of tears! tears! tears!
> Walt Whitman, *Complete Poetry and Collected Prose*, ed. Justin
> Kaplan (Cambridge University Press, 1982, p. 397)

'Not a sound this evening to bring in the human tears. I remember the sudden profuse shower one night just before the war wh. made me think of all men & women weeping.' (*Diary*, V, Easter Sunday, 24 March 1940, p. 274.)

124. *deeply interfused*:

> a sense sublime
> Of something far more deeply interfused
> Whose dwelling is the light of setting suns.
> William Wordsworth, 'Lines Composed a Few Miles Above
> Tintern Abbey . . . 1798', ll. 95–7, *The Poetical Works of
> William Wordsworth*, ed. E. de Selincourt (Clarendon Press,
> 1944, p. 262):

Cf. Introduction, p. xix.

125. *her semblable, her conspirator*: Baudelaire's address to the reader in the *Préface* to *Les Fleurs du Mal* was adapted by T. S. Eliot as the last line of 'The Burial of the Dead' in *The Waste Land*. William Dodge and the reader of *BA* are observers, audience, interpreters. Woolf, here

and in other works, frequently uses the word *conspirator* with the sense of breathing together as well as plotting.

126. *like Venus ... to her prey*: Jean Racine, *Phèdre*, II, ll. 3, 305–6:

> Ce n'est plus une ardeur dans mes veines cachée:
> C'est Vénus tout entière à sa proie attachée.
> *Œuvres complètes* (Editions du Seuil, 1962), p. 251.

127. *Canaletto*: Venetian painter (1697–1768).

128. *a criss-cross*: a letter written first down the page and then across.

129. *the pageant fade*: Prospero's farewell to his art: the actors 'are melted into air, into thin air' and

> And, like the baseless fabric of this vision, ...
> The solemn temples, the great globe itself,
> Yea, all which it inherit, shall dissolve,
> And like this insubstantial pageant faded,
> Leave not a rack behind.
> Shakespeare, *The Tempest*, IV. i. 166–80.

130. *England ... was then a swamp*: at the end of November 1940 Woolf began to write *Anon*, the first sentence of which runs:

> 'For many centuries after Britain became an island' the historian says 'the untamed forest was king.'

The paragraph continues to describe woods, birds, and the few early men. See Brenda R. Silver, ed., '"Anon" and "The Reader": Virginia Woolf's Last Essays', *Twentieth Century Literature*, XXV, 1979, pp. 356–435. The historian quoted here and adapted in Lucy Swithin's reading is G. M. Trevelyan, *History of England* (Longmans, 1926), p. 3. Silver observes that the passage describing Lucy Swithin's reading does not occur in the early drafts and was written two days before the opening of 'Anon'. For discussion see note 4.

131. *heart of darkness*: Conrad's story, 'Heart of Darkness' similarly opens with a scene where the distinctions between the present day and the primeval have vanished as Marlow prepares to tell his tale.

Appendix

Substantive emendations adopted or conjectured in this edition.

The first reading is the one printed in this edition. The italic entry immediately following the square bracket indicates whether this reading is that of the first British edition (*1941*), the first American edition (*A 1941*), or the present edition (*this edn*). When an emendation has been adopted in this edition, the original reading of *1941* is also given for purposes of comparison. When the present editor has allowed the reading of *1941* to stand but conjectures an emendation, the formula *conj. this edn* is used. The readings of the earlier typescript and the later typescript (see *A Note on the Text*, p. xxxix) are indicated by *ETS* and *LTS* respectively. Page and line numbers are for this edition.

14.4 beams] *1941*; beam *LTS*.
    The *LTS* reading is that of the quotation from Shelley, 'Stanzas –April, 1814', l. 2.

14.32 chemist's shop] *this edn*, *ETS*, *LTS*; chemist shop *1941*.

16.4 the placard on the Barn] *A 1941*, *LTS*; the placard to the Barn *1941*.
    Cf. 15.37.

16.24 green in the garden one moment; grey the next] *this edn*, *ETS*, *LTS*; green in the garden; grey the next *1941*.

19.9 old Swithin] *1941*, *LTS*; Mrs. Swithin *conj. this edn*.
    Lucy Swithin is nicknamed 'Old Flimsy' (19.5), and apparently also 'old Mother Swithin' (23.17). Despite the agreement of *1941* and *LTS* (the corresponding page of *ETS* is missing), 'old Swithin' is unidiomatic; it would be appropriate to an old man and perhaps also to an old woman-servant. The immediately following phrase 'the old girl' may have caused an anticipatory typing error which then persisted into the final typescript.

22.35 Sand and sandwiches clashed] *1941*, *LTS*; sand and sandwiches clashed *conj. this edn*; Sands and sandwiches clashed *conj. this edn*.
    Possibly another error persisting from *LTS* into the final typescript (again the corresponding page of *ETS* is missing).

In Virginia Woolf's handwriting it is often hard to distinguish between s and S.

23.18 her sharp look out of] *this edn*, *LTS*; her sharp look-out of *1941*.

24.17 'If you want] *this edn*; 'It you want *1941*.

29.33 'I was looking at the pictures.'] *1941*, *LTS*; 'I was looking at those pictures.' And he asked the usual question: were they husband and wife; then who painted them. He had already decided that one was different from the other. *ETS*; 'I was looking at the picture.' *Holograph*.

The holograph reading is from an unpaginated, undated sheet transcribed and printed by Mitchell A. Leaska (ed.), *Pointz Hall* (1983), p. 498. The following sentence, 'The picture looked at nobody', wittily takes this sentence up. Yet the reading of *1941* and *LTS* is defensible: Dodge might make a general statement even though he had been particularly looking at one of the two pictures; and at 31.28 Bartholomew Oliver begins to 'tell them the story of the pictures at which the unknown guest had been looking when Giles came in' – though the plural here is appropriate to the fact that he means to talk about both pictures.

35.21 What spring's touched] *this edn*, *LTS*; What springs touched *1941*.

36.30 it had begun] *this edn*, *LTS*; it had began *1941*.

51.13 Early Britons] *this edn*, *LTS*; Early Briton *1941*.

54.35 lorgnette] *A 1941*; lorgnettes *1941*.

Probably a logical emendation by the American copy-editor, a lorgnette being a pair of eyeglasses. There is no version of this passage in *LTS*.

58.16 *A-maying, a-maying*, they bawled. *In and out and round about, a-maying, a-maying . . .*] *A 1941*; 'A-maying, a-maying,' they bawled. 'In and out and round about, a-maying, a-maying . . .' *1941*.

65.18 against vine leaf] *1941*; against a fan of green vine leaf with a purple bunch pendant *ETS*, *LTS*; against vine leaves *conj. this edn*.

67.23 putting her hands to her hair] *this edn*, *LTS*; putting her hands to hair *1941*.

72.14 With the cutting of the clover this retreating and advancing –/ the swifts seemed to have shot beyond their orbits – / Will be] *this edn*; With the cutting of the clover this retreating and advancing – the swifts seemed to have shot beyond their orbits – /Will be]   *1941*; With the cutting of the clover this retreating and advancing – /the swifts certainly as they shot across the window seemed to have shot beyond their orbits – /Will be]   *LTS.*

75.19   *While   Commerce   from   her   cornucopia*] *this   edn, LTS; While commerce from her Cornucopia   1941.*

77.2   white stockings]   *this edn, ETS, LTS;* white waist-coats   *1941.*

78.8   *'A' done with rhymes. Rhymes are still a-bed.*]   *this edn;   A done with rhymes. Rhymes are still-a-bed.   1941;   A-done with rhymes. Rhymes are still a-bed.   LTS.*

79.11   *and the sheep crop rubies.*]   *this edn, LTS;   and the sheep-crop rubies.   1941.*
'Crop' is the verb meaning 'to bite off the tops of plants while feeding' (*OED* v. 3). There is no such noun as 'sheep-crop', and if it were a neologism of Virginia Woolf's it would not be governed by the plural verb 'are'.

79.26   *but it's her heart*]   *A 1941, LTS;   but its her heart   1941.*

81.35–82.1   the place of the lady's dressing-room]   *this edn;*   the place of the ladies' dressing-room   *1941;*   the place of Lady Harpy's closet   *LTS.*

90.15–16   *space between sections   this edn, LTS;   no space between sections   1941.*

98.12   Lynn Jones]   *A 1941, LTS;*   Lynn-Jones   *1941.*
The name is always so spelled elsewhere.

99.17   *as you think me – O what am I saying? But yes, I will speak the truth, before Mama comes – I too*]   *this edn, punctuated as LTS; as you think me. O what am I saying? But yes, I will speak the truth, before Mama comes. I too   1941.*

100.28–29   *if that's his name*]   *this edn;   if that's-his-name   1941.*
There is no version of this passage in *LTS.*

106.1   Oliver said nothing.]   *1941;*   Mr. Oliver said nothing. *conj. this edn.*
The thoughts expressed in indirect speech immediately before this sentence are those of Bartholomew Oliver, who, and not his son Giles, must be meant here (and so Oliver is not a slip for Giles, caused by the fact that Oliver is also a forename). Neither Bartholomew Oliver nor Giles Oliver is elsewhere referred to as 'Oliver'. There is no version of this passage in *LTS.*

109.10   Peek and spy?] *this edn, LTS;* Peak and spy? *1941.*

110.11   *and maiden faith*] *this edn, LTS;* *and the maiden faith* *1941.*
1941's reading is an error induced by the immediately preceding phrase '*the miner sweats*'. Virginia Woolf's adaptation of Shakespeare's line (cf. note 116) preserves the metre.

110.27–8   here and now] *this edn;* here and how *1941; not in ETS, LTS.*

111.9   megaphonic] *A 1941, LTS;* megaphontic *1941.*

118.25   I call that cruel] *this edn, LTS;* I called that cruel *1941.*

119.22   scurred] *this edn, LTS;* scrurred *1941.*
Cf. 123.33. Cf. Introduction xv, xxxiv

123.27   translation, 'to her prey …'] *1941;* translation, 'attached to her prey …' *LTS, conj. this edn.*
LTS's reading translates Racine's 'attachée' (cf. note 126), but *1941*'s reading follows Racine's word-order and may represent Virginia Woolf's second thought, i.e. to have William Dodge make his 'rough translation' in word-by-word form, and to leave the reader to recognize and complete the familiar quotation.

126.29   sheath] *this edn, LTS;* sheaf *1941.*

126.35   Here she rose. Isa followed her] *this edn, LTS;* Here she rose, Isa followed her *1941.*

FOR THE BEST IN PAPERBACKS, LOOK FOR THE

In every corner of the world, on every subject under the sun, Penguin represents quality and variety – the very best in publishing today.

For complete information about books available from Penguin – including Puffins, Penguin Classics and Arkana – and how to order them, write to us at the appropriate address below. Please note that for copyright reasons the selection of books varies from country to country.

In the United Kingdom: Please write to *Dept E.P., Penguin Books Ltd, Harmondsworth, Middlesex, UB7 0DA.*

If you have any difficulty in obtaining a title, please send your order with the correct money, plus ten per cent for postage and packaging, to *PO Box No 11, West Drayton, Middlesex*

In the United States: Please write to *Dept BA, Penguin, 299 Murray Hill Parkway, East Rutherford, New Jersey 07073*

In Canada: Please write to *Penguin Books Canada Ltd, 2801 John Street, Markham, Ontario L3R 1B4*

In Australia: Please write to the *Marketing Department, Penguin Books Australia Ltd, P.O. Box 257, Ringwood, Victoria 3134*

In New Zealand: Please write to the *Marketing Department, Penguin Books (NZ) Ltd, Private Bag, Takapuna, Auckland 9*

In India: Please write to *Penguin Overseas Ltd, 706 Eros Apartments, 56 Nehru Place, New Delhi, 110019*

In the Netherlands: Please write to *Penguin Books Netherlands B.V., Postbus 195, NL–1380AD Weesp*

In West Germany: Please write to *Penguin Books Ltd, Friedrichstrasse 10–12, D–6000 Frankfurt/Main 1*

In Spain: Please write to *Alhambra Longman S.A., Fernandez de la Hoz 9, E–28010 Madrid*

In Italy: Please write to *Penguin Italia s.r.l., Via Como 4, I-20096 Pioltello (Milano)*

In France: Please write to *Penguin Books Ltd, 39 Rue de Montmorency, F-75003 Paris*

In Japan: Please write to *Longman Penguin Japan Co Ltd, Yamaguchi Building, 2–12–9 Kanda Jimbocho, Chiyoda-Ku, Tokyo 101*

To the Lighthouse
Edited by Stella McNichol with an Introduction and Notes by Hermione Lee

Based on the author's childhood experiences, the novel tells the story of the Ramsay family on holiday in Skye and of a promised journey to the lighthouse that only takes place years later. Written with an astonishing and beautiful lyricism, it is told almost entirely through the reflections of its characters. '*To the Lighthouse* is the story of a marriage and a childhood. It is a lamentation of loss and grief for powerful, loved, dead, parents ... It is, less apparently, about the English class-structure and its radical break with Victorianism after the First World War' – Hermione Lee

Jacob's Room
Edited with an Introduction and Notes by Sue Roe

Set in the halcyon days of pre-war innocence *Jacob's Room* follows the progress of a young man as he passes from adolescence to adulthood in a hazy rite of passage. Wandering through the windswept shores of Cornwall to the sunscorched landscape of Greece, his character is revealed in a stream of loosely related incidents, thoughts and impressions. As Sue Roe writes in her introduction, 'Subtle, delicate and tantalizingly suggestive, *Jacob's Room* is the novel in which Woolf examines for the first time the relationship between memory and desire'.

also published

A Room of One's Own/Three Guineas
The Diary of Virginia Woolf: Volume 1
The Diary of Virginia Woolf: Volume 2
The Diary of Virginia Woolf: Volume 3
The Diary of Virginia Woolf: Volume 4
The Diary of Virginia Woolf: Volume 5
Mrs Dalloway
Night and Day
A Woman's Essays
The Waves
The Voyage Out